Life Blood

by

S. Jean Brenner

Argus Enterprises International Inc
New Jersey***North Carolina

Life Blood © 2011 All rights reserved
by
S. Jean Brenner.

No part of this book may be reproduced or transmitted in any form or by any means, graphic, electronic, or mechanical, including photocopying, recording, taping, or by any informational storage retrieval system without prior permission in writing from the publisher.

A-Argus Better Book Publishers, LLC

For information:
A-Argus Better Book Publishers, LLC
9001 Ridge Hill Street
Kernersville, North Carolina 27285
www.a-argusbooks.com

ISBN: 978-0-6155751-24
ISBN: 0-6155751-2-9

Book Cover designed by Dubya

Printed in the United States of America

Prologue

He sat at his desk chewing on the stump of a cigarette. He didn't crave the nicotine anymore, only the action. The phone on his desk broke the silence.

"Shit." He muttered and picked up.

"Mr. Styles, it's Detective Brown, we have a situation here."

He sighed. Situation meant another murder. They were gruesome. The first was a young girl, no older than fifteen—stabbed to death; her case along with three others had gone cold. Nobody could figure out anything. This one—was worse. Styles drove his silver Mercedes to the crime scene. Yellow caution tape surrounded the rundown apartment buildings. On the dirty ground near the dumpster was the body of a boy his face was covered with a dirty piece of newspaper.

"Any I.D?"

"Daniel Doe," Detective Brown answered, "I called the number found scribbled on a piece of paper in his pocket."

"Who'd you get?"

"Friend of the family," he answered. "His father had gone to a friend's house to play some poker and had given Daniel the number to call. He told us his son was going to visit a friend to play some video games."

"How old is the victim?"

"Fourteen."

Styles shook his head, "same as the girl?"

Brown nodded, "Stabbed to death, jagged edges in the torn flesh, exactly the same as Mary Walberg.

"I'm going to need the name of the person Daniel had seen that day."

Brown nodded and handed him a slip of paper.

* * *

He kept his eyes on the boy as he spoke.

"I don't know anything!" he demanded.

"I doubt that," Styles answered, "You were the last person to see Daniel alive."

"I didn't do anything to him!"

"You from around here?"

"Yeah."

"Got a nice place?"

"I guess. Look, this buddy-buddy crap isn't going to work for me, ok? He left my house Saturday night around 6 pm; he lives a few blocks down so he walked. Danny was my friend, I would *never* hurt him!"

Styles nodded, "Thanks."

Dr. Taylor Mandolin had just finished stitching up the body when Styles came in.

"What can you tell me?" he asked, trying to hide the sense of anguish he felt for the victim and his family.

"There are a couple of things I find puzzling," he answered, "he was almost completely drained of blood."

"What?"

He nodded, "There were two very thin shards of bone in the stab wound, it was defiantly the stabbing that killed him."

"A bone knife?" he asked.

"It's possible."

"This is a sacrificial killing," Styles said, "I've seen this before."

Mandolin nodded, "That was my guess as well—the body is drained of blood."

"It doesn't make sense," he answered, "Why would they dump his body in an alleyway?"

He shrugged, "that's your job. There was very little blood on his shirt; nobody knows what happened to the rest of it."

* * *

"Styles, it's Detective Brown again I just got a call from the coroner and there is a huge problem."

He moved the phone to his other ear. "What kind of problem?"

"Well, Mandolin wanted to run some more tests on Daniel Doe, and well—you're not going to believe this."

"Well?"

"He's missing."

"Missing?" Styles shouted, "What do you mean he's missing?"

"I mean, he isn't here, the freezer is empty."

Styled sighed, "Oh this just keeps getting better."

The crime scene photos were horrific. It was hard for Styles to believe that the pasty lifeless face had ever been the other boy in the photos, dark hair, and perfect blue eyes. Styles opened the file and peered at it re-reading, checking for anything he might have missed.

Daniel Doe, fourteen years old, high school student in Southern California, died of a stabbing in November. Body drained of blood and found in an alleyway by a construction crew. There were no fibers on his clothes, no DNA other than his own; there was no evidence of where he was killed or why he was drained of blood. No ideas why he would be moved to an alleyway. This guy was good. Family and friends were clean, nobody at his school knew anything and now his body was missing. Wonderful. Fourteen-year-old Daniel Doe was going cold.

S. Jean Brenner

I

The Bookstore

I had never actually thought about the whole reason behind my leaving. Now that I look back I feel selfish for abandoning my mother the way that I did. The liquor didn't help anymore and the house was a constant reminder of what I had lost. It seemed the only alternative was to run away. I was so sure that it would change everything—that everything would get better if I just left. I didn't know at that time exactly what was waiting for me just around that corner.

I got up slowly, dreading what I was about to do, not because I believed it to be the wrong decision but because I was leaving my mother—all by herself. I knew she could take care of herself but I didn't want to see her upset.

I dressed myself in dark wash blue jeans and a casual feminine blue blouse. I never liked that shirt but my mother had bought it for me, and I had never worn it more than a couple times. I decided I should wear it one more time—for her. I was hoping it would make her happy in a small way.

"I'm sure, Mom," I whispered, when we arrived at the airport "I just can't stay here any longer."

"I understand that it's too much for you, but are you sure this is the right solution?" She was doing a terrible job of not crying, and it was so hard seeing her that way. She had such a gentle looking face. Even though her hair was beginning to grow a bit of gray she still had that shiny lustrous black hair that I thankfully inherited from her. Unfortunately I didn't get her dark blue eyes. I got my chestnut eyes from my dad, which I still won't complain about. I decided I had to say some comforting words to her, at least so I didn't have to suffer through seeing her so upset.

"It's the only solution I can think of," I started "I won't be all alone, Mom. I will be near a lot of my old summer friends. And I won't be too far away either. I will see you soon."

She nodded and dried her eyes with the back of her hand. I fidgeted with the collar of my blouse. She didn't seem to notice it; she stared at my face and wouldn't avert her gaze.

"Please don't cry." I pleaded. I was in no mood to cry but it was difficult when my beautiful mother broke down. I had only seen her cry twice before. The last time was the divorce. She was still pretty torn up about it. My father, Ethan, never showed how much it really affected him and that's when he made her cry, when she felt like he truly didn't care. It had been almost three years and she was finally able to get up and go to work and live her life without my dad and now—*I* was leaving her too? I had second thoughts racing through my head. Should I change my mind and just get back in the car and go home? *No*, I thought, I *had* to do this. I sighed, trying to think of something else to say to her.

"I'll write you," I said, "I'll call. I won't be on the other side of the world you know, I can come visit you sometime, I promise."

I hugged her and forced a smile. I had to leave California, though I wasn't too excited about where I was headed. It was nice and I would be near some old friends but I was used to California and the warm summer sun. I was headed to North Bend Oregon a lovely small town full of woodland and rain.

Again came the thoughts of changing my mind and just staying in California. I hadn't even left yet and I already missed home. I was packed up with three suitcases and a duffel bag, not counting the things that were shipped to Ethan's a few weeks ago including my car. It was a very uncomforting feeling, getting up in the morning to an almost completely empty bedroom, the bedroom that had been mine since before I can remember. And it wasn't only home I would miss. I had a life here, though not many friends, I did have a job. My manager, Amber seemed very displeased by the move. I guess I was her best employee. I hated talking to people but somehow I was still able to sell those magazines, soaps and other things that were sold at half the price at liquor stores or the nearby supermarkets. I was truly hoping I could get a better job in North Bend.

After a few more hugs and a few more pleads for my mother to stop crying, I got on the plane and rested my eyes. It wasn't a very long flight, but it was long enough to cut blood flow from my thighs and make me feel all tingly and numb. I stumbled off the plane and gathered my bags. When I stepped out into the fog it was already slightly drizzling. I spotted Ethan climbing out of his silver Honda, the same one I remembered. He walked to me as fast as he could and pulled me into a tight hug.

"I'm so glad you're here, Jane."

I smiled nervously, "Me too, Dad."

"How's your mother?"

"She's fine," I said, "A little sad to see me leave."

"Come on," he said, "It's warmer in the car."

He turned on the car heater and drove down the old familiar streets. We didn't talk much but exchanged a few comments. When I got home, Ethan helped me carry my bags inside. I looked around at the old kitchen and the living room across the way. It made me feel like I was back somewhere from a past life. I hadn't been out to visit Ethan or my grandparents in a few years and it seemed like forever. It was all the same, the old wooden cabinets and the round table with the three nicely cushioned chairs, the white tile with pink grout, even the pale pink drapes on the window above the kitchen sink. The beige carpet in the living room and staircase. It was exactly how I remembered it. Even the smells were the same. I already missed my mom and didn't feel like concentrating on the old house. It was like my childhood came back to haunt me. Why did I think this house could help me *forget* the past? I needed to escape somewhere for a while before I tried to get settled in.

"I'm going to run down to the bookstore," I called to Ethan.

He emerged into the kitchen, "Don't you want to at least see your room first?"

"It's okay," I said, "I know what it looks like. I won't be long."

"All right, well I'm going to the store, to pick up some food for dinner. Maybe you can remind me how good of a cook you are." He smiled.

I nodded though I had no intention of doing such a thing. I hated cooking. My car was in the driveway like it had been for a few days. This time I was driving it in the rain and really had no idea where I was going. I tried to map out in my head what I remembered about North Bend and eventually was able to find Albany's bookstore. I ignored the spying eyes of the workers. Except for them the place was empty. I was alone which was a relief. I walked around to the fiction section and began flipping through books on strange happenings and unlikely romances.

I tucked my dark hair behind my ears and glanced at the dusty, green binding of a very thick, old-looking book. It was tightly wedged in the center of the shelf and I tugged at it, frustrated. The entire shelf shook and in an instant I saw it leaning toward me. I gasped, feeling the brush of flesh against my own and took in the sight of pale hands readjusting the shelf.

"You all right there?"

I looked up to see a pair of lucent green eyes staring into my own. I nodded, nervously.

"Fine," I answered, "thanks."

He nodded. "I couldn't let the shelf topple over on you like that now, could I?" He smiled, his perfect teeth catching my eye.

His gaze made me nervous. I had never had anybody stare at me that way before; it was so solid and emotionless. I moved my stare to the dancing particles of golden dust in the air. He had quick hands and moved the books as if they weren't lodged together. He was graceful. He handed me the book I had been tugging at.

"Sorry for being so impatient," I started, "I'm feeling a little anxious today."

He put his hand up, "No worries." He answered still smiling.

I didn't like people, I never spoke to people, but something about him aroused my curiosity. I cleared my throat.

"Well—umm—thanks again." I said and turned away.

"The name's Aidan!" He called.

I turned around and smiled.

"This is the part where you tell me yours." He added.

I giggled silently, "Maybe later."

He smiled and dropped his gaze for a moment, then looked back into my brown eyes, and nodded formally as if bowing then turned and left.

I stood up on my toes and placed the book on the top of the shelf, without worrying about dislodging the others. I found that I was no longer interested in it.

I shouldn't have, I told myself, *I shouldn't have been so friendly. God—what if he would have asked me out?* I shuddered and brushed my hair from my eyes.

I left the bookstore, still feeling nervous. I concentrated on the misty air and the small beams of sun pushing through the clouds. I stared at the ground watching the sidewalk lighten and darken when the clouds moved.

I felt eyes on my back so I picked up my pace but heard footsteps behind me.

"Hey," he breathed, catching up to me.

Oh god. I halted and sighed, turning around "Can I help you?"

He was silent for a moment; he seemed to be searching for the right words. Had he waited for me?

"I—uh—I just wanted to know if I could get your name…?"

I hesitated before responding, remembering the effect he had on me in the bookstore. *Don't be too friendly.* "Actually, I'd much rather not tell you."

He stared at me passively, "Why not?"

I averted my gaze, captivated by his green eyes and responded, "I don't like *humans.*"

I turned around again, pleased that I hadn't given in to his charm. I replayed my words and laughed silently. That should keep him confused for a while.

I quickened my pace to the parking lot and fumbled with my keys. I opened the door to my red Aveo and quickly started the engine. I turned up the air conditioner full blast—I felt hot, possibly because the blood had rushed to my cheeks. I took a glance back at Aidan who was still staring at me, almost gawking. I sighed and went straight home.

I opened the cupboard automatically without actually thinking about eating anything. I found nothing appetizing. I had to keep my mind busy with something other than home. Walking into the kitchen, I tried to remember why I had declined from my mother's offer to live with her in California. My mind found the path and I pushed back the memories and choked back tears. The roaring sound of an engine scattered my thoughts.

"Ethan." I thought with a sigh, "I am *not* making dinner tonight."

"Jane?" he called, walking inside.

I emerged from the kitchen into the entry.

"Oh good," he said, "You're home. Already raiding the fridge?"

"No," I lied.

I figured as long as he didn't know I was hungry he wouldn't ask me to cook. *Well if you're that hungry why don't you cook us some dinner?* He would say.

"Well—you look hungry."

"No," I answered dryly, averting my gaze from his dark eyes, "I—uh—picked something up on the way home from the bookstore."

"Mmhmm," he murmured, "Okay. Perhaps I'll just throw together some twenty minute pasta."

"Sure, Dad. I—uh—have unpacking to do."

"I ran into Mark Thompson," he said quickly before I disappeared up the stairs, "Do you remember him?"

"Yeah, sort of."

"He says 'hi' and maybe Rudy will be down later to visit you."

I nodded, "Okay." I answered, trying to sound interested.

I raced up to my bedroom before he could respond and locked the door. The room was empty except for the bed still with Ethan's blue cotton sheets. The walls were a light blue that matched the bed sheets. The rest of the room was an empty closet, an empty wooden dresser next to the door and dozens of boxes shoved in the corner. Along with a few trash bags filled with some of my dad's old stuff that he hadn't cleared out yet. I turned on the stereo Ethan had set on the dresser and drifted away into my mind. I began to feel an unnatural lethargic energy, forcing me to doze off.

"JANE!"

My eyes darted open and I sighed, opening my door.

"Dinner." Ethan said.

I sighed again and walked down the stairs, seemingly half asleep.

"You all right?" he mused.

"Fine," I answered, "just suddenly feeling hungry."

"Hmm, you don't say." He chuckled giving me a crooked smile and a playfully accusing look. He tried too hard.

I stared down at my plate, twirling the noodles over and over.

"I'm really glad you're here." Ethan announced.

My eyes locked into his. He was smiling so I faked a smile back, having no idea how to respond. I was usually so good at this, but with Ethan, with my own father I didn't know how to pretend at all. The rest of dinner was silent which wasn't unusual.

I missed my home in California a lot more than I expected to and was beginning to wonder if I could ever get used to North Bend. California was the place I had considered my home for over seventeen years. Suddenly, I was trapped in my father's world, a strange unfamiliar place, with strange, unfamiliar faces. North Bend was beautiful, I won't deny. Just a small coastal city literally on the north bend of Coos Bay with gorgeous sunsets and beautiful beaches but it wasn't enough to make me feel content. Ethan didn't know how to react to any of the things that involved me in even the slightest way. Clueless was an understatement. I guess I couldn't blame him; I wasn't exactly what you would call "normal."

The next day my dad had me help him move some boxes to the attic, it had been a while since I had gone to visit and my bedroom had become my dad's storage unit in the past year. I pushed the boxes against the wall and spotted a large redwood chest in the back corner

"Dad, what's in *that*?"

He followed my eyes, "Oh that old thing? Its empty, I'm sure."

"Don't you have a key for it or something?" I asked, eyeing a tiny silver lock.

He shook his head, "It belonged to my grandfather," he said, "I'm pretty sure it's empty, I had nowhere to put it so I moved it up here years ago, I had actually forgotten about it."

"It's nice."

"Yeah—it's old. So have you been around the block yet, saying 'hi' to all your old friends?" he made the waving motion with his right hand, "The Thompsons were really happy when they heard you were coming to stay with me."

I smiled not really listening to what he was saying. I gathered enough to respond. "Not yet." I said.

"Thanks for the help Jane; sorry to ask you, you have your own unpacking to do still."

"It's not a problem at all," I told him, "It is my room we're clearing out after all."

He smiled.

I climbed down the ladder and headed back to my room.

II

Becky

PEOPLE have always told me that I was eccentric, but eccentric is just a nicer way of saying different, and different is just a nicer way of saying "weird." So stop sugar coating it and cut the foreplay. I'm weird. Unique, original, whatever you choose to call it, I'm weird.

Heaven to me was the dozens of liquor bottles hidden in my parents' pantry, if parents you could even call them. Since Danny's death my mother had become very distant. She was so caught up in her son's tragedy that she only recently started caring about what I did again—just what I need—and my father just recently stopped hating her. Though they shared the same pain they were unable to comfort each other. I have decided that as long as I don't let myself get close to people then they can't hurt me, but that's just how it works isn't it? You can't help but get close to the people you want to keep as far away from you as possible.

I was planning on locking myself in my room for the remainder of the day, but something inside of me had made me terribly anxious and I ached to get out. As I headed for the door I heard a knock. I jumped startled and prepared myself to tell someone I wasn't interested in their product.

"Oh." I sighed in relief opening the door to see familiar gray eyes. "Becky."

Becky was like the sister of my soul. I met her one summer when I was out visiting my grandparents and we instantly clicked and since my parents' divorce and my living with Ethan I saw her more often than I ever hoped I would. She was the only person I was able to let myself love. Surprisingly enough, it was a relief that she never tried to cheer me up, and rarely asked me what was wrong, or what she could do to help, she just always knew. I meant to get around to visiting her since I'd moved in but had been preoccupied trying to get settled.

"Yeah," she laughed, "just me."

"God, I thought you were selling something," I said frowning, "Come in I guess."

"I don't usually ask you this but, are you all right?"

"Well—yeah—I'm obviously beside reality Becky."

"I know how reclusive you can be, but as long as you don't cut me out of your little world, I'll be okay." She laughed. I appreciated how she never pushed an issue. She understood that when I wanted to talk about something I would.

"I see you're on your way out…?"

"Yeah," I sighed, "I have no idea where I was going."

She smiled, "You'd end up where you always do."

I chuckled, "I guess Albany's is the only place where I feel like I can actually think."

"It's funny Jane," she started, "that you go to the bookstore to think and go to your bedroom to read."

"I don't have room in my mind to realize when things don't make sense."

"You can't keep beating yourself up."

"Oh, but I can."

"Jane…" She sighed, shutting the front door and sat beside me on the stairs, "Nothing was your fault."

"I know." I answered, "I'm very much sure of that Becky, but to be perfectly honest, that's what hurts. It hurts more to know that I had absolutely no control over it, to know that I couldn't protect him. I *had* to get out of California."

She embraced me. It was the only response I wanted, the only one I needed, and she must have known that. She suggested coming with me for a cup of coffee.

We sat down and I instantly launched into complaining about Aidan.

"So this totally annoying guy was harassing me the other day."

"What do you mean?" she laughed,

"Well, I was just minding my own business trying to find an interesting book and he felt it necessary to ask me my name about ten times."

"Okay, and this is bad how?'

"I have no idea who he is, and made it clear that I wasn't interested in finding out."

"Why not?"

"There was something about him that struck me as…odd."

She laughed, "Yeah you're one to judge what's odd."

I smiled, about to respond when I noticed Aidan across the room, staring at me with those enticing green eyes. I looked away trying to pretend I didn't notice him. I saw Becky eyeing the guy over by the condiments. She got up, pulling her top down showing more cleavage that I thought necessary. She flipped her long brown hair as she added a suggestive sway to her hips. I decided to leave her to it and secluded myself in the "new age" section flipping through books on Santeria and Wicca. It was quiet and for once I was able to put myself to rest and actually think. I saw a face in my mind, a face I hadn't seen in three years, the one I dreamed of every night with innocent blue eyes. I sighed, savoring the vision. My thoughts were instantly shattered by a familiar voice.

"Reading?" I heard.

"No," I answered, placing a book back on the shelf, "No, the book and I were just having a conversation."

"All right," he chuckled, "I asked for that one."

I picked up a random book and opened it to a random page, trying to ignore my irritating distraction.

"So what's new with you?"

"Why?" I asked, "It's not like you're actually interested."

"Why do you have to be like that?" he demanded, he sounded almost angry, "I'm just trying to be nice to you."

"Look, *Aidan*," I started, slamming the book closed, "I'm not interested in being nice all right. I just want to be left alone."

"Nobody likes to always be alone."

"Then does that make me nobody?" He opened his mouth to speak but I put my hand up, "I'm sorry," I said, "I just—I just want to be left alone."

"Well—can I at least get your name?"

I sighed, "Jane Doe," I said, and turned away.

I heard him mumble as he followed me, "Oh yeah—now that one is real original."

I smiled at the sarcasm in his voice and heard him pick up his pace as he followed me.

"Okay, just your first name then?"

"I just told you."

"Jane?" he questioned, "well is that…"

"Aidan—*please*!" I announced, turning around sharply.

"Fine," he mumbled, "nice meeting you."

I sighed and turned back around. I heard him grumble as he walked away and I was thinking about saying something to make him feel less offended, after all my not wanting to talk to people was nothing personal. I turned to look at him but he was already gone.

"Well—good." I muttered, at least I was alone.

I met back up with Becky and used my mess of packed boxes as an excuse to leave the book store and get away from Aidan.

* * *

I locked myself in my room with a random romance novel I had bought without even reading the title. I was more tired than usual but something kept me awake. I closed my eyes, simply waiting for sleep to find me.

Suddenly a feeling of dread washed over me and tore me from that trance between sleep and awake. I sprang up in bed as headlights cut across my window.

Daniel!

I raced down the stairs and opened the door. I saw him stumbling toward me. His mouth was open like he wanted to speak but all he was doing was crying. The light from the porch illuminated that sight that would haunt my mind for the rest of my life. His eyebrows were drawn together pressing thin creases into his forehead. He looked miserable, nothing like himself. There was this frightened look in his eyes, almost angry, in agony. I stood there in the doorway watching him stumble further into the light. I wanted to run to him but was paralyzed in my place. He had his hand clutching at his stomach.

"Danny?" He fell limply into my arms. I could feel panic creeping into my voice.

"Jane." He choked out my name.

I felt hypnotized at the sight of his hand gripping his stomach and the sight of the thin lines of blood running down his fingers. I lost my breath for a moment. I saw that look through my own tears, the one he would give me when we were really young and I would fall off my bike, telling me he was there and everything was going to be all right. I could see the color draining from his face, accenting the blue of his eyes, turning them to a light crystal hue.

"Oh god, Danny!" I ran my fingers through his hair, "Oh god please don't leave me. Please!"

I saw him weakly smile at me and I screamed his name when those gorgeous eyes of his closed. I cradled him in my arms trying to ignore the blood that was by then covering his hand.

My mother flew down the stairs in her nightdress and robe.

"Mom," I cried. "MOM!"

She pushed me aside and covered her mouth with her hand when she saw the blood on my shirt. I screamed as loud as I could, I screamed for long moments, letting out the feelings of pure agony.

I flew up in bed, running my hands through my hair. I sighed heavily and lied back down. "No more nightmares," I whispered to myself, "please!" The dreams were always different but when I awoke one thing was always the same—Daniel was dead. Every time I dreamed it was reminding me of all the ways I hadn't been there for him.

I tried to shut my eyes again but the dream just kept replaying. That beautiful boy in my arms, bleeding furiously all over my white shirt. How is it fair that things like that must happen? The pain in my dream was so real, the fear, the torture. I cried exhausting myself and finally fell back asleep. The last thing I saw was the digital clock reading 4:17 am.

I woke up to the phone on my nightstand.

"Hello?"

"Hey did I wake you up?"

"Uh—no. Don't worry about it, Becky. What is it?"

"Wondering about our beach trip today…?"

"Oh!" I cried sitting up, "Of course. I forgot, gimmie maybe thirty minutes."

"Okay see you then."

I hurried myself but Becky got there sooner than I expected. I grabbed a towel and hurried to Becky's car, leaving a note for Ethan, telling him where I was.

We laid out our brightly colored towels and watched the waves break. It was colder than I had expected being so used to the heat of California, but the sun was out, though low in the sky it was still there. It wasn't a crowded beach like California; we were the only people there. It seemed unnatural for things to be so quiet but I enjoyed it. Seagulls rode the waves in the distance and sometimes the clouds would come in and darken the sky for minutes at a time. The water was the color of smoke, but if the light hit it right you could really see the lovely blue color reflecting from the patch of sky not covered by the clouds.

Becky's perfect figure in her black bikini made me feel so self-conscious, and her dark round sunglasses seemed completely unnecessary I pulled my attention back to the breaking waves.

"So," she started slyly, "what about Aidan?"

His name made me jump and I turned quickly to look at her but suddenly recoiled. "Who?"

She laughed, "Yeah, he came to talk to me. After you left the last time we were at the coffee shop."

"What?" I sighed, "He just won't give up."

"He really wanted to know your name."

I groaned and turned my attention back to the horizon. "You didn't tell him did you?"

"Jane," she sighed, "Come on."

"So..."

"Well—when I told him, for some reason he got mad at me."

I burst into laughter, "Oh god!"

"What?" she cried.

"I'm sorry—it's just—I did tell him my name," I chuckled, "he didn't believe me. He thinks I'm messing with him."

"I wouldn't be surprised if you were," she said dryly.

"Why do you say that?" I asked slightly defensive.

"You don't like people Jane," she said, "that simple."

"huh." I mused.

"But you still like *him*."

"God, Becky. No not at all!" I broke eye contact, bringing my gaze to the sand as I ran my fingers through it, feeling the unexpected coolness.

She smiled, not at all convinced by my outburst, "I think you do."

"Well maybe you don't know as much as you think you do," I answered, keeping my voice even, "I just like his eyes—I mean; I guess he's sort of nice looking."

She laughed "Yeah *nice looking,* that's an understatement if there ever was one."

"All right," I admitted, "He's beautiful, but he's irritating."

She shook her head. "Well then I guess it would be okay for me to ask him out."

"What?"

"Well—you wouldn't mind would you? Since you don't like him I …"

"No, go ahead." I answered, trying to fight back the unexpected sting of jealousy.

"Uh-huh." She murmured, looking at me suspiciously.

"Well, honestly Becky, I can't say he isn't intriguing, I mean, nobody has ever been so persistent about knowing my name."

She chuckled, "I know."

"I need a new one."

"A new—name?"

"Yeah."

"Why?"

"One that fits me better, more original—like me."

"Fits you better?" she laughed, "Are you crazy? Jane Doe fits you perfectly."

"How?"

"Well—nobody really knows who you are—right?"

I thought about it for a moment, trying to keep my expression unreadable. "Maybe." I murmured.

Life Blood

III

Guilt

I felt I didn't exist. I died that warm night in May, I died the night when Detective Styles knocked on my door giving my family news of Danny's death. I clung to everything I could remember about him let go of everything else. Danny was different—like me in some ways. I've stopped trying to make sense of it, to make sense out of the fact that the only person who truly understood me was stolen from me.

Now I must admit that I would not have been entirely honest with myself if I were to say that I wasn't at least *attracted* to Aidan—that was a sure fact. He was flawless without a doubt but I couldn't let myself think about that. The *species* of men were as far on my agenda as possible. Summer break was almost over and I was not yet ready to think about anything but college and how I was going to get there with my math skills where they were, but being the person I am, I couldn't help but feel guilty about that afternoon in the bookstore. Had I just been a little too harsh?

A walk sounded nice. I thought out loud, evaluating my mood. "What *is* my mood?" As usual, I couldn't tell. Sometimes I truly felt insane. I already knew I was weird and clumsy, I had accepted that, in fact I had embraced it, but I often wondered that if I indulged in weird things for the reasons that I did if that may have made it possible that my life was just one delusion after another. The tragedy however, is that it wasn't. I would never wake up to the sound of Danny's voice I would never again look into those blue eyes contrasted with the clarity of his russet skin. I would never be able to confess my fears to him or tell him my dreams. This was my life—real. It was no bad dream.

I walked slowly through the woods near the house, not even checking to see if I was on the trail. I tried to think about nothing. Not that I had tried *not* to think about anything but I had actually tried *to* think about nothing. But nothing was—well something and it proved more difficult than I thought.

I sighed, pressing my fingers to my temples. *Bad attempt,* I thought, *okay think about something— insignificant.* For some reason, no matter what I thought about—a music video I had daydreamed through, or a romance novel that almost held my interest all of my thoughts came back—to Aidan. How stupid—or *insane* was I? I turned my attention to a small rabbit that hopped in front of me and froze. I was caught off guard by the fact that I noticed his fur was the same color as Aidan's perfect hair. No matter what I did I couldn't get him out of my head. I felt guilty, I felt bad for my sarcastic behavior when all he was doing was being nice. Or *was* he being nice? He was a guy after all and most guys aren't nice to girls just to be nice, but to get something in particular from them. Oddly enough Aidan did seem different somehow. My chest continued to burn and I thought the trees around me had begun to shake. It only took me a moment to realize that *I* was the one shaking and the ground appeared to be moving from the heavy rain, attacking the wood and leaves at my feet. I wrapped my arms around my body and headed back the way I had come.

I focused on the cold, not unhappy to feel miserable physically, because it kept my mind off Aidan and Danny. I realized I could never free my mind of Aidan until I apologized to him. Hopefully that wouldn't open a door of welcome into the life of Jane, if it did, I would be forced to close it without causing my chest to burn with guilt.

I continued walking aimlessly until I found a break in the trees and walked quickly to the house, trying to escape the cold. I secured myself in my bedroom and stripped of my soaking clothes and threw on a pair of gray sweat pants and a black tank. I focused myself on thinking about the rain—the woods, anything but Aidan. I put a CD into my stereo. Ethan had made me a mix of—something. Strange as it was I never listened to music, it usually made me feel sad. Not that I don't appreciate art, I have notebooks full of lyrics and I can quote the poetry of music, but could never get passed the blaring guitar, and pounding drums. I couldn't listen to the CD, but I needed it to tune out so I could more easily think of nothing. The vivid dream of Danny had torn a hole in my stomach, though I wanted to remember him, I didn't want to remember him like that. I couldn't think about Ethan either—I was obviously a terrible daughter, hadn't seen Ethan in three years and avoided conversation and concealed myself in my room. I needed to make an effort to let my father know at least a little bit about who I was. It wasn't easy though; he was too pushy with the questions.

It was the last day of summer break and the stress was building up again. I ate breakfast in silence and Ethan read the paper, occasionally glancing up at me. I avoided eye contact; it was uncomfortable to look at him it was like he was trying to read my mind.

"How's Becky?" he asked. Taking a sip of his coffee he looked up at me, "I noticed you two went out yesterday."

"She's fine." I answered soberly.

"Well—did you have fun?"

"Sure."

"Uh huh. You have school today?"

"Dad—it's Sunday."

"Right," he answered, "When you're like me and don't get days off, you forget."

I nodded, trying to smile. He dropped it there, perhaps realizing I was hopeless. Again I escaped to the bookstore. I sat in silence with a cup of coffee. The whole in my stomach was healing as the dream was fading. When I got home I devoted some time tackling the mess of packed boxes, still not completely moved in. I gathered my schoolbooks and a clean pair of clothes for the next day. Back home I didn't mind school—but here I couldn't go unnoticed. I felt like a virtual stranger in a small town. I slept well that night—no nightmares. I got up slowly; Ethan must have already left for work. I cramped my long limbs into the tiny shower. I didn't worry with my hair; I threw it up in a ponytail, and dressed myself in a simple pair of blue jeans and a T-shirt. I grabbed my school bag and left the house. I ended up early so I sat in the car reading until people started flooding the campus. I tried to hide myself in the sea of students but it still seemed like people were staring. I wished I could have turned invisible or blend in with the walls. I rushed to my first class with my head down. When I opened the classroom door, I felt my breath explode.

"Thank god!" I mumbled, and took the seat next to Becky.

"Oh hey," she said, with the biggest smile on her face, "I was hoping we'd end up with at least one class together."

I smiled, "I was terrified we wouldn't". Considering the fact that math wasn't exactly my strongest subject—I could probably use some help.

The day dragged. Every class seemed like a whole day. I knew I couldn't go unnoticed, people stared at me like I was an alien, they asked me my name or tried to start conversations, but I avoided it as best I could. It was finally lunch and I dreaded it; luckily Becky found me and kept me company. Of course she insisted as always that she take a thousand unnecessary pictures of me. I tried to hide my face.

"Oh come on," she laughed cheerful as ever, "you look adorable."

"Hey." I heard.

I turned to see Aidan.

"Oh hi," Becky answered.

He was talking to *her*?

He glared at me but wouldn't keep eye contact; he didn't sit with us but chose a table by himself.

"You know for somebody who tries so hard to talk to me, he certainly likes to be by himself."

"What?"

I cocked my head toward Aidan.

"Oh," she chuckled, "Why don't you just go talk to him?"

I didn't even answer.

"He's new here too," she continued.

I noticed he wasn't looking in my direction so I took a minute to stare at his perfect face. I had honestly never seen anyone so beautiful. His hair hung messily in his face in an intentional kind of disorder. His face was flawless and pale; it contrasted wonderfully with the piercing green of his eyes. He looked up and I immediately broke my gaze.

I looked at Becky; she was staring at me making the blood rush to my cheeks. Her smile told me that she didn't know what to say and I was meant to read her mind.

"What?" I whispered.

She shook her head, "what did you do, he's glaring at you."

"Still?"

"Yes."

I knew it was probably the worst time for me to look in his direction but it was like my eyes weren't attached to the rest of me. I looked over, and sure enough he was staring at me—glowering. He didn't stop with the death stare so I looked away.

I was relieved when I finally got to my last class, realizing that the first dreadful day was almost over. I had walked slowly, so I rushed to the nearest seat I could get to before the bell rang. I cringed and gritted my teeth when I saw Aidan sitting right beside me. That burning guilt started eating away at me and that mental wound in my stomach began to throb. I decided I should at least try to make conversation and move into an apology.
"Hey."
He stared at me.
"Oh, you're talking to me now?"
"Well…"
"Don't bother."
He sat there silently; sometimes he would clinch his hands into fists or pass me a glare. I was only trying to apologize but I guess I had asked for it, and he *was* after all leaving me alone which is what I had wanted in the first place.
"I'm sorry." I whispered. I wasn't sure if he heard me but he turned to stare at me.
"Yeah," he answered, sarcastically, "I'm sure you care *so* much more than you did a couple days ago."
"Really, Aidan…"
The bell rang and he bolted out the door before I could say another word. Oh well—I *did* apologize at least. My heart was pounding; it irritated me to realize he made me so nervous. He was so mean, but I can't say I didn't deserve it.

The next day was the same. Aidan seemed harsh. It made me uneasy. He didn't have that curious innocence in his face; his eyebrows were pulled together, forcing wrinkles in his ivory skin that seemed permanent. I just kept my eyes on my paper, sometimes I could feel him staring at me and my ears would burn and my heart would race. He made me feel so self-conscious.

I saw Becky talking to him after class and as soon as he saw me he left.

"What was that about?"

She shrugged, "nothing really," she said, crossing her arms in front of her chest, "he just came to talk to me."

"I see." I answered dryly.

"He likes you."

I laughed loudly once, "yeah."

"Really," she answered, "I explained to him that you wanted to apologize I let him know that you really *are* sorry."

"Great, Becky." The tremor in my voice ruined the intended sarcasm.

Becky talking to him might have done something because the next day in history he was completely calm again.

"Hi." he said cheerfully, passing me a glimpse of his beautiful smile.

"—Hi." I choked out.

"I didn't realize you knew Becky for so long," he started politely, "she mentioned you were summer pals since the first grade."

I nodded. He was making conversation and was perfectly polite; maybe I had only imagined his harshness the day before. Maybe I was insane.

"Well—she's nice."

"She is."

Sounded to me like he liked Becky not me.

I didn't talk to him much, which shouldn't have surprised him, but as the days passed he seemed as if he had actually taken offense. I would often catch him looking at me with a miffed look in his face. I tried to ignore. When he talked to me I responded, what more did he expect?

IV

Lost

I was lying in bed, letting my mind wonder; I sank into my memories of home and began missing my mother like crazy. I did promise I'd call didn't I? It took a bit of courage to pick up the phone, I was terrified that I would start to cry and miss her so much I'd come running home. I sighed and dialed the number.

"Hello?"

"Mom?"

"Oh, Jane!" I instantly heard the smile in her voice, "How are you?"

"I'm okay."

"Just okay?"

I smiled, "Well, I miss you and things here are a bit different then what I'm used to, but Becky is making it easier to adjust."

"I'm glad to hear that, I miss you so much. How's the school?"

"It's fine."

"Meet any nice boys?"

Oh god, the question I was dreading. "No." I fibbed.

"Are people nice?"

"Most of them," I answered, "I haven't had any problems." That was the truth wasn't it?

"Of course you haven't had any problems. You're nice and beautiful, Jane."

Sometimes I felt like my mom didn't know me at all, but either way she made me feel better.

"Umm—yeah I guess. How have you been?"

"Lonely," she chuckled, "It isn't the same here without you."

"Well—maybe Becky and I can take a road trip to come visit you, over Winter break, I should come home for Christmas anyway and it isn't like Becky's mom would notice."

"That sounds great."

"I'll celebrate with Dad early, that way he doesn't feel too left out. He'll be partying with all his work buddies."

My mom laughed, I loved to hear her laugh, "Sounds great. I have some things around the house to take care of so I'll talk to you later ok?"

"Sure. I'll call you later."

She never said bye, which was a relief in some way. Saying goodbye always made things feel so—final.

I found the next day that going for a walk sounded like a good idea, anything to clear my mind. It was surprisingly relaxing, I almost fell asleep as I wondered aimlessly into the trees—again, ignoring the trail. I was hardly even aware that it had started raining. I pulled the hood of my raincoat up and decided to turn back. I noticed that the trees in every direction looked exactly the same. I sighed. This would be interesting.

I looked behind me and noticed that the rain had turned the dirt to mud, washing away any footprints I may have possibly left. I walked like I had last time, looking for that same kind of break in the trees. I moved quickly, searching for a way out, chances were I was getting myself more lost that I was already. It was starting to get dark, which made me nervous, but I stayed calm, looking for the trail. The rain hadn't stopped and I was unusually frightened. I had never been afraid of the dark but as I walked I could swear I felt eyes on my back. My mother always teased me about my "active imagination" so I concentrated on that, telling myself that I was alone. I ignored the rustling sounds behind me, but they persisted, becoming louder as they approached. I began walking faster and that rustling sound came again. I broke into a panicking sprint, only trying to avoid running into the trees as I scraped my ankles on rocks and branches. Something caught my foot and I fell, crying out in pain as I felt the muscles in my ankle tearing loose. The shards of pain overwhelmed me for a moment and I couldn't catch my breath. I heard that same rhythmical resonance, and squeezed my eyes shut. I could feel that the owner of the sound that was following me was right in front of me.

"Jane?"

My eyes darted open to meet a white face and eyes that almost appeared to be glowing. I was mute for a moment, paralyzed, but I'd recognize that voice anywhere.

"Aidan?" but my voice caught in my throat and rather than sounding baffled, it came out pleadingly.

"What are you doing in the woods?" he asked.

"What are *you* doing in the woods?"

"Oh my god, Jane!" he whispered, kneeling down and looking at my ankle.

"I'm fine." I told him.

"I'll carry you."

"Ha!" I burst out, "You most certainly will *not*. I can walk."

"Jane, your ankle is broken—you *can't* walk."

"Watch me!" I scowled at him and stood up. The pain shot up through my leg causing my stomach to turn with nausea. I tried to pretend that I didn't feel it but it was causing my breathing to quicken and the look of agony on my face was impossible to hide.

"Yeah," Aidan laughed, "Now don't complain."

He sighed and lifted me into his arms. I gasped.

"Put me down!" I screamed.

"Don't be a baby." He snapped back.

I growled in my chest. "Put—me—*down*!" I screamed, but to be honest, I couldn't mean it. He was strong and his skin felt comfortingly warm and soft and as strange as it seemed—I almost wanted to be closer. It made me angry that I fell weak to his beauty that way. I was so lost in my thoughts, and confusion that I didn't even realize that I was already home. He set me softly on the porch. I tried to glare at him but he was smiling and I felt like I had the air stolen from my lungs.

Ethan opened the door. "OH! Jane, where have you been?" he demanded.

"I just went for a walk in the woods." I said, turning to look at him, "I think I broke my ankle."

"All right," he replied "I'll be right back." My father disappeared inside the house

I looked over at Aidan, but he was already gone. I shook my head and pressed my fingers to my temples, trying to make my vision stop spinning. I saw him emerging from the shadows.

"You don't have to hide," I told him.

He smiled.

"Um—thanks." I said, trying to return the smile.

Aidan quickly disappeared into the shadows again.

Ethan came back outside with a splint and a wrap. I could see by the light of the porch that my ankle had already begun to swell and turn black.

"I don't think it's broken," Ethan said, "but you twisted it something terrible."

I winced as he wrapped the splint tightly and helped me wobble inside. That's what you get for having a doctor for a father everything needs special treatment.

I glanced behind my shoulder to see if I could catch one more glance at Aidan, but there was nothing. He was so weird and passive and quiet—unnatural considering the way he had acted in the bookstore.

That night I didn't sleep well. As soon as my ankle stopped hurting, Aidan crowded my mind. That guy who had never been much more than a minor annoyance had carried me home. What was he doing in the woods? And how did he know where I lived? Maybe I was being paranoid, after all, I was in the woods as well, and this town isn't that big. I'm sure everybody knew everybody; there aren't many secrets in North Bend.

That's the way it works, you can't help getting close to the people you wish to keep as far away as possible

A few days later I surprisingly found myself talking to Aaron Raines, the boy who sat next to me in English, History and Science. There was something about the way he was nice—it was pure. He was comforting to talk to. He walked with me to the lunchroom and sat between Becky and me. Aidan walked passed me like he did every day, but this time he didn't ignore me or glare at me, he smiled and sat across from me.

"How's your ankle?" he asked.

"Fine." I lied.

"What did you do to your ankle?" Becky interrupted.

I just shook my head.

"Well you certainly did a number on it." Aidan chuckled.

"Really, it's fine," I answered, not looking at him. His direct gaze made me nervous. "It only hurt for an hour or so."

He probably knew I was lying but I kept the act up anyway.

Aaron laughed quietly. "Do things like that happen to you a lot?"

"You have no idea," Becky laughed back, "she's been a tom-boy her entire life."

"I never had any sisters," I said, poking at the cold pasta on my plastic tray, "except maybe for you, Becky." I glanced at her.

"I know," she answered, "still true."

I stared at my tray, not making eye contact with anybody.

The lunch bell rang and Aaron walked me to English. "Are you okay?" he asked, trying to get me to look at him.

I averted my gaze from my shoes back to his gold eyes. "I'm fine, Aaron, why?"

"You seem—distracted. Is your ankle bothering you?"

"I'm fine."

He nodded as we walked inside and took the seat beside me.

"Did you read the chapter?" he whispered.

I giggled, "I read the book."

"Seriously?" his eyes widened.

I smiled and nodded.

"And?"

"Well, I hated it actually—Steinbeck was never one of my favorites."

"Actually—I was asking what happened in chapter four."

I chuckled, "Basically nothing—like most of his work."

He sighed.

"Relax," I laughed, "Mrs. Webber will go over it."

He nodded.

Mrs. Webber did go over it briefly, and to his relief, didn't pop a chapter quiz like she often did. I was dreading history next. Aaron walked with me but Becky wasn't there yet. Sitting next to Aaron was better than the other alternative. Before I had even seen him enter the room, Aidan had stolen the seat right beside me. I looked over at Aaron who looked even more confused than I did. I could tell his feelings were hurt.

"You can sit here," I told him, gesturing to the seat at my other side.

He shook his head. "It's all right."

He moved closer to the front of the room, three rows in front of me. Becky was late for class, so the only empty seat was the one to the left of Aaron. I glared at Aidan briefly then covered my face with my hands. I felt terrible; remembering the look Aaron had given me as soon as Aidan sat down.

"Hi." He said, shattering my thoughts.

I wanted to ask him why he did that being sure he'd know what I meant, but I didn't say anything.

"I hope I didn't upset him."

"Aaron." It wasn't a question.

"Yes," he answered, "Nobody has been very friendly to me, save for maybe Becky."

I chuckled.

"What?"

"It's nothing." I answered but couldn't help but to laugh again.

"Really—what?"

"It's just funny—Becky is friendly to anybody of the male species."

He smiled, revealing his perfect teeth, "Figured you'd say something like that."

"Did you?"

He just smiled. "How's your ankle."

Way to change the subject. "I told you already—it's fine."

"Are you sure?"

I nodded. Ethan had tried to wrap it up for me again but I insisted it didn't hurt anymore.

"You can tell me if it's bothering you."

"Aidan, please!" He was the only thing bothering me.

Class dragged, it was purely lecture and I had my mind set completely somewhere else, somewhere quieter.

"Are you all right?" Aidan's musical voice scattered my peaceful daydreams, crashing me back to the reign of terror.

"If I were to tell you yes I am guessing you're going to ask me if I'm sure."

He smiled. "I'll take that as a yes."

After class I bolted out the door faster than Aidan had the day before, but Aaron caught up to me in the parking lot.

"You know," he started, slightly out of breath, "People are saying some pretty strange things about that guy."

"What guy?" I asked, being sure of whom he was talking about.

"Only the guy who *stole* my seat in history today."

I chuckled at his sarcasm, "Aidan." I said.

"Yeah, whatever."

"What are they saying?"

"Ask Rudy Thompson."

"Rudy?" I exclaimed, remembering him from years ago he used to live a few houses down from Ethan, I hadn't thought about him since Ethan said something when I first moved in.

"Yeah," he answered, seeming not to notice my enthusiasm, "He's got a few people thinking he's nuts but there's something about the Summers kid Rudy actually seems afraid of."

I twisted my lips to one side and gave him an awkward stare. He laughed quietly.

"Don't look at me that way," he chuckled, "You make me feel—exposed. Like you're reading my mind or something."

"What?"

"You have a way with your eyes Jane."

I smiled, taking it as a compliment.

"Really though," he said, "talk to Rudy, and you may want to steer clear of the new kid, he doesn't seem to like anybody."

"Really?" I asked dryly.

"Well, he doesn't seem like he *wants* to like anybody. He's pretty reserved."

I remembered him in the lunchroom by himself, and how Aaron had chosen a seat as far away from him as possible.

"So?" I said, "I'm reserved, too, you know…"

"I know." He answered, "It's different, Jane. Just talk to Rudy."

"I'll talk to him soon," I said, "Becky has a date Friday night and wants me to help her pick out a new outfit, so it looks like I'll be out shopping."

He nodded, "Well—just talk to him when you can."

I nodded.

I was on autopilot the entire drive home, planning my weekend in my head. I really didn't want to talk to Rudy. I wanted to like Aidan, because of how difficult it is for me to get close to people, it's even more difficult to discover when someone is genuine and Aidan had rescued me twice. Once when the shelf in the bookstore almost collapsed on my five foot four body and again in the woods when I sprained the hell out of my ankle. He was so kind and curiously innocent. I didn't want to think about what Rudy would say. Hiding neighborhood kids gone missing in his garage. I laughed at this thought—the quiet, breathy laugh that escapes when I think something should be funny but actually fails to amuse me. Knowing Rudy, that's exactly what he would say.

I didn't like him much as a kid. He was one of Danny's friends. My lovely brother never failed to see the good in people. Rudy just seemed a little—weird. I'm sure I have no right to say that, but weird in a completely different way than myself—superstitious kind of weird. But at the same time it was always nice and fun to be around him. He was a comforting kind of company.

The next day at school I daydreamed through every class. It took me until history when Aaron sat next to me with a huge grin on his face to realize Aidan wasn't there. I was somewhat relieved. Aidan was oddly shy but also very determined to talk to me. I couldn't tell if he actually liked me or was simply intrigued by me as I was by him.

I heard Aaron mumble something.

"Huh?"

He laughed, "You know, you may want to pay closer attention in class, when Mr. Cornally pops a test you're going to be in for it."

I half smiled, "probably."

When I got home, Ethan was in the living room. I heard a grumble and the familiar sound of a bottle cap hitting the T.V.—sports.

"Dad?" I called.

"Oh, you're home."

"Yeah," I opened the cupboard, "I'm gunna heat up some lasagna, sound all right?"

"Sure kid. Thanks."

I was in a good mood for some reason, perhaps looking forward to the weekend. I didn't even mind cooking. I brought Ethan his dinner in the living room, not even checking to see what he was watching. Whatever it was, his team was losing.

I slept well that night. Aidan wasn't at school that Thursday and after school I changed into my comfortable clothes, prepared for a long day shopping with Becky. Shopping was definitely not my thing but it couldn't be all bad; I could do some shopping myself with the money from my mom. A job hadn't even crossed my mind since I arrived. My job back home selling magazines was slightly less than ideal, considering I hated people—didn't especially like magazines either.

V

Shopping

"I'M driving." I said to Becky.

She laughed, "I do *not* think so."

"Okay, Becky," I started, "you're going shopping and *dragging* me with you—I'm driving."

She sighed but smiled, hopping out of her red truck and into my tiny car.

"I should be driving," she said, switching on the radio, "You don't even know where we're going."

"I will once you tell me."

She directed me to Pony Village Mall, across the street from the school. I tried to avoid the huge sign reading, "Used Books," and followed Becky into some clothing store, with a name I didn't even bother to read. She tried on several different outfits, mixing and matching but after an hour she still hadn't found anything that suited her.

Surprisingly enough I had a good time, and got a little shopping done myself. Becky eventually settled for a pair of dark, tight-fitting blue jeans, and a red, strapless evening top that brought out her gray eyes and accented the red highlights in her brown hair.

"You look great!" I told her, and I meant it. After all, she had a beautifully shaped body.

We stopped at the little coffee house across from the store. As I expected, Becky flirted with the waiter, trying to get free food. He didn't seem interested.

"My name is Rodger," he said, "I'll be your server tonight."

"Rodger huh?" Becky sang, looking up at him and cocking her head slightly, "I'm Becky, I'd like to serve you—Sunday night if you don't mind."

The blood rushed to my cheeks *Oh good god, Becky—for one night could you NOT be yourself.*

"How about we just start you off with something to drink instead."

She sighed and nodded.

I ordered water, making eye contact only enough to be polite. He smiled at me and locked his gaze into my own. As soon as he left, Becky instantly complained.

"How do you do that?" she asked.

"Do what?" I answered, opening my menu.

"He was *totally* checking you out!"

"Oh please!" I chocked, "Maybe if you weren't so forward guys would find you more—unattainable. Guys like that."

"I'm not a slut, you know."

I burst into laughter, "Oh god, Becky, I know that. I wouldn't be friends with you if you were."

She nodded. "So—chicken sounds good."

"You always say that," I answered laughing.

"Well, chicken always sounds good."

The waiter didn't make eye contact a single time the rest of our stay. It was actually a relief.

We went back to my place and Becky stayed for a few minutes, answering Ethan's questions about school since I wasn't.

The plans for Saturday were to not have plans. Maybe I could actually try to talk to Ethan over dinner or something. Friday was a typical day at school. I listened to Becky's chatter about her date later that night that she apparently couldn't wait for, and ignored her snapping pictures of me whenever I happened to chuckle at something she said. When I got home I caught up on some homework and went to bed early.

I awoke the next morning, absolutely thrilled to see the sun shining through my window. I raced down stairs in a much better mood than Ethan had expected, he was home reading the paper.

"The sun's out!" I sang, pouring a bowl of cereal.

He looked up from his paper smiling. "You seem overly happy about that."

"It's been a while." I laughed.

"So what's Becky up to today?" he asked.

I smiled, "Not sure" I answered, "I was just thinking about running down to Albany's to do some reading and catch up on some homework."

He nodded.

"I won't be home late." I said.

"Sounds good, honey."

I realized that when I was willing to talk to my dad, he wasn't nearly as nosey, I guess he figured when I didn't talk to him I was up to something. I ended up at Albany's and took Aaron's advice about paying closer attention to our History assignments. I brought my book and read through the chapters and lectures I had daydreamed through. The coffee on the table shuddered and I realized that the chair across from me was no longer empty. I smiled.

"I knew I'd find you here." She laughed.

I looked up from my book. "How was it?"

"What? Oh—Anthony?"

"Yeah—your date, how'd it go?"

"Oh it was perfect."

"Really?"

"Yeah, if you enjoy human suffering."

I tried not to laugh. "Oh no."

"I don't even know how to describe him."

"That bad?"

"Well you know me, Jane, and you know how much I love theatre."

I nodded.

"Well—he did too, so he tried to convince me into being in one of his—*films*."

"I don't understand," I said, "Sounds like a good opportunity for you."

"Umm—not *that* kind of film."

I was silent for a moment until it processed. "OH!"

"Yeah," she sighed, "he didn't tell me he worked for *that* industry."

I sighed, "Well what did you say?"

"Simply told him I wasn't interested, for some reason, he seemed surprised."

I raised my eyebrows.

"Yeah I come across as forward," she said, "But I have more self respect than that. I can get pretty self conscious sometimes."

I smiled lightly. "We all do, Becky."

We ordered coffee and Becky went on about Anthony, letting me leave my non-existent love life out of the conversation. I thought a lot about Aaron and was in a way hoping that Becky could spend a little more time with him, maybe even like him. He was her age after all and pretty decent. Becky always found the "wrong guys," such as Anthony, a few years too old for her and in the adult entertainment industry. She would be happy with a guy like Aaron.

I watched as Becky licked at the whipped cream from her coffee, getting it all over her face, which caused her to curl and twist her lips.

"Becky, stop it!" I snarled, "That guy over there is looking at you. You don't want to give him the—right idea."

She laughed but I wasn't joking. I handed her a napkin.

"You know, Jane—you should lighten up a little."

"Lighten up?" I demanded feeling slightly insulted.

"I'm sorry," she said, "That came out wrong, what I mean is—well maybe you should get out more."

"What do you mean?"

"There's a—party."

"No way!" I interrupted, "No way, Becky, no parties!"

"Come on, Jane." She pleaded, "Just one party. Just make an appearance it won't be so bad. It's Halloween time. You love Halloween."

I shook my head and sipped at my coffee. "I don't know," I said, "I don't think so."

"Come on," she continued. "My little bookworm…? For me?"

"I'll think about it," I said, "But don't hold your breath."

"You've never even been to a party so how do you know you won't like it?"

I chuckled "Well, that part is true," I said, "The last party I went to you were turning eleven."

We both laughed.

"Well I'll call you," she said smiling, " It's Andrew Gallagher's party."

I hesitated for a moment "Who?"

"He sits across from me in History."

"Oh, dark hair? Usually half covered with that gray baseball cap?"

She laughed, "Yeah it used to be blue."

"Yeah. don't count on it."

"Okay, okay, I'll just call you tomorrow, but right now I gotta get home to finish up some homework of my own."

I nodded and she leaned over and kissed my cheek.

"Don't waste away into your mind now Janie."

Being interrupted by Becky never bothered me, but when I was interrupted again, I was horribly annoyed.

"Jane?"

I looked up from my book. It took me a moment to recognize him. His face had lost most of its roundness and his hair was a shade darker than I remembered, and slopped with hair gel.

"So good to see you. Do you not remember me?"

At last I smiled and nodded.

"Of course I remember you. Anyway, you look so different!"

He laughed. "Not *that* different."

I closed my book and leaned forward a little, still smiling. "Gosh, Rudy, how are you?"

"I've been good," he answered, "I haven't seen you at school at all yet."

"Yeah." I answered.

"You're a reader, I see."

"Always kind of have been," I said, "just never cared as much when I had Danny to keep me company."

He frowned, "Yeah," he answered, "Sorry about that. When I heard I locked myself in my room for days."

I nodded. Trying to hide the pain.

"Sorry," he mumbled, "I'll change the subject. I'm actually glad I found you here," he said, "Aaron Raines said something about you being friends with the new kid."

"Friends?" I asked, "Aidan Summers hardly talks to anybody. He's more reclusive than I am."

"Haven't you talked to him at all?"

"Not really," I said, "But Aaron seems to highly dislike him."

He laughed, "Yeah, people have been talking."

"People?" I asked "Or you? Because Aaron said…"

He interrupted me with his laughter, which seemed loud and unnecessary. "Aaron says a lot," he answered, "But in this case he's right—I certainly have my suspicions."

"What kind?"

"Just that something isn't right with the new kid."

I sighed. He had a name. "Aidan." I said.

"Yeah whatever, he just seems…" he paused and pulled his lips to one side, trying to find the right word, "odd?"

"Odd?" I mumbled, "That's hardly a crime." And hardly a reason to be afraid of him, as Aaron had said.

"I don't know," he said, taking the seat across from me as if he didn't hear what I said, "My grandfather used to tell me stories as a kid. My mom always hated how he did that. But I loved his stories so much."

"What kind of stories?"

"There was this one he would tell me over and over. The legend of The Hunters."

"What does the legend say about hunters?"

His voice lowered to an extremely serious tone. "The legend *is* the Hunters," he started "I'm not talking about men in hats and boots shooting deer."

I didn't respond.

"The Hunters are said –well by my grandfather at least, to have certain—abilities."

"Such as?"

"Such as extremely keen eyesight in the dark like a wolf or a cat."

I just stared, suddenly intrigued.

"Their eyes tend to be electric looking, like a piercing color of blue, green or gold."

I smiled. "I like stories like this."

"Well that's the thing," he said, "I don't tell these stories for entertainment. I tell them as more of a warning."

I looked at him solidly and my eyes narrowed, "what?"

"I think these stories hold truth. I think the hunters may actually exist and the most frightening part is what they hunt."

"What *do* they hunt?"

"Us," he said, "Humans."

Again my eyes narrowed. *He's got a few people thinking he's nuts.*

"Are you saying that Aidan…" I paused, "Rudy, come *on*."

"Please, Jane," he retorted, putting his hand up, "I thought of all people, at least *you* would believe me."

"Ok—I'm weird, Rudy," I said, "not crazy."

I picked up my books and stormed quickly out of the bookstore. He didn't follow.

Becky's suggestion about Andrew Gallagher's Halloween party was beginning to sound like a good idea, anything to get my mind off Aidan and the things I didn't want to think about. Aidan may be different, but he wasn't some nocturnal monster. Rudy now had *me* thinking he may be a little nuts.

Becky called me like she said she would.

"So is there anything I can do to convince you to come to Gallagher's party with me?"

"Actually, Becky, I was thinking about it—it might be fun."

"Really?"

"Really," I laughed, "Don't sound so surprised."

She chuckled quietly, "You were just so sure earlier that you didn't want to go."

"I guess I changed my mind," I said, "I'll drive over myself, in case I want to leave."

"Sure." She said, "See you later tonight then."

VI

The Party

    I was actually looking forward to this party, I always loved getting dressed up. It was fun to be someone different for a night. I was just a little concerned about Becky. Hopefully she would cover most of her lovely curves. I dug through a few more of the boxes in my closet, still not completely unpacked. I found the costume I had worn a few years ago. It had been a while. I went through a time when I believed that Hallows Eve should be respected for the true holiday that it was, but though I still felt that way I was at the point where I was able to have fun like most people.
    I lied in bed and read for a couple of hours until Becky called. She was coming over to help me with my makeup as if she actually expected me to care.
    "You're so beautiful, Jane," she said, "You really should express the fact that you realize it."
    "Realize it?" I laughed, "Who said I realize anything? I'm average, Becky, and I'm okay with that."
    "You're hopeless."
    I was dressed before she got there in my tight black corset and knee length black skirt. I added the fishnet stockings and the red high heels that matched my red hooded cape. I opened the door and Becky smiled.
    "Wow," she said, "You look amazing." She hugged me.
    "Wow yourself." I said smiling.
    She was dressed in a red, tight fitting tank top with sparkly red bra straps slightly showing. She had on matching red, velvet pants that flared at the bottom,

clunky platform shoes and red devil horns. She was covered and still beautiful.

I let her do my makeup like she wanted. She was having a ridiculous amount of fun with the cat eyed contacts she had bought me and the false, sparkly eyelashes.

"From innocent little bookworm, to evil sexy vampire."

I laughed. "Vampire?"

"Sure," she said, "What were you planning to be?"

I chuckled, "I honestly don't know."

"Well here," she started, handing me a box she had in her purse, "tooth caps," she said, "The glue never works right so I bought you some denture paste, it doesn't taste too bad to be honest."

"Oh god, Becky, you bought me fangs?"

"Yeah but—not the silly plastic ones you can't talk with."

I smiled, "okay."

She was going a little too far. She had even painted swirled designs around my left eye with eyeliner and silver glitter.

"Oh yeah." She said reaching into her purse again.

I shook my head, what now? She handed me a fake velvet chocker with a plastic spider charm. It actually looked really neat once it was on. I stood up and looked in the mirror of my vanity I never used. I heard Becky snap a picture.

"Oh my god, you didn't!"

She laughed, "lighten up," she said, "You look great!"

Becky turned her hair into a beautiful mane of light brown curls, and had the tips temperately dyed red to match her costume. Her eyelids were covered in red glitter and her lips were painted the same color. She even added the designs around her eye with red and silver.

"Time to go." She announced.

I didn't realize how long it had taken her to get us ready.

"Already?"

"Yeah," she laughed, come on."

"Wait—when is it over?"

She smiled, "Calm down," she said, "for you it's over as soon as you leave, for everybody else it's over when the last person passes out."

I sighed, but smiled, "All right, Becky, promise me you'll be careful."

"You worry too much." She laughed.

"Humor me?"

"Okay," she chuckled, "I promise."

Becky knew the way so I followed her down the dark streets. I drove slowly, nervous over the constant rain. When we finally got there, Becky didn't even wait for me, just rushed over to Jared Emery, her newest crush from her gym class. I guess his body was something to look at because his face wasn't very attractive, it was very narrow and he had a large nose. Becky looked over her shoulder and signaled me to follow. I followed behind, still feeling like people were staring. I eventually lost Becky in the crowd and found myself alone looking for the house. I finally spotted the cement steps leading to the house. They were lit by jack-o-lanterns set on the steps. I gripped the railing, barely able to walk in the heels I had on. I stumbled before the next step, but regained my balance until I put my foot down and realized the heel of my shoe had slipped off. I instantly fell backwards, giving a short cry. I suddenly felt as if metal clamps had closed around my arms. I felt myself lift up and I was set gently on the ground right in front of the porch. I looked up to see who had rescued me.

"You're a walking accident." He said."

"Oh." I breathed, placing my hand on my chest, feeling my racing heartbeat, "Aidan."

I was at the moment, glad to see him. "Quick hands," I said, still gasping for breath.

"Only when there is a need. Are you all right?"

"Fine. Thanks to you."

He flashed me his perfect smile.

"I didn't even know you were behind me," I said.

He didn't respond. I realized at that moment that I was always so distracted by his eyes that I hadn't noticed the rest of his face very much. It had a rounded shape to it but a lovely, masculine build to his jaw line and chin. He had medium brown hair with golden highlights, hanging slightly in his face, but not enough to cover his insanely gorgeous eyes. He smiled at me again and I lost my breath.

"You look—beautiful." He gasped.

I felt myself flush horribly. "Loving the Dracula costume," I said, "we match."

I took a moment to study how the costume hung on his figure. He was slender but with more muscle mass than I had noticed before. The tuxedo he had on looked high quality, and terribly expensive. I tried not to laugh when I noticed an "Allan's party rentals" tag showing at the color of his red, satin lined cape.

He chuckled and held back his cape bowing formally. He actually fit the part flawlessly.

"Vladimir Dracula," he said, with an accent, shattering the English syllables.

I laughed and responded with a curtsy, "Elizabeth?"

He smiled, "You know your history, Jane."

"Sort of."

He was exactly the thing I was here to distract myself from.

"So what's it like in there?" I asked soberly, "anything going to jump out at me when I walk in?"

He smiled in almost a shy way. "I don't think so," he said, "but I just got here less than half an hour ago." He glanced at his watch "I was just leaving."

"Oh?" I was instantly relieved, maybe I could use this party as a distraction after all. "Why?" I asked.

"Well—" he paused, "I don't care for the atmosphere. People here are avoiding me even more than usual if that's possible." The sarcasm in his voice was unsettling, "half the people here have started taking drugs and Andrew is already drunk."

"Oh wow. I'm not sure I want to be here either."

"But Becky...."

"I know," I muttered, "She tried so hard to get me here."

"To be honest, I'm surprised to see you here."

"I'm surprised to see *you* here."

I made eye contact and he smiled, bowing his head. He moved his eyes up to look at me without lifting his head. Pressing wrinkles into his forehead. I noticed he was lacking the fangs so I smiled back, slightly showing off.

"You should stay," he said.

"Why?"

"Well," he laughed almost silently, "They're having a costume contest later and you look so amazing."

I smiled, "Becky would *crush* my hopes." I said "Along with everyone else's."

He laughed, "She looks great I'll admit," he said, "But honestly, Jane, you don't give yourself enough credit."

Costume contest—even more of a reason for people to stare.

"I'll make an appearance," I said, "But I don't plan on staying long,"

"Well," he answered, "Can I at least get you a drink?"

"Sure." I laughed, "Why not right?"

"Right," he said laughing, "Be right back."

I stepped inside, the room was dark and flashing black lights made it hard to see anything, there were people everywhere and I lost sight of Aidan in the sea of skeletons and wolf masks. I tried to tune out the pounding music. I spotted Becky dancing with Jared with a drink in her hand; if you could even call what she was doing dancing. She made me laugh. I looked away when I noticed some guy smiling at me. He walked over to me.

"Hey," he breathed. He smelled like whiskey and marijuana.

I half smiled, trying to hide my nervousness. He was dressed like Indiana Jones. He took off his hat and smoothed back his shoulder length, light hair.

"You wanna dance?" He sounded completely dazed.

"Mmm, dancing really isn't my thing."

"Well—there's an empty bedroom upstairs if you'd like to show me what *your thing is*."

I groaned, disgusted and turned away.

"Oh come on, sweets," he purred, "I'm not gunna hurt you."

Just then Aidan came back with my drink. He noticed I was being bothered but all he had to do was stare at the guy and he got nervous and left.

"Thanks." I sighed and drank the entire cup of punch, which I could easily taste the vodka in.

He laughed, and handed me his, "want another?"

"Oh no thanks," I answered, "I have to drive remember?"

He nodded, "Right."

"I owe you one," I said, "For rescuing me again."

He chuckled, "It was nothing."

I shook my head when I saw Becky, turned partway around, kissing Jared. He fell over and landed on top of her, spilling his drink all over her velvet pants. She stood up laughing. So much for keeping her promise. I'd have to come back later for her. I planned to relax in a café for a while until she was ready to leave. I headed for the door.

"Hey," Aidan breathed, "I don't think I could tempt you into a movie, maybe dinner?"

I forced a synthetic smile. He *had* asked me out. Oh god. I couldn't imagine what it would be like sitting in a restaurant beside someone so beautiful. I would look painfully average compared to him. It made me cringe.

"I don't know, Aidan. It's late."

"You said you owed me," he answered.

"And *you* said it was nothing."

"And we both know you have to come back for Becky."

"Like this?" I waved my hands up and down; reminding him we were in costume, looking for a way out.

"Yeah," he laughed, "We won't be the only people dressed up, it *is* Halloween after all. People dress up at work—good for business." He smiled.

I knew I should say no, but against my better judgment I nodded.

"I'd like that, Aidan."

Damn!

I stepped outside and felt him place his cape over my shoulders.

"You look freezing." He said.

I remembered I was wearing that black corset. "I'm all right." I said. The fact that I could hardly breathe in it had actually made me feel hot.

He walked with me to my car.

"Don't you drive?" I asked.

"Oh I live just a couple blocks away," he said, "I walked here."

"I see." I answered, trying to sound interested in what he was saying.

"I'm guessing you want to drive?"

"Right."

"Do you know your way around?"

"I'll know where to go once you tell me."

He smiled, "Can't argue with that."

I turned on the dome light and pulled down the visor. I used the mirror to take out the contacts and put them back in the case I had left in the glove compartment. I pulled out the fangs, tasting the mint flavored denture paste.

Aidan slipped off his black gloves. It almost looked like he had put makeup on his hands they were so white.

"They're having what they call Flashback Week at the theatre," he started, "showing old horror movies. What did you think of *Halloween*?"

I laughed, "Loved it," I said, "A classic."

He nodded, "sound good?"

"Perfect!"

"You know," I started, "you have an obsession with rescuing me. You're not stalking me, are you?"

He laughed, mirroring my smile and shook his head. "You're different." He said.

"Yeah as if I haven't heard that before."

"No." he laughed, "That's not how I meant it. I meant, different than you were in the bookstore, the first time I rescued you, but—good different."

"You're different too," I said, "but also the same."

"So why did you come to North Bend?" he asked.

"I lived in California but my parents divorced and I couldn't stand living there anymore after my brother died."

"Your brother died?"

I nodded. "Three years ago," I said. My chest burned. "Murdered, and dumped in an alley way."

"I'm sorry." His voice seemed to be caught in his throat, "that's awful. Did they catch the person who did it?"

I shook my head. "The bastard fled. They *still* haven't found him."

He was silent.

"What about you?" I asked, "Why did you come here?"

"My family wanted to move here. For some god unknown reason."

"You don't like it here?"

"Oh the place is fine," he said, "The school is fine too. It's just the people; they seem to find me—intimidating."

I chuckled.

"What?"

"Intimidating doesn't even begin to cover it," I said, "You captivate peoples' attention, Aidan."

"Have I ever captivated yours?"

"You have." I answered, "After saving my life a number of times."

I heard a breathy, silent laugh shake through him. "So—what kind of movies do you like?"

"Scary." I said.

"You're different," he said, "and this time I do mean it that way."

I nodded. "I know."

VII

The Hunters

AIDAN was right. Most everybody who worked at the theatre was dressed up, and I got quite a few compliments on my costume. It was very uncomfortable walking around dressed up, everyone stared. The theatre was mostly empty except for the people working there so that was a relief. The room was dark and lit by lights on the stairs that I still almost tripped on. The red seats were uncomfortable and my shoes stuck to the floor. I would have much rather been at a café—by myself. I daydreamed through the movie to the point where I wasn't even sure what was going on. I had seen it before so it was no big deal. Any questions he asked me about it I could answer without a problem. I kept my eyes on Aidan more than the movie screen. He had that strange stone-cold hardness to his face. His gaze was locked onto the movement on the screen.

After the movie more questions came to my mind.

"So why did you act that way the first day of class?" I asked as we walked out of the theatre.

"I don't think I know what you mean."

I realized immediately by the look on his face and his tone that the question had bothered him.

"Never mind," I said, "It was probably my imagination."

He nodded. "Do you need to get home?"

"I'm tired," I said, "But thanks for getting me away from the party."

He smiled.

"Should I take you home?"

"Back to Andrew's," he said, "I left my jacket there."

I nodded. "Sure. I need to make sure Becky can drive."

He laughed. "I can guarantee Jared can't"

I chuckled. "Oh you saw that?"

"Who didn't see that?"

When we got back to Andrew's, Jared was passed out on the bathroom floor. I helped Aidan carry him to the couch. It took me about ten minutes to find Becky in the crowd. I interrupted her, dancing with some older guy dressed as a Jedi. At least she was conscious.

"Oh, hey," she said, "This is Kyle."

"Kevin," he corrected, lending a gloved hand.

I shook his hand.

"Becky, are you sober?"

She laughed, "You're leaving already?"

I nodded.

"I'll be leaving here soon." She yelled over the music.

"How soon, Becky?"

"I don't know." She said, "Go ahead; I'll call you in the morning."

I sighed, "Kevin. would you…"

"I'll make sure she gets home safe."

I nodded. "Thanks."

I bolted out before anybody could say anything. I turned back around and glanced at Aidan walking down the street in his brown leather jacket, with his vampire cape slung over his shoulder. I started slightly trembling when I remembered we had actually gone out. Why the hell couldn't I say no to him? I wanted to say no, I had tried to say no. Instead I had daydreamed through a movie with him. I couldn't understand how those words had slipped.

I'd like that, Aidan.

Those words weren't even in my head. I tried to worry about Becky my way home, that would have been the normal, logical thing to do, but I couldn't. Aidan crowded my thoughts again. Thankfully I was able to sleep that night, without any nightmares disturbing that sleep, and only woke up because Becky had called me.

"Hey, are you all right?" I asked.

"Depends on your definition of all right."

"Becky!"

She laughed. "I'm fine," she said, "Just one wicked hangover."

"Oh my god." I growled, "I'm coming over."

I drove to her house with some chicken soup and aspirin. She was still in her pajamas with makeup smeared under her eyes. I couldn't understand how she *still* looked attractive.

"Where were you most of the night?" she asked.

Oh god. "Around." I handed her the soup.

"Thanks Janie," She said, "how was your date?"

"What?"

She laughed loudly. "Oh come on! Half the party saw you leave with Aidan and Mr. Jones was pretty upset."

"Mr. Jones."

"Yeah," she laughed, "Mr. *Indiana* Jones."

"Oh god!" I shrieked.

"Ah come on," she laughed, "His name is Mike, and he really isn't half bad when he's sober."

"Becky!"

"Calm down!" she demanded, "I'm not saying I like the guy," she said, "He's a mess and a half, destined for trouble the whole works, I was simply saying that underneath it all he's pretty nice."

"He doesn't like Aidan."

"That surprises you?"

"Well—I guess not. It's nothing new."

"Everybody is intimidated by him, some people are even afraid of him."

I remembered the size of him. He wasn't a big guy, and didn't have much muscle mass.

"Why?"

"I don't really know," she said. "Ask Rudy."

"I did. Do you know what he said?"

"Okay," she laughed, "I was kidding."

"Not funny, Becky."

It was hard to ignore what he had said. I was confused after all and a lot of the things Rudy had mentioned were actually beginning to sound logical. Of course I knew it was ridiculous. Aidan was not a— hunter, but either way there was something about him that I was determined to discover.

I decided to go to Albany's and see if I could find any books on the hunters after no luck with the Internet on Ethan's ancient computer. Every book I found on mythology and creatures of the undead had not one thing about the hunters Rudy had talked about. I found encyclopedias of folklore and myths of creatures such as vampires and werewolves but the only thing I could come up with was that Aidan had some kind of strange life, like gypsies or something. Couldn't I have just thanked him for saving me and leave it at that? I felt so ridiculous buying into such stories. But I was sure that Aidan wasn't behind me at Gallagher's party when I had fallen and I couldn't remember him being anywhere near me when I almost killed myself in the bookstore. Rudy had mentioned something about their eyes but I was beginning to believe that Aidan wore contacts because his eyes often appeared to be amber or sometimes terribly dark. I was dazzled by the striking green, which had to be the work of contacts.

I was more frustrated than necessary, it was becoming an obsession. After seven cups of coffee, I had found nothing but my caffeine limit. I was completely wired. I figured I'd go home and check the Internet again. When I got home, Ethan wasn't there. Probably got called in for some emergency.

I walked to the door with my keys in hand and gasped, realizing the door was open. I stepped inside and heard strange moans coming from the living room. I dropped my keys on the kitchen table and peeked around the corner.

"You won't leave here alive." I heard. The voice was distantly familiar.

"Rudy?"

He turned toward me. His face was twisted into a mask of pure fury.

"Oh my god!" I cried when I saw a boy on the floor. He was bleeding and coughing.

"No, Jane!" Rudy called, "He's crazy, I saw him sneaking into your house. I was trying to protect you."

He grabbed the boy by the neck of his shirt and shoved him against the wall. I swallowed a scream when I noticed it was Aidan with his extraordinary eyes.

"Rudy, what the hell is wrong with you?" I screamed.

Aidan's head was nodding and he was covered in blood. He looked only half conscious.

"Jane, I tried to tell you before, he isn't human."

"What?"

"He's a hunter; you *have* to keep him away from you."

"Rudy, you're my friend," I said, "and I would *hate* to call the cops on you."

"Jane—"

"Get the hell out of my house Rudy. NOW!"

"Jane. please!"

"Three numbers, Rudy, that's all it takes."

"Fine," he growled, letting go of Aidan causing him to slide down the wall and end up on the floor again.

"But do me one favor," he said, "Keep yourself safe. Avoid him."

He stormed off, completely livid.

I rushed to Aidan but he put his hand up.

"I'm fine." He choked.

"Oh my god, Aidan, what's your definition of fine?"

He managed to smile. I helped him to the couch.

"Lie down." I said.

"Really I'm fine."

"Okay, then humor me and lie down."

He obeyed and I went to the kitchen to get him some water and damp rags to clean him up.

"Jane."

I turned to see him standing there.

"Oh for the love of god, Aidan, would you please lie down?" I hissed.

He was covered in blood.

"Jane—look."

He took one of the towels from me and wiped his beautiful face and arms, the blood came off and there were no marks. No bruises, no scratches. I was baffled.

"I could have torn him apart with my bare hands, but all I could think about was you and how you would never forgive me."

Before even asking how or why he had gotten into my house I tried to ask ten thousand other questions, but nothing came out.

"What?" he asked, "What are you thinking?"

"At this point—I'm—trying to figure out—what you are."

He gave me a crooked smile and bowed his head.

"Oh, Aidan," I mumbled and touched his shirt, realizing the fabric was in ribbons.

"Oh." He sounded like he was suppressing laughter.

"Aidan how on Earth do you find this funny?"

"Really Jane, I'm fine."

"What happened?"

He chuckled, "Uh, business end of a garden rake."

"God. What is wrong with him?"

"Actually that was Eric," he said, "I'm guessing Rudy's older brother?"

I nodded.

"It's because of Rudy, Eric is alive. One more swing and I would have killed the guy."

I couldn't answer.

"Thanks," he said smiling, "For rescuing me."

"Aidan, why…?"

He put his hand up and sighed. "I was trying to protect you."

"From?" I asked, "and—why me? Why were you here, you live by Andrew don't you?"

He nodded, "There isn't much to do when people avoid you," he said, "So I walk sometimes. Just to clear my head."

I nodded, "So what do you mean protect me?"

"Your dad left," he started, "Apparently he had forgotten to lock the door."

"What?" I demanded, "No—Ethan would never forget to lock the door."

"He did, Jane," he answered, "I thought I saw a burglar entering your house but when I opened the door that's when Eric came at me with the rake. Rudy stopped him but pulled me inside and starting hitting me—among other things."

I stared open mouthed. "Why would Rudy have been in my house?"

"He was yelling at me telling me I wasn't going to leave here alive," he said, "Saying that I better not hurt you. He thinks we're friends and when he saw me walking down the street I guess he thought I was coming to visit you so when he noticed the door was unlocked he hid inside until I walked by."

"Friends?"

He nodded.

"Are we not friends?"

He smiled, "That's one thing Rudy *was* right about," he said, "You should avoid me."

"Why?"

He sighed.

"You were the one who was so persistent about wanting to know my name. You could have simply done what I asked and left me alone."

He chuckled, "I know," he said, "but I couldn't help myself. I was so intrigued by you. I didn't mean to captivate you that way, or interest you if I have."

"You interest everyone," I whispered, "except maybe for Rudy."

"I'd love to be your friend, Jane, but I don't think Aaron Raines would like that too much."

"Why does *that* matter?"

"Because you don't want to lose him. Be careful Jane—who you rescue."

I tried to respond but he was gone. One second there the next gone.

After everything that had just happened I wanted to walk back into the living room and see him standing there, smiling at me.

"Jane?"

I spun around and thrust my hand to my chest.

Aidan laughed, "I'm sorry."

"You're still here."

He smiled. "I couldn't leave without thanking you properly."

I shuddered as he pulled me into his hard chest and wrapped his arms around me.

"Thank you," he whispered in my ear. I felt his cold, perfect lips touch my check. "If you were to wish it, Jane—you would never see me again."

"I do not wish that." I whispered, my voice hardly coming out.

He smiled and gave me that same formal nod I had seen in the bookstore where he seemed to be bowing and then—he was really gone.

I fell into the soft chair behind me to catch my breath. I could still feel the tingle from his kiss lingering on my skin. I was trembling. I had never felt anything like I felt when I was close to him. But maybe Rudy was right; maybe something wasn't right about Aidan. But he hadn't hurt me had he? He was trying to rescue me again; he was more like a guardian angel than a nocturnal predator.

It looked like Rudy still lived in the same house, I was tempted to go over there and yell some sense into him, but I figured it was better just to calm down first and straighten out my thoughts.

*   *   *

"Wow," she giggled, "Aidan Summers."
"I know."
"So does he like you?"
"I'm not sure. Maybe."
"Do you like him?"

I didn't want to respond, I wanted to keep myself out of the conversation.

"maybe."

I shuddered after answering. She probably knew I was lying. She was all grins; very interested in the gossip she would later get to share.

"Becky, really," I started "I don't even know if I'm going to see him again." Again she knew I was lying, she knew me too well.

When I walked out of class with Becky, Aidan was leaning against the wall with his arms crossed in front of his chest. Becky smiled at me and skipped away.

"Hello." He sang. His voice was once again musical and perfect like it had been the first time I met him.

"Hi." I stammered. I wasn't expecting him to be waiting outside my classroom.

"I have decided to do what I want," he said, "I have decided that I want to be your friend, even if Aaron and Rudy don't like it."

"Good." I answered, "So are you ever going to tell me how you do those insane things you do?"

He chuckled, "What do you mean?"

"Like can you fly with that vampire cape you wore…?"

He laughed loudly but I was only half joking.

"Is that a theory of yours?"

I shook my head. "No." I said, "I don't know what to think."

He shook his head

"At the party," I started, "you weren't standing behind me were you? When I fell?"

"Of course I was."

"I was alone, Aidan," I answered, "How did you know I was in danger?"

"Jane," he sighed.

"I really want to know how you do those crazy things."

"You need to stop listening to Rudy," he chuckled, raising his eyebrows at me.

I sighed. "Probably."

After every class Aidan was there waiting for me. We were mostly silent; I knew he wouldn't answer my questions anyway. People stared obsessively. It was almost like the first day here all over again, or Gallagher's party. I ignored their glances as Aidan walked me to the cafeteria. He sat down and signaled me to sit across from him. I glanced over my shoulder at Becky and Aaron who seemed to be pleasantly debating and kept looking over at me. I sat down and started picking at the chipped nail polish I was wearing.

"So why...?"

"Hold on," he chuckled, "Don't you think it may be my turn to ask the questions Jane?"

"If you can think of one."

"Hmm—well," he paused, "How do you know Rudy?"

I laughed. He was trying too hard, I was painfully boring. "He lives a few houses down," I said, "he was really good friends with my brother when we were kids."

"How old was your brother when—when it happened?"

"Fourteen." I answered.

"You said three years ago," he answered, "That would have made you fourteen."

I nodded. "My twin." I whispered.

He sighed. "I'm sorry," he said, "you ask the questions."

"I was just going to ask why you acted that way the first day of class. You seemed almost—angry at me."

He chuckled. "It wasn't that," he said, "I was just in one of my moods and in some ways I was upset with you for ignoring me but—apology accepted, everything is fine."

I smiled. He was overly charming.

"Also," I started, "those green eyes of yours—contacts right?"

He laughed quietly, "Now why would you think that?"

"They seem—unnatural."

He leaned forward and I shuddered almost thinking he was going to kiss me. I was completely lost in his eyes for a moment, lost in the piercing green color that was clearly natural. I could see the tiny specks of other colors and the refection of myself. I felt Becky's gaze stabbing into my back.

Finally he leaned back and locked his gaze on his folded hands in front of him.

"Wow," I whispered, "some eyes!"

"They often absorb the colors around them, that's why they may sometimes look dark or even violet on occasion as I have been told."

I nodded and smiled. It made sense. Maybe I was just being ridiculous.

"But your cuts," I said, "when Rudy and Eric attacked you."

"The rake didn't cut passed my shirt, I backed away and Rudy really isn't very strong. The reason I looked so dizzy and disoriented is because the smell of blood makes me sick."

"Uh huh." Not possible. There was blood all over him, there had to be at least one tiny mark, one small cut or light bruise, there was nothing.

I started slowly picking at my nail polish again searching for something to say.

"Now what are you thinking?" he asked

"Why do you always want to know what I'm thinking?"

"Well, what good are thoughts with nobody to share them with?"

I smiled.

"It's just that you're always so passive," he said, "It's so hard to read you."

"Can't be that hard."

He chuckled, "Oh it is. You hide so much"

I looked away from his eyes again.

"Like Becky, for example," he started, "She's contemplating coming over here, just to see what's going on."

"How do you know that?" I said not turning around to look at Becky, "Maybe she is just daydreaming about something completely out there."

"Well that's obviously possible but I don't think so."

"How do you know?"

"She's just one of those people," he said, "who is easy to read. You have to admit yourself, Becky isn't really too hard to figure out."

I smiled "But I am?"

He shook his head.

"Why?"

"I don't know."

"I have a question."

"More questions?"

"Well just one—maybe two."

He nodded.

"What were you doing in the woods that night?"

He chuckled, "I told you," he said, "I walk. I don't sleep well so sometimes I just walk all night."

"How did you know how to find me?—um two questions."

He smiled again and dropped his head for a moment.

"And at the party," I said, "and the bookstore."

"That's more than two."

"Aidan…"

"All right, you want the truth?"

"Of course."

"I have this thing—where I can feel when danger is close. When there is a strong possibility that someone may be hurt. I don't know how it happened; it was just— one day I woke up with this odd new feeling. And to think of you being hurt…" he shook his head and lowered it again.

I was silent for a moment. "How does it work?"

He shook his head, "I don't know," he answered, "I usually can't feel it unless it involves you."

"Me?"

"Yes."

"Why?"

He laughed, "You obviously are, as I have said before, a walking accident."

"Just a little clumsy," I answered.

"As an understatement."

I glared at him.

"You know, Jane—my knight in shining armor act shouldn't have made you want to talk to me."

"It didn't," I answered, "*you* talked to *me*, remember?"

"I'm just saying that Rudy was right—well about one thing—you really should avoid me."

"Why?"

"I'm not a very good friend."

I sighed, "Aidan," my face burned when I said his name, "you're strange."

He smiled, "I know," he answered, "But you should, and *that,* to answer one of your first questions is exactly why I acted that way in class."

Again I felt angry over the fact that he affected me so strongly. I tried to ignore.

"Maybe I will then!"

He nodded, "It's probably better for you."

"Okay, so now it's suddenly better for you to *not* talk to me?"

"I'm sorry." He said.

"Don't worry about it," I snapped, "At least you warned me this time, so don't be mad when I don't talk to you."

"It's not that I *want* you to avoid me…"

"Make up your mind, Aidan."

"It's just that it would be best," he said, ignoring my response. "It's just that—well as a person I like you—enough to be good friends, but I would let you down, it's in my nature. So logically you *should* avoid that. I don't want to hurt you."

"Maybe this time I'll do what I should."

"Be careful who you choose to rescue Jane."

I glowered at him and when the lunch bell rang Aidan was gone before I could blink.

Ignoring him proved to be easier than expected. When I didn't speak to him, he didn't speak to me, that simple. He still sat next to me in history, but there was obvious tension and coldness between us. Aaron seemed pleased by that and always took the seat at my other side.

"Do you know if Becky has seen Jared lately?" he asked at the beginning of class before Aidan had taken his normal seat.

"I don't know," I giggled, "After the party they sort of stopped hanging out."

"Oh."

"Why?"

"No reason. Just curious."

"Mm hmm."

"Okay—so I kind of like her."

I smiled. "I kind of hoped you did."

"Did you?"

I nodded, "You'd be good for her. Becky needs a decent guy like you."

"Oh. Well—what about you and Rudy?"

"Rudy?" I cried, "What *about* me and Rudy?"

"Oh I don't know," he said, "he's always liked you."

"I'm not exactly on speaking terms with Rudy right now." I snarled.

"Why?"

"Long story."

He nodded, realizing by my tone that I didn't want to talk about it. I could feel Aidan's eyes on me and I tried to ignore. He was so close that all I would have to do is move a few inches to touch him. I wished I could touch him, wished it would have been normal. He was too perfect—and beautiful—and dark. He was also irritating and confusing. I couldn't believe that I even thought for one second that he could like me. I always knew I was too average for somebody like him, but yet he had rescued me. If it was just that he cared about *people* he would have stayed at Andrew's and watched over Becky, instead—he took me to a movie. I shook off the thoughts of him. Nobody should make me tremble and lose my breath that way, him least of all.

VIII

Miranda

BECKY stopped by after school. She mentioned some girl she had met in her French class, and how fun a shopping trip with her and me would be.

"Becky why would I go shopping?"

"Because I'm your best friend and you love me." She chuckled and batted her eyelashes playfully.

"Well, who is this girl?"

"I told you," she started, "A lot like you in the being shy department."

"I'm not shy," I told her, "I'm reclusive."

"Whatever. Her name is Miranda and she just moved here and doesn't really know anybody so I told her I would take her shopping I was going to see if I could drag you with us."

"Why?"

She averted her gaze staring at my bookshelf.

"Becky," I whined, "no more plotting."

"It's the only way to get you to do anything that involves meeting people."

"I thought you understood that."

"Oh I do," she said, "but this may be more difficult than the party."

"Just tell me."

"It's been really sunny lately—or haven't you noticed?"

My mind had been elsewhere. I hadn't noticed at all.

"And we were thinking about heading down to the mall and buying new swimsuits for a beach trip."

"What? You want me to wear a swimsuit?"

"Yes."

"I don't think so."

"Come on. Jane," she pleaded clasping her hands together "Just come."

"I'll go with you to the beach I'll even go shopping with you I just…"

"No shorts and a T-shirt this time, Jane. Please."

I sighed. I hadn't seen Becky in almost two years and she had given up many dinner dates and movie nights to stay in with me. I guess I owed her.

"Okay," I sighed, "but no bikinis."

She squealed and wrapped her arms around my shoulders.

Miranda was a tiny blonde girl who looked about three years younger than she actually was. She was pretty and chipper like Becky. Her voice was small and high-pitched but not enough to be irritating. They chattered the entire time. They would occasionally toss a few comments at me but I did my best to just smile or use my one-worded answers. I had no idea what Becky meant when she said Miranda was shy. She introduced herself with a hug and a huge grin.

Becky tried on at least seven different bathing suits until she found one she liked. I almost hated how everything looked good on her. She ended up buying a black bikini with white polka dots showing off her new belly button piercing.

I ended up giving into Becky and Miranda when they insisted that I buy the one piece with the holes in the sides. At least it came in my color. I was relieved I could wear red; it was my comfort color, oddly enough since I shied away from attention, but being normal was never something I strived for. My suit was low cut and I kept pulling it up.

"Stop it," Becky laughed, "A little bit of cleavage is a good thing, be thankful you have some."

Miranda was lengthy and thin. She looked great in green, even she kept trying to get me to stop pulling my suit up. I frowned, not wanting to be that exposed. I would already be drawing attention to myself, being with two attractive girls and wearing bright red.

It was still sunny by the weekend and Becky seemed overly thrilled that the beach trip was still on. I was tempted to put on my old pair of shorts and my black tank, but I had to do this one thing for Becky. I put on my red swimsuit and examined myself in the mirror, not unpleased with the way I looked but uncomfortable. I put on a pair of black form fitting sweatpants over the suit at least until we got to the beach. I pulled the top up again and covered my pale skin with sunscreen. I grabbed my towel and headed to Becky's truck.

"Where's Miranda?"

"Meeting us there," she answered.

I nodded. This was not exactly my ideal day off. I hated to ruin Becky's fun so I smiled as often as possible and engaged in conversation. Eventually I forgot about the discomfort I was feeling. That lasted only until I got out of the car and stepped onto the hot sand. Miranda was sitting on the curb waiting for us, her golden hair in a thin bun fastened with a green clip that matched her bathing suit. She was all smiles and chipper. She was as into this as Becky was.

It was sunny and warm but not as warm as it would have been back in California, the sun was still lower in the sky than I expected but the sky was blue instead of that light gray color I was used to. No rain clouds to make me nervous either. It was nice.

I listened to their babble about the newest "hottie" in their French class. My mind was elsewhere. I managed to tune in when I heard Miranda mutter something about how he's a senior. I took the opportunity.

"You know Becky, it wouldn't be too bad to go for a guy your age."

"What do you mean?"

"She has a point." Miranda chimed in.

"Yeah like—Aaron for example?"

"Aaron? As in Aaron Raines?"

"Yeah, what's wrong with Aaron?"

"Well nothing, it's just…"

"Then there's no problem?"

"He's just—a little too—I don't know. Geeky?"

I laughed, "Oh come on, Becky," I demanded, "He's a sweet guy, and he likes you."

"Does he?"

"Oh like it's *not* obvious. Come on!"

She smiled. "I don't particularly like his type."

"Type?" I was almost offended, "What do you mean type? You know Becky most people would consider themselves lucky to have a guy like him."

"Then why don't *you* date him?" she was angry now.

I sighed. "Never mind." That definitely didn't go as planned.

The tension lessoned when I was willing to talk to Becky about things that interested her more, like Jared Emery.

"Oh god," she laughed, almost synthetically, "That guy was so drunk at Gallagher's I'm surprised he remembers me being there. I don't think he remembers knocking me over."

I laughed, "Becky I didn't think *you* remembered that."

"Okay, I wasn't that wasted, Jane."

"You were wasted enough, Becky—definitely."

Miranda joined in, "I didn't hear about that." She sounded like a little girl in a toyshop.

I smiled at her, "Just Becky's wild streak shone a little brighter than usual that night."

"Apparently," Miranda answered, "Would have *loved* to see that."

Becky insisted on staying late and lighting a completely unnecessary bonfire as soon as it got dark, but no rain bothered us even after the sun set.

"You trying to burn down the nearby houses?" Miranda chuckled.

"Oh, this is fun, admit it."

"Sure," I said, "But where are the marshmallows?"

I was only joking but sure enough—Becky had two bags full. Again I sat mostly silent except for an occasional laugh or one word response as Becky and Miranda gossiped. It was only until the subject reached *me* that I joined the conversation—mostly to try and change the subject.

"So did Jane tell you anything about *her* new man?"

"What?" Miranda shrieked out, "No not a thing!"

"That's because I don't *have* one."

Becky was persistent, "But you went out with Aidan, didn't you?"

"It was one time," I answered, "I wanted to leave that awful party and I had to come back to make sure you were all right anyway."

"Aidan?" Miranda cried, "Aidan Summers?"

I nodded.

"Wow," she laughed, "To think..."

"What?"

"Nothing," she answered, "It's just that he's so gorgeous. I was silly to think he'd like me when you were right there."

"WHAT are you talking about?"

"Told you," Becky murmured.

"Told me what?"

"Why do you think people stare, Jane?" she asked, "Because you're from outer space?"

I looked away, staring at the flames and charring wood.

"You're beautiful," she added, "I wish you knew that."

I shushed her, "let's keep me out of the conversation." I said.

She let out a short breathy laugh, "sure sure."

She dropped it there and I daydreamed through her babble, looking for shapes and pictures in the fire. For whatever reason I wasn't seeing Danny's face in the flames like I normally would have—I was seeing Aidan's. I sighed and looked away at the waves. The water was dark and not as beautiful without the sunlight sparkling across it or the sunset reflecting. The fire was much more interesting. Becky was busy taking pictures of Miranda. She posed playfully and took the camera taking pictures of Becky too. Those two were definitely too fun-filled for their own good. I laughed quietly.

"You awake over there, Jane?" Miranda hissed playfully.

I glanced at her and smiled. "Yeah," I said, "But I should be getting home. Ethan won't be happy if I stumble in near dawn."

Becky laughed cheerfully still full of energy like she always was, "Sounds like your dad," she said, "sometimes I wish my mom would tell me no, would at least mean she notices me."

I didn't answer. That topic was uncomfortable for the both of us.

Miranda left after about ten more pictures and a few more hugs. Becky drove me home chattering the entire time. I wasn't listening to much of it.

"I love driving." She said. I had no idea where that comment came from since I wasn't listening but I took the opportunity to reply.

"Really?"

"Yeah, it's relaxing."

"Oh, well I was kind of thinking about a road trip."

She laughed, "You feeling okay?"

"No I'm serious," I laughed smacking her arm, "I mean, not *just* for fun, I wanted to go visit my mom."

"OH," she answered, "That sounds more like you."

"Hey, I'm not *that* boring, Becky."

"I didn't say you were boring," she giggled.

"Well, what do you think?"

"When?"

"Winter break. You can spend Christmas with us."

She smiled wide, "Great! I'd love to."

I wondered when was the last Becky had a real Christmas. I decided not to ask.

"Can't wait to wake up Christmas morning in California."

I smiled, "It not like it would be snowing." I laughed.

"Not entirely my point," she answered, she wasn't smiling anymore, "I've just always dreamed of waking up to the smell of apple pie and cider, to the sounds of Christmas music from the stereo in the other room—anything like that."

"I guess my family's more normal than I thought."

She laughed, "Your family defines normal, even if *you* don't."

I laughed, "Glad you're excited."

Becky stayed over and we were up half the night planning our road trip. She seemed even more excited about it than I was.

"What should I get for your mom?" she asked still smiling as usual.

"I'm not sure; I'll take care of that."

She laughed, "No, I want to get her something that's *only* from me."

I giggled and shook my head, "suit yourself."

"So—does your mom make apple pie and eggnog and cook ham and all of that."

"Yes."

"That's so amazing. Does she still do the whole stocking thing, or are you too old for that now?"

I laughed again, "To my mom, I'll always be six."

She almost started jumping up and down, it was so funny. I wished then I invited her over for Christmas before.

We would have to leave before Christmas Eve to make it there in time, meaning I wouldn't even spend that night with Ethan. I was sure he would be celebrating with his work buddies and the Thompsons, so I wasn't too worried about leaving him. He didn't seem at all surprised, I didn't even have to tell him.

I served myself dinner silently as I always did.

"So," Ethan started, always the first to break the silence, he sipped his coffee then continued, "Are you going to spend Christmas with your mom?"

It was almost like a sudden relief but I didn't tell him I had already planned on it. It was good to know I wouldn't have to break the news to him and hurt his feelings.

"I was thinking about it." I said. "What do you think?"

He smiled, "I won't be alone if that's a worry of yours."

It wasn't.

"But," he continued, "If you do want to stay here this year, I wouldn't tell you no."

I smiled, "Mom wants to see me, and I think Becky would like to come along."

He smiled, "Great, that girl needs a friend like you."

I nodded. "I know."

IX
Winter Break

BECKY and I had decided to leave the 22nd that way we would make it to my mom's by Christmas Eve so Becky could wake up to the smells of Christmas like she was dreaming about. We took my car and for the first hour of driving Becky didn't once hold still.

"Is your mom mad?" I asked.

"What?"

"Your mom," I repeated, "Is she mad you're leaving her?"

"No," she laughed, "Of course not she's with her new boyfriend, Cal or Carl or whatever his name is. She goes through them so fast I can't keep track."

Becky must have been getting a bit of that from her mom.

"Just making sure I'm not causing any waves doing this for us."

She smiled, "It's worth it even if you were."

I laughed silently. I started imagining what it would be like to be back home for a while with my mom. I couldn't hold in the smile, I was more excited than I realized. I hadn't noticed before how much I missed her.

* * *

The drive was brutal, Seventeen hours and clearly we didn't have time to stop for longer than a few minutes at a time. We stopped at a gas station to fill up and grab a few snacks.

"I think it's my turn now," Becky said laughing. "To drive."

I had been driving for six hours I was more than willing to let her. "Thanks."

I fell asleep in the passenger's seat while Becky drove but every bump she hit would jolt me back awake.

"Jane, look!" she yelled.

I bolted up to see a sign saying *CA 300 miles.* She woke me up for *that?* I put my head back again and tried to get some sleep.

Becky was like a rock when I took over driving again. Nothing woke her up. So the road trip wasn't going to be the fun part of this plan. I kept my focus on my mom hoping it would take my mind off the cramping in my legs.

Leaving in the evening proved to be a good choice, it looked like we would get there about 10:00 in the morning Christmas Eve.

"Becky." I said loudly enough to wake her up. She barely even stirred. "Becky! We're here!"

She bounced up instantly. "What?" she groaned, "We're still on the freeway." She rolled her head back down against the head rest.

"For about fifteen minutes," I said.

"Really?"

She didn't even sound tired anymore, all of her energy instantly returned.

"Oh I can't *wait* to meet your mom," she said, "I can't wait for Christmas dinner. Oh it's going to be so fun."

"Oh yeah," I laughed, "Right up until my mom pulls out the family albums."

She laughed, "Oh that's going to be the best part."

"Thanks," I joked, "That's encouraging."

It was like my mom had a time clock perfectly in her head and ran out to the parking lot as soon as she saw the car pull up. She didn't wait two seconds before pulling me as hard as she could into a hug.

"Mom." I choked out, "Have you slept at all?"

She laughed and let me go. "You must be Becky." She said.

"Nice to meet you." Becky said chipper, lending my mom her hand.

"Oh don't be silly," my mom said, "You're practically family." She gave Becky a hug that looked just as tight as the one she gave me.

My mom grabbed the bags out of the trunk and never once stopped smiling. "I'm so glad you're here."

"So am I." I told her, "I promised to visit and here I am."

"Oh but it's better than that," Becky chimed in, "Here *we* are—on Christmas Eve."

I laughed, "True."

"You look tired." My mom said, "Take a nap and I'll wake you up in a bit."

"Oh there is no way we could go to sleep." Becky yelled, "This is too exciting."

She was running all over admiring the bells and wreathes my mom had put up. She even had to touch all the little ornaments on the tree and climb up and down the stairs looking at the garland my mom had wrapped around the banister.

"Speak for yourself," I chuckled, "You were passed out for over eight hours."

She just turned and smiled at me, following my mom into the living room.

The smells brought me back and I instantly felt a sense of comfort and happiness wash over me.

"I hope you don't mind if I take a nap," I said to Becky.

"Not at all, I was just about to ask your mom to show me some old photo albums."

I stuck my tongue out at her, but she just laughed. "Would it be okay if I used your shower first?" she asked.

"Of course." My mom laughed, "You don't need to ask."

I led Becky upstairs and showed her where the bathroom was, I talked to my mom for the hour Becky was in there. We talked mostly about school but nothing too important.

"How's your dad?"

"Oh he's great to tell the truth," I said, "Didn't seem disappointed or surprised that I was leaving him on Christmas."

"Well that's a relief," she laughed.

Becky came down stairs in a pair of sweat pants and a black tank. "You know it's a little colder than I expected from California."

I laughed, "It's Winter."

"Thanks Jane," she said sarcastically, "I wasn't sure of that."

I laughed, "Come here in the summer," I said, "You'd kill to be cold."

We sat on the couch looking at old pictures until my eyes felt too heavy to stay open.

"I'm going to take a shower myself," I said, "Then I'll be in my room."

"Okay Honey. I'll wake you up in a bit."

"Thanks."

My room was exactly the same, except everything was empty. The old bed sheets hadn't changed, it was still the purple and pink floral and the pale pink curtains were still up as well. I decided to focus on my room after I got some sleep, that way I could enjoy it more.

My mom came in and woke me up around six.

"Jane? You want something to eat?" she asked peeking inside.

"Oh my gosh!" I said sleepily "I would. Thanks. Did you have a nice talk with Becky?"

She laughed, "For about an hour until she fell asleep on the couch."

I smiled. "Figured."

I woke Becky up and told her it was dinner time.

"Great," she said stretching, "Did your mom cook?"

"Of course." I laughed.

My mom had to ask if Becky wanted anything else to eat.

"No favorites," she answered, "anything is fine."

"Fried chicken is fine then?"

She laughed, "I love chicken."

"Perfect."

"Come on," I said, "I already have the table set."

"This is like a story book." She whispered.

"What are you talking about?"

"You sit at the table for dinner," she said, "It's not like that at my house. We fend for ourselves and I usually eat in my room."

"Well this is the way our family eats so it's the way you'll eat." I smiled.

"Did you just call me family?"

I laughed. "Come on, Becky, like you didn't know I always saw you as my sister."

She laughed, "I love this place."

After dinner my mom let me open one gift from her.

"Tradition," I told Becky, "One gift on Christmas eve and the rest in the morning."

"The rest?"

I laughed, "My mom has this tendency to buy me a million gifts."

"And don't think I forgot you, Becky." She said.

"No way!" Becky squealed, "You got me a gift?"

"More than one," she said, "Open this one."

She handed her a red bag. Becky practically tore through it to find a beautiful red sweater.

"I wasn't sure of your favorite color," she said, "I know Jane likes red, I thought you might too."

"I love it," she said, "it's so beautiful."

She put it on right away over her black tank top. "Oh and it fits." She said. I could tell she was trying not to cry. I didn't realize how touched she must have been. I felt selfish for not realizing how wonderful I had it.

My mom gave me a long crushed velvet dress. It was black with red around the neckline and cuffs.

"I want to see you in something a bit more—feminine this year." She said.

"Thanks," I said and leaned over to hug her, "I love it."

And I did, as much as I hated dresses, I would definitely wear it for her.

In the morning Becky came in my room to wake me up.

"Jane!" she yelled, bouncing on the bed, "Jane, wake up! It's Christmas." It reminded me of Danny when we were little. So much I almost heard his voice instead of hers.

"Becky it's barely light outside."

She laughed, "The sun came op an hour ago," she said, "get up."

I rolled over and smiled at her still with my eyes closed. "You are unbelievable." I said.

"So we have to open presents in our pajamas right?" she shrieked, "Then get dressed for Christmas breakfast and Christmas dinner and Christmas guests."

I just started laughing. "Don't get too excited," I said, "We don't have many guests coming over."

"That's okay," she said, "I'm having my first real Christmas, I won't be picky."

I smiled and crawled out of bed. Becky raced through brushing her teeth and barely pulled a comb through her hair before racing down the stairs to see my mom still rearranging the stockings by the fireplace.

"You're up early." She sang.

"Thank Becky for that." I groaned walking down the stairs slowly. My mom laughed.

"Are you going to fall asleep between gifts Jane?"

I smiled. "Hope not."

The stockings were stuffed with candy, makeup, gloves, socks and other things my mom thought I would like. Becky was ecstatic. She poured everything out and plowed through it like a child. She made me laugh.

We opened about five gifts each, mostly clothes and of course my mom had to continue to restock my bookshelves. Becky gave her about ten hugs and kept giggling and tearing through packages.

"You know we got something for you mom." I said.

"You did?"

"Oh my god!" Becky yelled, "I can't believe I forgot. I'll be right back. She raced upstairs and came back down with a green gift bag and a package.

"This one's from Jane," she said handing her the bag.

I had bought her a red sweater. Funny, it was almost the same one she bought for Becky.

"Oh I love it," she said, "Now we can match."

Becky laughed, "Okay now open mine."

Not even I knew what she had bought. She wouldn't tell me.

"I wrapped it myself."

I had never seen my mom's face light up the way it did when she saw what Becky had done for her, I thought she was going to cry.

"It's a scrap book," Becky said, "That's Jane, her first day in North Bend. I don't remember what she was laughing at."

"Probably you." I teased.

She flipped through all the pages of pictures as Becky explained what was going on and who our friends in the background were.

"There are a lot of blank pages," she said, "So you can continue it later on."

My mom smiled and hugged her, "I don't know what to say."

"Say you like it," Becky answered still sounding happy and cheerful.

"Like it?" she choked, "I love it, it's beautiful. Sort of like a gift for all of us."

"Did I steal your thunder, Jane?" she whispered. She wasn't smiling though; she actually sounded worried.

"Don't be silly," I said, "I'm glad you can make my mom react that way."

She smiled and sighed, "Good. So am I."

We didn't have many guests over like I told Becky. Mr. and Mrs. Hunter from next door stopped by for a while and brought us cookies. My mom's old friend Leslie stayed for dinner. I hadn't seen her since I was about ten. She had to go on and on about how big I got and how beautiful and grown up I looked. Becky jabbered the whole time and couldn't get over how good the breakfast quiche was. Immediately after breakfast she was looking forward to Christmas ham with all of the other things she dreamed of. I loved doing this for her. I knew next year had to be like this too.

We stayed four more days after Christmas and Becky stayed in the guest room but would sneak through the hallway and come into my room anyway. She would just sit with me and talk until we fell asleep. It was like really having a sister. I wished we could just adopt her. She and her mom would probably both be happier that way. I brushed off the thoughts, it wasn't a logical idea.

I was dreading the drive back home but kept my mind off of it by visiting with my mom as much as possible. We spent the last few days with her expanding the scrap book Becky started. I had a lot more fun with it than I thought I would. My mom promised she would put all the Christmas pictures in and send us copies for our own books.

X

Five Dozen Roses

BECKY was fidgeting with the radio while trying to drive.

"Becky, stop that." I hissed, "Keep your eyes on the road."

"I'm fine, Jane." She said, but didn't switch the station again.

It was getting warmer outside and even in the car I could feel it. California was never as cold as it should have been in the winter, I'd never seen snow. Despite it all I was enjoying the warm weather anyway and leaned my head back and closed my eyes. I thought sleep was impossible on a bumpy freeway but I ended up completely unconscious for quite a while and when I awoke Becky was switching the radio stations again.

"Here," I said, reaching over, "Tell me what you want and I'll switch the stations, keep your eyes on the…" A loud sound interrupted and I turned just in time to see a truck collide into the front of the Aveo and to hear Becky scream, just before my vision went dark.

When I awoke, at first there was no sight. Smell yes. The smell of smoke, leather and gasoline. For a long time I couldn't open my eyes.

"Becky?" I tried to say but my voice was muffled, nothing was coming out. "Becky." I tried again. Still nothing. I couldn't hear her breathing, I couldn't hear her crying, I couldn't hear her at all, and I still couldn't see anything. I tried with every ounce of strength I had left to pry my eyes open.

It was then that I finally came to and instantly felt the blood rush to my head. I noticed with great shock that I was hanging by my seatbelt upside down in a completely thrashed Aveo. I tried to call Becky's name again but still no sound came out.

I looked down to the black seatbelt tightened around my body and pushed in the red button. I fell hard onto the roof of the car. I tried to calm my heart and stop my tears as I crawled through the broken window of the car. I took one deep breath and pulled with all my strength across the glass which had been blocking my way out. Pain ripped up my chest but I kept pulling until I found myself lying on the cracked road with the sunlight dancing over the hills and trees around me. I tried again to call for Becky but before I got the chance, I lost consciousness still with her name the last thing I tried to say.

I roused to a beeping sound, a constant rhythmical beeping sound. It was almost maddening. I couldn't open my eyes, though I tried over and over again. Where was Becky? Where was I?

"How is she?" I heard. It was female voice, one I didn't recognize.

"She'll be all right," a man replied, "She's suffered a minor head injury, a few cuts and scratches, mostly from the broken glass other than that, nothing too serious."

It took me long minutes to remember the last thing I saw. A blue truck and my arms in front of my face. The last thing I heard, a loud bang and Becky screaming. The car crash, the shattered window, and Becky. My God, where was Becky?

"I'm so sorry." I heard. That voice I knew, I would know anywhere. Thank God. I tried to open my eyes. I pulled them open only enough to see a blurry vision of her face.

"Jane!" She was crying.

"Becky."

"Oh god you're awake."

"Becky."

"I'm so sorry." she took my hand, "I'm so sorry, the truck came out of nowhere, I didn't even see it—I—."

"It's ok." I said.

"Are you hurting?"

"I'm fine." I couldn't feel anything yet.

"I was so scared for you Jane." She said, her voice still trembling "They wouldn't let me see you until they bandaged me up."

"Am I...?"

"You hit your head," she answered my unasked question, "But you will be fine. They promised me you will be fine."

"They?"

"The doctors," she said, "Where do you think we are?"

I saw she had a bandage on her for head and bloody piece of gauze wrapped around her left hand. I moved my sight passed her and realized I was in a white room on a white bed. I closed my eyes and moved my hand to my forehead. Oh god. I tried to sit up but could only make it a few inches. I was defiantly in a hospital room.

"Someone brought you roses," she said, "More roses than I'd ever seen."

"Did you tell anyone?" I asked.

"Rudy called," she said, "I told him. He's coming to pick us up. Your car is—well…" she paused. "I didn't tell anyone else." She retorted.

"The car is what, Becky?"

She sighed, "Not exactly—drivable."

"Oh, man, Ethan is going to *kill* me!"

"Jane, I'm so sorry…I…"

"Becky, never mind," I said, "I'm not too worried about that right now, we are both alive, that's what's important."

She nodded.

"So did Rudy send the flowers?"

"I don't know," she said, "Unless he told someone, it would have to have been him. Here." She handed me a red envelope. In it was a white card with red roses on it. It had beautiful handwritten words.

Jane,

Feel better. I want to see you at least one more time. I'm sorry about the roses, I couldn't resist. I hope you like them. Love,

Aidan.

Aidan? Aidan sent me roses.

"Who's it from?" Becky asked, "Rudy?"

"No."

"No?" she questioned, "Really?"

"Really," I answered handing her the card.

"Whoa!" she laughed, "Nice. You made an impression."

"Becky, stop it," I giggled. I noticed laughing hurt quite a bit.

"Sorry," she said, "Are you okay?"

"I'm fine," I said, "I'm a bit sore."

"The car is really a mess but I swear I'll pay for it," she retorted, "I'll do anything I have to; I'll pay for the doctor bill too. Jane…I'm SO sorry."

"Becky it's fine. We're both alive; that's a lot better than where we could be right now. Stop crying, please. You're going to make me cry."

She smiled, "I was just scared for you."

"I know," I said, "I was scared for *you.*"

"For me? Why?"

"I didn't know where you were," I said, "I tried calling for you but I couldn't speak, I couldn't see you or hear you. I didn't know if you were—all right."

She nodded, "I should be the one lying there," she said, "Not you."

"Becky, stop that!" I hissed. I managed to sit up the rest of the way, "The truck came out of nowhere, it wasn't your fault."

She nodded, "You were right though. If I had my eyes on the road it might not have happened."

"Stop blaming yourself, honey; it's all going to be okay."

"Take a look at your gift," she laughed.

I looked around and saw what Becky meant by more roses than she had ever seen. She meant it. They were everywhere around the room in ten different vases. There were at least sixty. My god, if he couldn't resist couldn't he have settled for one dozen rather than—five? Becky smiled.

"I know what you're thinking," she laughed, "He went a bit too far right? But it was sweet. He likes you."

"Yeah—maybe."

"I'm making you take at least one vase full home with you, and the card, too."

I Smiled. "You're hopeless."

She mirrored my smile and shook her head "You feeling okay?"

"I told you already, I'm fine," I said, "I'm sore but I'm fine."

"Then let's get you out of here."

* * *

They unfortunately made me stay the night in the hospital and Becky insisted on sleeping in the chair beside the bed. It was almost evening when Rudy got there. He had to hug us both about ten times. I groaned.

"Gently, Rudy," I whined, "Please."

He smiled weakly, "My god, I'm so relieved to see you. You shouldn't drive anymore."

"It was me," Becky said, "The truck came out of nowhere, I swear."

"Nobody is mad at *you*, Becky…right?"

I nodded, "Not at all."

Becky had to make sure the radio was turned off. I wasn't able to sleep; all I could think about was how mad

Ethan would be and the throbbing in my bandaged arm was very uncomfortable. I wouldn't have been able to drive.

When I got home I thanked Rudy about a hundred times and gave him a kiss on the cheek before he headed home.

Ethan was already sleeping. I cleaned up the plate and cold noodles left on the table. I guess I had forgotten about the fact that my dad would have to have dinner by himself. Becky stayed over and we talked about how we would break the news to Ethan in the morning. She insisted on accepting full blame. She stayed the night so we could both tell him in the morning. I was more tired than I expected to be and it wasn't difficult for me to fall asleep quickly.

It was a relief that my dad took it so well. There was no yelling.

"Well, thank god you're both all right." That was the first thing he said.

He also said he'd let me drive the old Camry that had been sitting in the garage for about a year, but if *anything* happened to it, I wouldn't be driving anymore.

"It really wasn't her fault," Becky said, "Really it wasn't. It was my fault."

Ethan nodded and put his hand up. "All right," he said, "You both need to be more careful."

I couldn't stand talking about it anymore and just spent the rest of the day in my room to rest. I was still very sore and tired. I was hoping to feel better the next morning.

XI

The Clearing

THE entire next week at school I never once stopped thinking about Aidan. In history class I tried not to glance over at him when I felt him staring at me. I turned my face away but my ears burned and my cheeks were flushed.

It would be for the best.

What could that mean? So he wasn't a very good friend—obviously I didn't mind. I didn't expect that from many people. I tried to focus in class with a little bit of success, more success than expected. It still bothered me that he didn't want to talk to me and I knew I shouldn't be complaining. This is what I had wanted in the first place and if I got any closer to him I would only end up hurt in the end. But he also sent me roses, five dozen roses. And the fact that Rudy didn't tell him had me even more confused. I sat silently through lunch listening to Becky's babble about the guy in her French class flirting with her. I smiled and tried to act amused, she wasn't fooled.

I glanced over at Aidan and chocked on my breath when I saw that his table was empty. For some reason the cafeteria seemed very still and quiet. It felt very normal. Aidan was like a rose in a field of weeds and without him nothing was quite as beautiful. Everything in the room was hazy.

"Are you okay?"

I turned to Aaron and cleared my throat. "I'm fine."

"Are...?"

"I'm sure, Aaron," I retorted, putting my hand up, "I'm fine."

But I wasn't fine. I was confused and frustrated. I wished I could just forget about him. When I got home I locked myself in my room and ended up falling asleep. Ethan didn't even wake me up for dinner. A knocking at my window is what woke me up near dawn, according to my slightly off digital clock on my nightstand. From the series of strange dreams that had disturbed me that night I felt extremely anxious. I stared at my window almost wishing there was somebody there so at least I would know what I was up against. I heard the sound again and I jumped when a shadow skipped across my ceiling. I realized it was the wind slapping the tree branch against my window. I felt ridiculous. I sighed and rolled over but couldn't get back to sleep.

I closed my eyes and pictured Aidan. Suddenly I felt unnaturally lightheaded and tired, and that—was the first night that I dreamed of him.

It was like being lost in the woods again, only I wasn't in the woods. I didn't know where I was. My surroundings were red. I saw Aidan smiling at me. I took a step toward him, but it was as if the ground moved with me. In this red haze, he was completely unreachable. He threw his head back laughing, but there was no sound, I tried to run but my muscles wouldn't move. I was desperate to get to him as if he was in danger and I was the only one who could save him. He stared at me and I was frozen stiff, paralyzed. I saw his eyes transform into the horrific golden eyes of a cat. I awoke screaming. Ethan naturally raced into my room.

"Jane!"

I instantly felt his panic, "Oh, I'm sorry," I murmured, "I'm fine, Dad, I swear."

His eyes were full and terrified yet his thoughts were unreadable. It reminded me of the look he had given my mother when she told him about Danny. My heart sank. If Danny had awoke screaming, I would have run to him.

"Just a nightmare," I said, "I don't even remember it at all. I'm fine."

He nodded and slowly closed the door, peeking at me until he couldn't see me anymore. I rested for about half an hour before getting up for school.

When I pulled into the parking lot I saw Aidan climbing out of a blood red mustang. *Sexy car.* I parked as far away from it as possible. I tried not to look at him but it was hard not to. His face was blank until I saw him look over at me. Our eyes met and I looked away. When I peered back at him he wasn't there. I rushed to my first class, relieved as always to see Becky.

By the time that dreaded History class came around I was already too anxious for the day to end. Aidan ignored me as usual. When Mr. Cornally called on him for the answer to the question I wasn't listening to, I couldn't even hear Aidan's words, only the velvet softness of his voice. It was unnatural. Those hunters came to my mind again and the thoughts that maybe I should talk to Rudy, it would be a good time to yell some sense into him.

"Jane?"

That voice, so distantly familiar. I turned halfway, almost meeting his eyes.

"What are you thinking?" he whispered.

I sighed heavily and turned away. "So you ignore me for I don't know how long and now you suddenly want to know what I'm thinking?"

"I wasn't ignoring you."

"What?"

"In case you haven't noticed, you've been the one avoiding me. Avoiding eye contact—conversation."

Was this true? "Aidan," I shuddered at the sound of his name in my voice, "Don't talk to me."

He laughed.

"I'm sorry," I said increasing sarcasm, "Was I making a joke?"

"Oh, come on, Jane," he answered still with a smile in his voice, "You're the one who was mad when I said we shouldn't talk, that it was better that you avoid me."

"No, Aidan." I answered, "I am irritated by your inconsistency, if you want me to ignore you then for the love of god—let me!"

"I don't want that," he answered, "You just *should*. I told you I'm not a very good friend; I wouldn't want to let you down."

"You're stranger than me, Aidan."

"Maybe." He laughed that happy laugh that I remembered, "I wanted to know if you would like to go somewhere with me after school today? There's something I want to show you."

Again came that horribly annoying urge. I couldn't say no. This time I gave up the fight and didn't try.

"Okay." My voice was emotionless

"Okay," he echoed sounding extremely happy, "If you're worried about being let down, I'm warning you now."

"I expect it from everybody."

He nodded.

I instantly regretted my decision when the last bell rang. I raced to the parking lot as fast as I could.

"Hey."

I turned around, "Oh—hi."

Did he just appear out of thin air again?

"You didn't wait for me outside your class," he said, "Did you forget?"

"No," I answered, "Just wanted to get out of the rain."

He seemed to believe me but with him I could never be sure. He had just appeared again out of nowhere there were a lot of things I could never be sure about. How did he do that? I decided to actually see if could get an answer out of him.

"Where did you even come from?" I asked.

"What?" he laughed.

"I mean—you just—appeared just now."

He shook his head, "Really, Jane? Rudy is definitely seeding some crazy ideas in your head. I walked, ok? Same as you."

"Mmhmm."

"So are you going to make me give you directions again?"

I shook my head, "I can let you drive," I said, "If it's far away. But what about your car?"

"I'll come back for it," he answered smiling, "You seem highly distracted, Jane, is everything…"

"Fine." I retorted before he finished his sentence, which was a dead giveaway that I was not fine. I was terribly nervous. What if he had some plan to lead me to a secluded place and perform some kind of "hunter" ritual on me, or drink my blood? Was I simply being ridiculous? I was letting him drive me some unknown place—he hadn't even mentioned where it was, and I was letting him because I was in no mood to fight him over it. Besides, his voice made me nervous so his giving me directions wouldn't have done much good, I wouldn't have been able to listen. I got out and walked around to the passenger's side door. When I got in he already had the key in the ignition. He turned and smiled at me as if he were enjoying some sort of private joke. *Oh god*, I thought, *He's going to do something. He's going to kill me!*

I couldn't decide why I was suddenly having these thoughts, why I suddenly didn't trust him at all. I sat silently trying not to think about my worries. But I couldn't refrain from asking him one thing.

"Aidan?" I started; he turned to look at me, "The roses…"

He chuckled, "Yes, I'm sorry about that, I couldn't resist."

"Yeah, so I read."

He chuckled again, "did you like them?"

I had to think about it for a moment, "I did." I answered, "But—how did you know? That I crashed."

"Rudy, of course."

"What—no. Rudy said he didn't tell anyone."

He sighed, "Okay," he said, "You caught me."

"Aidan—you didn't."

No response.

"Did you—follow me?" I instantly felt enraged.

"I'm sorry," he said, "I have this incredibly annoying urge to protect you. I *only* followed you to make sure you were all right. Unfortunately I wasn't able to save you from the crash."

I couldn't speak.

"I really am sorry," he said, "Nothing creepy, Jane, it isn't like I stared through your windows or watched you sleep. I only followed a bit behind while you and Becky were driving. That's all."

It took me a moment to reply, "Really?"

"Yes." He said, "I swear."

I sighed, "I don't know why it's so impossible to stay mad at you?"

He smiled. "One of my gifts."

I stayed silent again after that waiting for him to speak. He drove passed my street onto a road, lined with trees on both sides.

"Heading to the other side of the woods," he said, "I want to show you where I was walking. There's something I want you to see."

I nodded. He pulled over to the side of the road and rushed to the other side to open my door for me as if I was waiting for him to. He offered me his hand; it looked very warm and welcoming. I hesitantly took his hand and was confused at how it didn't feel warm or welcoming at all. It felt cold, and timid. I removed my hand from his cold fingers and rubbed my knuckles across my jeans as if that could remove the sensation. He stood there just staring at me with those radiant eyes of his, smiling. I wanted to say something, just to break the uncomfortable silence but I had nothing to say. I wanted to hear his voice again. When he didn't speak I tuned into the sounds of the birds and the wind, the rustling of leaves and tiny animals.

"Come." He finally said.

It was amazing how his voice hadn't sliced through the other sounds, shattering the serenity I had opened up to. It sounded like part of the woods, like it belonged. It was perfect. He walked slowly into the trees and signaled me to follow. He was so light when he walked. My boots sloshed loudly in the mud, when he made almost no sound at all. He pulled back some branches and moved a little farther into the deeper parts of the woods. Maybe this was his plan, maybe this was a way for him to keep me from escaping, if I didn't know my way back, and yet—I followed, wanting to trust him. The trees were full and green but some of them still burned with the colors of fall. I couldn't focus much on the beauty around me when the beauty in front of me had shown interest in me. Again he pulled back a few branches and revealed a circle of completely clear land

"Most people don't just walk into the middle of the woods," he started, his voice still adding to the whipperwheel like another part of the choir, "The trail leads around this. *Most* people follow it, Jane." He smiled at me and raised his eyebrows. My body became chilled, my god he was adorable! I still couldn't speak, I couldn't find any words. In the center of the clearing there was a boulder, surrounded by a circle of smaller stones. It looked like some—Aztec place of ritual.

"What is this?" I asked.

"It's an old place of sacrifice."

"What?" I whispered, "Sacrifice?"

He nodded, "There are stories of a tribe, some say a coven or cult who would bring certain people here and open their throats. They would drink their blood then throw their bodies to the wolves."

"Why?"

"I don't know," he answered. He sounded distressed, "It's what they do. They hunt people."

He must have been talking about the hunters. Oh god, I was right the entire time. I noticed then that the larger rock was stained strange shades of brown—blood stains. I never should have trusted him.

"Jane?"

I realized that I was trembling and my teeth were chattering.

"Are you okay?" he actually sounded sincerely concerned, "Do you want my jacket?"

"No, Aidan." I said. I wasn't cold, "No, I'm okay."

He nodded. He opened his mouth to speak then closed it again and patted my arm.

"Thanks." I said.

"For?"

"Not asking me if I was sure."

He smiled.

"Why did you take me here?" I asked.

"I guess to show you where Rudy gets his superstitions. Some things about his stories may hold truth and I am simply warning you to stay out of the woods—especially at night."

"You said they drink peoples' blood."

"Yes."

"And Rudy mentioned acute night vision and strange abilities."

"Yes."

I almost laughed, "You people are talking about vampires!"

He chuckled, almost silently, "I'm sure some people might call them that, but since vampires are mythical creatures, we stick to "hunters.""

My god, this entire town was mad, Rudy wasn't the only one.

"You believe in them?"

"Like I told you," he answered, "to an extent, this wouldn't be here for no reason. It's just an interesting thing to see and hopefully a good reason to stay out of the woods."

"If you knew, Aidan," I started, "If you knew that the woods were so dangerous especially at night, then why you were there that night? When you rescued me?"

He smiled, "Most people like I said follow the trail," he said, "Which isn't that far into the woods. First of all—I'm not like most people, and second, I told you about my ability to sense danger."

"I wasn't sure I believed you." I confessed.

"Do you now?"

I nodded. "I think so."

"Anything else?"

I glared at him but answered, "Actually yes. You mentioned wolves."

"Yes?"

"Why didn't I see them that night? Why didn't they bother us?"

"It wasn't really late yet," he answered, "Wolves usually become active deep into the morning; it was just after sunset when I found you."

I nodded. I was *definitely* being ridiculous.

"So have you yelled at Rudy yet?" he asked, "I'm guessing you wanted to."

I growled deep in my throat, "I'm not on speaking terms with Rudy right now. But when I am I will definitely yell at him!"

He chuckled dryly as if he was completely unamused. "He was only trying to help," he said, "You really shouldn't be too hard on him. He came into your house looking for you because he thought I was with you. He feels like he needs to knock some sense into you. I came in thinking he was a burglar, and that's when he attacked me."

"You're not angry?"

"Not really," he said, "He's a decent guy—he was caring about you, that's all."

"Yup," I muttered, "Stranger than me."

He smiled again—flawlessly.

"Well; thanks for showing me this," I said, "It is interesting, and I will stay out of the woods."

He nodded once. "Good."

Without warning I felt his cold skin on my own and realized he was tracing the veins in my hand. I shuddered.

"You have very beautiful hands." He whispered. His mood had completely shifted. He was serious and calm now, very thoughtful and passive.

I couldn't respond. I didn't trust him. He started playing with my fingers timidly, it felt amazing. His skin was so smooth. He frightened me and although I knew I should have been running, I only returned his touch, moving my fingers with his. My heart was pounding at even the smallest touch. He moved to interlock his fingers with my own. I stared at his flaccid smile, mirroring my own. Why was I letting him hold my hand? Why was I letting him near me? He was silent again; I couldn't even hear him breathing so again I tuned in to the chorus of the woods waiting for his perfect voice to chime in.

"Thank you." He whispered seriously.

I didn't answer.

"For letting me take you here," he continued, "For trusting me."

I nodded. I guess he didn't notice my nervousness, didn't notice the fact that I didn't trust him at all, that I was almost frightened of him.

"Should I drive you to school?" I asked, "To get your car?"

He smiled as if I was joking, "I'll walk," he said.
"To the school?"
"Yes." He answered, "Then I'll drive home and—probably walk some more."
"Aidan," I sighed, "Will you just let me drive you? Please?"
"You don't need to do that."
"No; really," I pleaded, "It would make me feel much better if you just let me drive you."
He shook his head, suppressing laughter, "Fine," he said, "But only because you agreed to come here with me."
I drove back to the school, trying to think of something to say. We were both mostly silent.
"Thanks Jane." He leaned over and kissed my check, but lingered a moment and kissed it again.
"Good night, Aidan."
He slung his school bag over his shoulder and shut the door behind him. It wasn't too late so I satiated my obsession once more and drove to Albany's. While sipping at my coffee and skimming through a romance novel a familiar voice caught my attention.
"Hey," he said. I turned around.
"Hi," I answered. I recognized the voice but not the face. "Do I know you?"
"Yeah," he laughed, "Gallagher's party."
Oh GOD! "I can hardly believe you remember me."
"How could I forget?"
I shrugged. I did—quite easily. I recognized his light colored hair, almost to his shoulders and his gray eyes. Mr. Jones.
"Oh right. Mike is it?"
"Yeah." He nodded, "Are you busy?"
"Actually, I am sort of."
"Well—let's go to dinner."
"I don't think so, Mike."
"Ah, come on."

"I have to get home."

I closed the book and grabbed my bag. I headed for the door but he grasped my arm. "Come on," he said, "It'll be fun."

I yanked my arm away from him. "Really, Mike," I snapped, "I have to go."

He followed me out to the parking lot and I remembered what Becky had said about him being nice, she was a terrible judge of character. He grabbed my arm again and suddenly his face was flushed and he looked furious. He must have some anger management issues because he started raising his voice and speaking almost venomously.

"All I wanted was one dance," he growled, "Now, I'm offering you dinner and you walk out on me."

"I'm sorry," I said, "I just can't tonight."

"But you can!"

He was yelling now, causing a few people in the parking lot to stare, seeing if he was an abusive husband or something. I opened my car door, and he pushed me with the heels of his hands into my shoulders causing my door to slam closed. I gave out a moan and turned back to face him.

"Do not dismiss me again."

"What is wrong with you?" *Okay, Jane, shut up!* Bad time for confrontation.

"Mike, please," I begged, "Can't we do this some other time?"

He took a step back. "Another time?" he echoed.

I nodded.

"Tonight is better."

"I come here all the time," I said, "Come down here another time." I instantly regretted telling him that, being sure he *would* come back another time.

A different voice interrupted me. Said my name the way he always did.

"Jane?"

"Aidan!" I called.

Mike took another step back. Aidan gave him a slight nod and a glare. Mike glanced at me once more and left.

I let out a long sigh. "Thanks."

"Are you okay?"

I nodded. "My ribs are a bit sore," I said, "he shoved me against the car, but I'm fine."

"I should kill him."

"Nah, I don't think he's all that dangerous."

He looked at me shocked.

"Found me again."

"Well maybe you're right," he said, "He probably wasn't planning on hurting you, I was just walking aimlessly and ended up here, I didn't sense danger the way I sometimes do. You're just born for trouble."

"You got here fast."

"Did I?"

I nodded. "Where are you headed?"

Suddenly before he answered, I gasped and pressed my back against my car as hard as I could, staring into the golden eyes of a snarling canine.

"Aidan." I hissed.

He gasped, "Oh, it's all right," he said quietly, "Simply stay calm."

He took a step toward it.

"What are you doing? Are you crazy?"

"Shh. It's fine, Jane."

He led out his hand.

"Aidan, you idiot it's going to bite your damn fingers off."

"Jane, *please*! Be quiet!"

The animal was suddenly very still but still quietly growling in his throat. Aidan began petting its head and it instantly became calm. I was still backed against the door of my car.

"Go on." He whispered, waving his hand.

The wolf turned and pranced away.

"My god," I whispered, "How did you do that?"

"Animals can sense fear," he said, "As long as you don't show them you're afraid they won't bother you."

I had a hard time believing that. Another one of those unnatural things again. It was one of the things about him I wanted to ignore, to suppress any crazy ideas it may seed in my head. I changed the subject.

"Can I give you a ride home?"

Surprisingly he nodded. "I think I've walked enough tonight."

He got in the passenger's seat and settled comfortably

"I still don't think I understand why you're not angry at Rudy," I said, taking the car out of park.

He smiled the way he did when he was happy. "Actually I found the whole trying to kill me thing quite entertaining."

"Why?'"

He turned his head, then chuckled, "Well because if Rudy knows so much about the hunters and he believed me to be one then he should have known that he wouldn't have been able to kill me."

"Are you saying you're a hunter?" My hands started to shake.

"I didn't say that, Jane."

"But you are."

He didn't respond. I almost took that as confirmation.

I drove passed Andrew's house to a small suburban neighborhood. He lived in a small house at the end of a cul-de-sac. It was pale, beige stucco with a tiled roof. There were vines covering the left side of the house and part of the roof. The porch was dimly lit by lights in the grass. It was comfortable looking. I stopped in front of his porch still searching for something else to say.

"Why don't you just tell me what you are?" I asked.

"Just stay out of the woods, Janie." He said. He squeezed my shoulder and twisted a strand of my hair between his fingers. With a smile and formal nod, he opened the door. "Stop listening to Rudy," but before I could think of a response he was already at the door of his house. When he opened the door light flooded out and he appeared to be speaking to somebody inside. He turned and waved at me, I waved back and he shut the door—gone.

I stayed there for a moment staring at his house, wanting to see his face one more time before I went home. I couldn't think about anything but what we talked about.

I didn't say that, Jane. But he didn't say otherwise either. And because he told me once again to stop listening to Rudy I knew at that point that I *had* to talk to him.

XII

Are You Going To Tell Me Now?

ANOTHER dream distressed me that night, the same as before, flawless and beautiful, unreachable Aidan. Ethan came in again when I awoke screaming and I had to assure him again that I was fine.

School dragged, I didn't speak to anybody. I hardly even acknowledged Aaron or Becky. Again it didn't occur to me until history class that Aidan wasn't there. Skipping school on a Friday? Why bother? Mr. Cornally called on me, probably realizing I wasn't paying attention.

"Miss Doe?"

"I'm sorry," I said, "What was the question?"

"Wake up," he hissed.

I flushed horribly and put my head down. When school finally got out I rushed home to start on some homework, then gathered my courage to talk to Rudy. I knocked on the door and not two seconds later he opened it. He was silent.

"Hey." I said, trying to keep my voice even.

"Hey."

"I'm not here to lecture you," I said, when I noticed the tremor in his voice and how he avoided eye contact.

He nodded, "Well, come in, Jane."

He moved aside and instantly I felt that dreamy sensation of the past and it made me miss Danny terribly. The house was familiar, although only distantly. It reminded me of Danny when he was alive—happy. It was built a lot like Ethan's house. The door leading into a small, tile entry way and the kitchen slightly to the left, where a little round table sat in front of those windows with the old, pale yellow drapes. There were flowers everywhere. To the right were the stairs, I had never been up there as a kid, but nothing that I could see was any different than I remembered. From the corner of my eye I saw Eric at the top of the staircase, perhaps to see who was at the door. When he saw me he avoided eye contact and disappeared around the corner. I didn't bother with him; I got straight to the point.

"I wanted to ask you a few things," I started, "Without you forgetting that I am utterly infuriated."

His eyes tensed and he turned toward the kitchen. "May we sit?"

I nodded.

We sat at the little round table and he moved aside the vase of flowers. I folded my hands in front of me trying to think of how to start.

"I'm guessing this is about the Summers kid," he smiled, "just to break the ice."

I had forgotten how much I liked Rudy at times.

I pressed my lips together, "There is something different about him, yes, but I am not buying into your vampire superstitions."

"Vampires?"

I nodded, "That's what they sound like to me."

He shrugged.

"I just wanted to know what you know about the hunters," I started, "I want you to tell me what you know because there are a few things that have me concerned."

"Ah, you saw the clearing."

No response.

"Figured you would stumble across that sooner or later."

"A coven of people," I said, "Who hunt other people—my guess is that they are insane, thinking they are vampires or—something."

"They're sane," Rudy answered, "just not entirely human." He was suddenly serious and actually sounded frightened. He really *was* trying to protect me.

"That isn't possible." I said.

"Do you think people just make up stories off the top of their heads?" he asked, "Nobody is that creative, Jane, everything comes from somewhere."

"Most of the books I read are pretty out there." I answered.

"I tried to warn you before and you wouldn't listen, do you want to listen this time?"

I nodded.

"The legend of the hunters is old and not one you will find at a local bookstore. About forty years ago my grandfather was in his twenties and traveling the world studying cultures and their religions. He was an anthropologist of cultures but obsessed with theology. Religion was his true passion. There were several cultures he found intriguing, such as the African tribes in the forests and the Arabics in their clothing styles, but the strangest things he saw happened here in Oregon. People went missing and my grandfather was determined to find out why. The police and even the FBI were stumped. Sometimes bodies would turn up in alleyways or dumpsters."

My stomach ached when I remembered Danny's case.

"There were even a few cases where the bodies went missing after being sent to the morgue. Those cases ended up cold—the bodies were never found. Eventually my grandfather did find out what was going on and when I was young he used to tell me the story. For some reason it never frightened me, it was like a bedtime story, my papa was a hero in my eyes and I would ask him to tell me the story so often that I eventually knew it word for word. There were a lot of details he left out but I do know that he talked about how he sought out the mysterious people in the woods who called themselves "The Sevren." He explained to me how they hunted people. Only certain people, pure people, the most loved and happy. They would sacrifice them with bone knives or axes and spill their blood on the alter in the clearing you have seen. The members would drink the blood of the victims, taking in their beauty and the essence of their lives. It is an incomparable pleasure to them, even the children.

"There was a woman who had fallen in love with my grandfather—my grandmother. A woman who was a member of this cult. She promised him that if he would love her she would send her people away from the woods and they would never again harm another human. He agreed seeing as he was in love with her as well. She did what she promised and sent her tribe away. The tragedy in the story strangely enough is that my grandfather may yet be alive."

"What?"

"He went missing. Along with my grandmother and disappearances have been happening again."

"How do you know that?"

"Please don't tell anyone," he said, "You know my dad is a cop right?"

"Oh—right. I'd forgotten about that." "Nobody wants this to alert the media."

"Who's missing?"

He shrugged, "Even if I knew I couldn't tell you."

I nodded.

"So The Sevren are back…?"

He nodded. "I believe so yes."

"He had a friend who worked with him sometimes and came here to help him farther study The Sevren before he went missing. Clyde Wingfeild, an anthropologist and a historian. He came to my grandfather's house one night terrified and bleeding everywhere. He told him that he was attacked. He explained that a man had broken into his house and attacked him while he slept. He would have believed he was dreaming if it wasn't for the blood. He shot the man with a pistol he kept in his nightstand but he was only momentarily hurt, it wasn't until he smashed his head through his bedroom window that he died. They are almost impossible to kill. It was only a week later my grandfather went missing. My mom thinks her father is a big fish—but I believe him. And you should too. If the Summers kid is one of The Sevren –he's broken the pact and there will be hell to pay. Be careful, Jane, they are stronger than us."

I just stared at him for a moment.

"Vampires." I whispered.

"What? They aren't vampires."

"Sounds that way to me."

"They may have some of the same abilities but vampires don't exist."

"Exactly," I stood up, "Thanks. Rudy, but I don't think that listening to your stories is the best idea."

I walked toward the door and heard him behind me.

"The night you hurt your ankle," he called, "The night you got hurt and Aidan rescued you."

I froze in the doorway and turned around. "How do you know about that?"

"Why do you think the wolves didn't bother you that night?"

"What?" My voice swelled with sarcasm.

His voice dropped, "Why do you think nothing worse happened?" He looked at me sadly. He appeared somber, yet distressed at the same time, "Why do you think you're alive?"

I sighed, "Rudy, Aidan isn't a vampire. okay?"

He opened his mouth to speak but I stopped him, "or *hunter*."

"You *have* to listen to me."

"No Rudy, I really don't," I said, "Aidan can't—control the wolves."

I ignored and started walking home, he didn't follow but he called to me.

"I saw what he is, Jane," he yelled, "What he was doing, and it was terrible. Please just keep yourself safe!"

I sighed. I had gone to see Rudy for a reason and when he told me what I was expecting to hear, I walked out on him. I guess I owed him as much so as to at least listen to him. But I couldn't get his story out of my head. My stomach was turning. Danny had died a mysterious death and his body was found in an alleyway. His case went cold. My brother's death was matching Rudy's story. The Sevren were in Oregon, that's what Rudy said. Danny died in California. I felt ridiculous for reading so much into it but there had to be some explanation and I couldn't beat myself up for wanting to believe *something*—anything!

I walked to the edge of the woods but hesitated before walking into the trees. I couldn't decide who to trust, Rudy or Aidan. Aidan had told me to stay out of the woods, but I know Rudy wanted me to go into them—hopefully to find something that would prove him right. Either way—it was daytime and I was very much expecting Aidan to appear out of nowhere if I was in danger. I inhaled deeply. I was hoping to prove that Rudy was crazy.

I hadn't even made it to the clearing if I could have found it at all before I stopped dead cold in my tracks. I tried to focus on breathing regularly. Hunched over on his knees like an animal, I saw him there, chewing on something. That's when I noticed the feathers tightly gripped in his hand—his perfect hand. I gasped before I could stop myself and he instantly turned to look at me. His mouth was smeared with blood and his eyes were dark, yet still I knew as I would know any time, any place—it was Aidan. He was frozen stiff for a moment. I took a couple steps back. That's when he stood up and dropped the bird carelessly on the ground. I turned and ran. I ran faster than I can ever recall running before, my muscles burned. My stomach turned and I was stopped only feet from my porch, sick in the flowerbed. I scrambled to my feet and shut the door behind me locking it clumsily. I leaned against the door, heart pounding, trying to get control of myself. That's when I heard a knock on the door and that voice. The way he said my name never seemed to sound exactly like my name.

"Jane?"

"Go away!" It was impossible to hide the fear in my voice.

"Jane, please," he begged, "You have to listen to me."

"Rudy was right about you!" I called back.

If he wanted to hurt me he would have done it already—wouldn't he?

"Jane, I'm sorry," he called. He sounded miserable, "I had to."

"Just go away!"

"Open the door. Please!"

"No!"

"I'm sorry—I was so hungry!"

"Then cook a damn cup of noodles, Aidan! Go away!"

"You don't understand!"

"I don't want to." It didn't make sense, who eats raw birds like a cat?

"Would you just let me in?"

"Why the hell would I let you in?"

"Trust me, please."

"I could never trust you," I answered, "You told me yourself you're not a very good friend."

"Yes, I said that," he answered, "but when have I ever given you reason to be afraid of me?"

I looked back on everything. The only thing Aidan had ever done was save my life and take me out to a movie.

"Listen to me," he said. His voice had suddenly become very soft and kind. My heart sank, "I need you," he whispered, desperately, "I know it sounds crazy but I need you to listen to me—please."

I remembered the cold, soft kiss he had planted on my cheek the day I had saved him from Rudy. He had this power over me, this kind of dominance over my thoughts. I sighed and unlocked the door. When I opened it he was standing there, perfectly clean and beautiful again with those enticing green eyes of his. I stepped aside and nodded, but couldn't bring myself to make eye contact.

"Thank you." He breathed.

"Are you going to tell me what you are now?" I whispered hesitantly,

"Do I need to?"

I jerked my head toward him but quickly averted my gaze again.

"Maybe not."

I sat down on the couch in the front room and he sat beside me. I gasped and pulled my hand away when I felt the coolness of his skin.

"I'm sorry." He whispered. He was sweet and innocent again.

"You just surprised me," I said, but didn't move my hand back to let him get any closer.

"Don't be afraid," he said, "I swear to you, I'm not going to hurt you."

"What does that mean?" I asked, "Does that mean you will kill me so fast I won't feel the pain?"

He pulled his eyebrows together and looked at me puzzled. "Jane—"

"I'm sorry," I said, "Just please Aidan—if you're one of them, tell me."

"One of who?"

"You know who."

He chuckled and shook his head. "Rudy," he mumbled, "ah Rudy."

"What?"

"My personal opinion is his grandfather was senile," he said, "I don't think The Sevren exist."

"You know the story?"

"I—heard."

"You were spying?" I yelled.

"Not exactly," he retorted in defense, "I have good hearing and yes I walked by and could hear from the open window, I couldn't help but to listen to what he was telling you."

"What other abilities does your kind have?"

"My kind?"

"Yes. The—well you know."

"Well, the wolves."

"It's true?" I questioned "You can really control the wolves?"

"I wouldn't say I can control them," he said, "But they listen to me, they trust me. And my *kind* as you put it has nothing to do with that ability; I don't know where that one came from, much like my ability to sense danger. It's just something I have inside me."

"What about the bird?"

"I told you," he said, "I was hungry."

"You ate the bird? Raw?"

He shook his head.

"Oh my god," I whispered, "You—"

He nodded, "It's what we do."

"Blood?!"

He nodded, "I cannot explain everything to you right now, but I promise you, I will. I would never hurt you Jane—or any human."

"Then you aren't a true—*hunter* right?"

He put his hand up, "Another day."

I nodded.

"I just had to make you let me in," he said, "I had to tell you to your face that I don't intend to ever hurt you but I also want you to know that I can."

"That's just it then," I said, "That's why you didn't want to be friends."

"Now you understand," he said.

He stood up and turned away. I put my hand on his shoulder, concentrating on the softness of his leather jacket.

"Tomorrow?" I asked.

He turned around and held my face in his hands. He very lightly touched his lips to mine.

"Soon, Jane," he whispered, and then gone so quickly, leaving a lingering sweetness on my lips from his kiss.

I couldn't sleep that night. Usually thinking of Aidan put me to sleep but this time my daydreams kept me awake. I heard that sound again, the eerie tapping of the tree against my window. I rolled over trying to ignore. I realized then that it wasn't that squeaking noise I heard before but a rounder more rhythmical rapping. I turned back to the window and turned on the lamp on my nightstand. I inhaled deeply trying to calm myself so I wouldn't wake Ethan.

"Jane!" I heard, in just a loud enough whisper to hear.

"Aidan?"

"Open up!"

I sprang up and opened the window. "Are you crazy?"

"I hope so," he chuckled.

I smiled and he crawled from the oak tree into my bedroom.

"Don't wake Ethan." I whispered.

He nodded. "I had to see you," he said, "I don't think I'm entirely ready to explain myself yet but for some reason—I had to see you."

"You *must* be out of your mind." I said, but I couldn't help but smile.

He sat down on the edge of my bed and I sat beside him. He moved slightly closer and began brushing his fingers across my neck. I shuddered as I did every time he touched me. *I need you.* I replayed those words in my mind so many times the syllables began to run together and the words became meaningless. I wondered what he could have really meant, that he needed me to believe him or that he actually needed me with him and by his side.

"Stay." I whispered. It was half caught in my throat.

"I'm not going anywhere."

It was puzzling to suddenly have this desperation for him to touch me. I felt as if the coolness of his skin turned mine to silk, he made me feel almost un-solid—like mist. I could only ask myself why I was feeling this way. This boy who was once the source of no more than pure irritation somehow brought tenderness from me that I never thought I could feel since I lost Danny. My mind raced and I continued to feel weightless.

"You're beautiful." He whispered.

I couldn't respond. I felt him touch my cheek and brush his fingers across my lips, which forced a cold gasp from my chest.

"Are you okay?"

His voice was like velvet.

I moved closer, still trying to veil the sudden affection I felt toward him.

He groaned quietly. "You're tempting me Jane."

I wasn't sure what he meant but when I remembered the bird I grew nervous. "My blood?" I almost regretted asking, "Or my body?"

"Well, neither would be safe for me to take."

He moved away.

"Stay," I whispered, "Please."
He nodded, "You need your sleep."
"I'm not sleepy."
"Will you sleep if I lie beside you?"
I nodded.

He curled up next to me and instantly I felt nervous yet warm and tired. He put his arm around my waist and I quietly gasped.

"I'm sorry." He muttered as he moved away from me.

"No, it's okay," I whispered back "I don't mind."

And it was true, I didn't care if he constricted me to death—I would die in his arms.

I did fall asleep eventually even though I had tried to stay awake to savor the time that he was actually there with me, and when I awoke I was alone. Sure that I hadn't been dreaming I whispered, "Aidan?"

"I'm here."

I turned to see him beside the window leaned against the wall with his arms folded in front of his chest. I jumped when I saw him and he laughed.

"I'm sorry," he said, "I got my car, I'm driving you to school."

"I wasn't planning on going to school."

He smiled, "Go to school Jane."

I nodded, "Just need a shower," I said.

"I'll wait." He answered, still smiling.

I hurried into the bathroom and showered as quickly as I could. I pulled a brush through my hair and didn't worry with the blow dryer. I got dressed and skipped back to my room. He was there, still leaned against the wall smiling at me as if he hadn't moved at all. My memory never did his beauty justice. All I could think about when I looked at him was what he was and why after all that had happened I wasn't afraid of him, why I only wanted to be closer.

XIII

Abraham

SCHOOL wasn't the same that Monday, I felt like a different person. After every class Aidan was there, waiting for me. He was different when he was at school. He seemed more normal, more like a kid. When it was just the two of us he sometimes acted like a seventeenth century nobleman.

Aaron tried to steer away from the subject of Aidan in conversation and chose a seat as far away from him as possible in history class. During class, Aidan was silent but sometimes he'd steal a glance or smile at me. He drove me home after school and I tried my hardest to make conversation.

"What are you thinking?" I asked. The most real and logical question in my head.

He glanced quickly at me and smiled.

"Trying to figure out what you're thinking."

"Oh."

I couldn't think of what to say next.

"Are you afraid of me?" he asked.

I didn't even hesitate before responding. "No."

"You should be."

"Why?" I snapped, "You promised you'd never hurt me."

"I did," he answered, "It's just that the logical, safe thing to do would be to fear me."

I shook my head, "I'm not afraid of you."

"I know," he answered, "I'm just saying you *should* be. I know by now—that's never changed your mind about anything."

"Why would you *want* me to be afraid of you?" I asked, "You said before that—you needed me—to believe you remember?"

"More than having you believe me, more than having you close to me, Jane, I want you to be safe."

"You've saved my life more than once already."

He nodded, "Let's hope I am never the cause for anybody else needing to play your knight in shining armor."

I sighed. *He promised he'd never hurt me.*

"You've never killed anybody before, have you?"

"You know I have, Jane, I told you I have."

"But—the bird."

"I simply promised that I would never hurt another human again."

I nodded, "Am I safe with you?"

He nodded, "For now—yes."

I glanced in the rearview mirror and peered over my shoulder.

"What is it?" His voice had completely transformed from the tension a moment before, he sounded completely content.

"That car." I answered, "It's been behind us since we left the school."

"Hmm," he grunted, glancing quickly over his shoulder at the black Mustang, "Strange. You don't recognize it?"

I shook my head, "No. Should I?"

"No." he answered, "I'm just expecting Rudy to do something stupid again."

"You would never hurt him would you?"

"I let him beat the crap out of me Jane, without moving to fight back—what do you think?" he chuckled. His emotions were inconsistent, as usual. The most unnatural thing about him. I just nodded.

"Right." I said.

I looked behind me again. The car was still following us, even after we had turned.

"Where are you going?" I finally asked when I noticed he had passed my street.

"Testing this guy." His voice was quiet, and swelled with tension again.

"Can you actually see him?" I asked, glancing over my shoulder again.

"Stop turning around!" he snapped, "He'll figure out what I'm up to."

"Can you see him?" I asked again.

He nodded, "barely."

"Well…"

"Please." He demanded, cutting my sentence short, "Don't ask any questions. I promise everything will be all right."

That was a dead giveaway he was worried. I was thinking that maybe he could read the stranger's mind or something of that effect. *Should* he be worried?

I leaned back in my seat and closed my eyes. It was strange, I could barely even make out a shape behind the tinted windows of the car but Aidan seemed like he actually knew who it was.

"Aidan?" I whispered.

"Shh." He whispered, "Really, Jane, I'm trying to concentrate."

Concentrate on what? I didn't ask. After about fifteen minutes of silence Aidan turned and the Mustang kept going straight. I thought I saw the stranger's shape in the car turn and stare at us as he drove by. Aidan sighed and pulled over on the side of the road and put the car in park. He squeezed the bridge of his nose.

"I did the only thing I had tried to avoid." He said.

I didn't answer.

"All I wanted to do was keep you safe, and now I have endangered you."

"What?"

"I didn't want us to be friends because I wanted you to be safe, but if I leave you now, you will *never* be safe."

"Aidan. What's going on?"

"The license plate of that car…" he paused.

"Yeah?"

"Did you see it?"

"I saw there was a 7 and I think a—B?"

He nodded, "Yeah, tacked to the end of the letters S-E-V-R-N."

I froze for a moment but recoiled, "It could be a coincidence."

He shook his head.

"I thought you didn't believe in them."

"Yes, I said that," he answered, his voice dropped, "I lied."

"You lied?!"

"Yes Jane, I lied, let's not make a big deal about it all right? I know the Sevren exist, I know for a fact."

"Because you're one of them!" I yelled it out instantly after his response.

"No," he yelled back. "No! Never!"

"Then why are they a problem?"

"Because they are being led by a man who is more powerful than me, stronger than me, and I have history with him."

I wasn't sure if I should say anything, wasn't sure if it was a good idea to ask any questions. I tried to let him get a hold of himself before I said anything, but the word was being forced from my mouth. It was hard to find my voice at first and it was scarcely a sound when I finally asked, "Who?"

He sighed and squeezed the bridge of his nose again. He answered in a choked whisper, "My father."

It was silent for a long time. I couldn't bring myself to ask for an explanation, just the look on his face told me he was in agony.

"I'm taking you home." He finally said, starting the car again, "But I want to stay with you tonight, just to make sure you're safe."

I didn't answer but I nodded to let him know it was okay with me.

"If you don't ask me to talk about it tonight, I will tell you tomorrow; just please not tonight."

I nodded again, still unable to answer.

When I got home Ethan was there. As soon as I opened the door he called my name.

"Jane?"

"Yeah, it's me." Who else?

"I thought you were home earlier because I saw your car. Did Becky drive you to school this morning?"

"Yeah." Easier than explaining Aidan.

Aidan was in my room waiting for me. He smiled as soon as I walked in. I dropped my book bag on my bed and sat beside him.

"I shouldn't leave my car in your driveway," he said, "That wouldn't look good."

"Yeah, I don't want to give my dad any reasons not to trust me."

"I'll go park down the street and come right back."

I nodded, "okay."

I watched out my window as he pulled out. He drove like a lunatic. I realized he drove much slower when I was in the car with him. I sat back down and waited for him. I didn't feel safe by myself, I didn't feel safe, knowing that The Sevren were back in North Bend. I tried to ignore, tried to push that from my mind until Aidan would explain. He appeared again out of nowhere. I jumped.

"Aidan!"

He laughed, "I'm sorry."

"No, you're not."

"You're right" he said, still laughing, "I couldn't resist."

I shook my head, "How did you do that?"

"Do what? You obviously weren't paying very close attention and your window is open."

"Uh huh."

"You give me too much credit." He shrugged his shoulders and sat back down beside me, "So—promise me you'll sleep tonight Jane."

"I'm promising nothing." I looked away from him, staring out my window at the gray sky.

"Yeah—should have guessed as much from you."

"What's *that* supposed to mean?" I snapped, bringing my eyes back to his.

"Exactly what I said," he answered, smiling, "I wasn't insulting you."

"Mmm hmm."

He smiled again and put his arm around me, pulling me into his chest. I couldn't decide why I was letting him so close to me, why I trusted him after what had happened.

* * *

"If you don't mind," he started, "I would like to know some things about you."

"Such as?"

"Such as—your mother."

"Okay," I answered, "My mother, Carol. She's very attached to me. She's the type of person my dad fell in love with when they were young. The problem was—Ethan grew up, my mother didn't."

"Kid at heart?"

"You could put it that way," I answered, "She's crazy in my opinion. She *relieves* stress with extreme things like sky diving and parasailing."

He laughed. "Not your thing."

I let out a long sigh and chuckled, "definitely not."

"And your dad," he started, "Why did he come here?"

"He actually grew up here," I answered, "My grandparents lived here, that's how I met Rudy and Becky, I had been out visiting my grandparents every summer, after they died, and my parents' divorce my dad moved here so I still saw my old friends every summer. Now that I live here I see them more often than I thought I would. I hated this place at first, but it seems I fit in better here than I did in California. I didn't have many friends there. Everyone I've ever *truly* cared about besides my mother—lives here."

"Well, then it worked out for the better."

I smiled. "Yeah—I guess it did. People still stare at me like I'm an alien, but I'm getting used to it."

"You notice that?"

"Of course I notice it. I'm the new girl at North Bend High. The average and reclusive girl that nobody can get any type of answers from. You're the only one I've told things to that involve my life, except maybe Becky and Rudy."

"Well, then I should return the favor right?"

I nodded, "Sure, I'd love to know about the mysterious Aidan Summers. You're famous at school you know. People make up stories about you."

He laughed, "I bet."

"So what about *your* mother?"

"My mother was—crazy," he said, "Not crazy in the good way like your mother. She was a little off her nut if you know what I mean. Both of my parents are dead."

"Oh my gosh, Aidan I'm sorry."

"No it's really all right. I live with my uncle Walter, who is a professor and a genius."

"How did your parents die?"

"They were murdered," he answered, he seemed to be able to talk about it without a problem, "My father's business partner was a thief and destroyed my father's wealth before he killed him—and my mother. I came home to find them dead."

I stared at him. "Not really a good time for sob stories," he said and forced a synthetic smile, "You'll hear all about it later, I promise."

I pulled my lips to one side and narrowed my eyes. He laughed.

"Take your moments," he told me, "I'll wait."

I nodded and took a towel and my pajamas into the bathroom with me."

"I'll be right back."

"Take your time," he said, "Ethan won't see me, I promise."

I did what he said and took my time, I washed up then stood there, letting the water hit my face. I had the feeling that his not talking about things meant that he had lied to me about more than his knowledge of The Sevren, like the fact that he was one of them. I shook off the bad thoughts reminding myself that he would explain everything to me soon. I changed into a nightgown my mother had given to me one year for Christmas. It was a silky white sleeveless almost see through but not enough to be indecent. Aidan was in my room; I wouldn't be caught in something ridiculous. No more old, holey shirts.

When I walked in he was there, still in the same exact place I remembered like he was a statue. When he saw me he smiled and lightly blushed, which I had never before seen him do. I sat beside him.

"Are you going to sleep tonight?" He asked.

"Mmhmm."

He smiled, "good."

"I have one condition."

"Of course you do."

"You have to lie with me," I said.

He nodded smiling. He moved closer and touched my shoulder. Those feelings and thoughts came rushing back to me, the feelings of nervousness and fear, the thoughts that I shouldn't trust him—that I hardly knew him. He stopped when I locked my gaze into his. With those beautiful green eyes of his I could clearly see the truth behind his previous words he had spoken before.

"You're beautiful." He whispered.

Coming from the boy who was looking at his shoes when speaking so softly, so hesitantly, it wasn't the most flattering of compliments, especially when every glance he had passed my direction had revealed to me his thoughts long before now. But yet I could not help but to tremble, and my heartbeat sped up. I leaned in closer and ran my fingertips across his cheeks. I couldn't stand being so close to him without touching him. There was this hungry desperation for him that frightened me. My hands were quaking and my face was hot.

"Are you afraid?" he asked.

"I don't know."

And this was the truth of course. I had never even thought of feeling this way, and that was only the half of it, I had no idea who—or *what* he was. Still, as I felt the cold, timid press of his lips to my cheek I didn't even hesitate to turn my face and meet his perfect lips with my own. I couldn't let myself give in too strongly and I pulled away gently, but I knew he was nowhere near finished. He placed his hand on the back of my head and pulled me close, kissing me passionately yet tenderly as he did everything else. It was no doubt the kiss I had always dreamed of and the feeling I had always tried to imagine. I felt nervous so I wrapped my arms around him, desperate again for his touch. He returned my embrace and I gently kissed his neck. He pulled away and stared at me. His eyes looked tense and focused.

"Are you okay?"

He nodded. "Lay with me."

"I want you to kiss me again."

He leaned forward and kissed me briefly. I held on and parted my lips but he pulled away harshly.

"I'm sorry, but you're testing my self control."

"Then let it go." I hummed.

He chuckled quietly, "not tonight." He kissed my cheek. "Lay with me."

I nodded and curled up in his arms, pressing my face into his chest. As I closed my eyes to rest there was one thing I was sure of, the one thing I had tried to deny since the very first day I had met Aidan—I was completely, undeniably, in love with him.

There was no way of turning back now. It was real and he knew it, how could he not? I slept soundly, I didn't know if Aidan had been sleeping but I ran my fingers through his hair and he smiled. I touched his cheeks and he opened his eyes.

"Morning." He whispered. He twisted my hair around his fingers, "I didn't know you had curly hair."

"I don't." I answered, tucking the ringlet behind my ear, "you mistake my tangles for curls."

He smiled and shook his head.

"What?"

"Nothing." He said, "You act so modest."

"Do I?'

He raised his eyebrows at me still smiling. He was undeniably adorable.

I blushed and turned away.

"It's tomorrow," he said, "and I promised to explain."

I nodded.

"I need you to believe me. I need you in general, that simple."

"You need me?"

He nodded, "Yes. And I would rather you not go to school today, simply because it would make me feel better for you to stay within my sight at least for a day.

"I tell you I need you, and if I ever want you to need me in return you deserve to know the truth."

"You lied to me?'

"Yes, Jane, and I'm sorry," he said, "I understand that It's going to be hard to believe anything I say now, but that's what I need you to do, believe me."

"Okay..."

"It seems like a very long time ago yet I still remember it as clearly as possible. I was young and still lived with my mother and father. My father was a very skilled surgeon and was very wealthy. His fortune however was beginning to diminish thanks to his partner. Mathius Castlebar. Castlebar was a thief but at the time, my family trusted and respected him.

It wasn't easy for my mother and I when my father became ill one spring. I got a job at a restaurant and my mother stayed home to take care of my father. It was late one night when I was still at work preparing to close when I found myself getting into deep conversation with a man who said he was a science professor at some big university, said he was planning to discover the secrets of life and death and how they can not only be created but be reversed. I was fascinated. We talked until the streetlights at the corner of the street went out. We both noticed it immediately and that's when he realized he needed to be getting home.

"Before you leave," I asked him, "Are you teaching a class right now—about your theories on life and death?'

He smiled, I could tell he was pleased by my interest, "I am not actually," he answered, "but I would never turn down a young person willing to learn.'

Those words led to a very good friendship. Walter Redline was his name and he was truly a genius. I told him about my desire to learn about life since my mother had always been a little mad. She was convinced that I was photosensitive as a child, though the sun is harsh to my fair skin, she kept me concealed inside always and the only time I was able to work was evening shifts when the sun was hardly out. At the time I had believed her, yet I still knew her to be mad and I thought that Walter might be able to help her. For months I studied with Professor Redline and he really had some incredible things to teach me.

"You are gifted," he told me, "If anybody can find a cure for death it is you.'

I continued my studies, inspired by the story of Frankenstein and other books about scientific wonders. I could cure death—how miraculous. I knew I was close, I could feel it in my blood and my bones, my studies were almost at an end.

I was out one night on my way to work, it was dark and I cut through an alleyway as a shortcut to the restaurant. A man stopped me; he held a knife to my throat. I offered him my wallet and anything else he wanted. I tried to step back from him but he pushed me against the wall and pressed the knife harder against my neck. My limbs were shaking and my teeth were chattering. Before I could even take another breath to speak, I passed out in the darkness. When I awoke I was sweating, the heat was intense. I couldn't open my eyes at first but I knew I was not alone, I felt the presence of another.

"Are you all right?"I heard.

I opened my eyes only to be horror stricken by the sight—of the sun!

"The sun!"I cried, "Good Lord, get me out of the sun.'

I covered my head with my arms.

"My god, "I heard the voice say, "you're ill.'

I began sobbing into my hands and whimpering "the sun the sun" over and over. Again I lost consciousness. When I came to the first thing my eyes met was a beautiful face, the face of a woman. She had round brown eyes and dark shiny hair. She looked kind and innocent. My vision was blurry and my eyes closed again.

"Where am I?"I asked, "and why am I here?'

"You were screaming, "She said, "you were screaming at me to get you out of the sun.'

I couldn't answer. Suddenly I heard her gasp loudly.

"Good lord, "she cried, "what on Earth happened to you?'

I was afraid of how I must have looked. I knew from what my mother had told me that my skin was black and shriveled. I felt her touch my neck and was surprised at a sudden sting in my skin.

"What?'

"You're cut, "she said, "you're cut badly. What happened?'

"I—don't know. I was robbed last night. I don't even remember how I got away.'

"I'm surprised you're alive, "she said, "You're lucky your throat isn't slit.'

I felt the cut where the mugger's knife had begun to rush through me before I lost consciousness. That's when I remembered Professor Redline and how I had to get home to him. I was only months away from my discovery I had to get home to finish working.

"I have to go!"I yelled out. I tried to lift myself from the bed but instantly fell back onto my pillow.

"You're sick, "she said.

"No, "I tried to yell but my voice seemed caught in my throat, "you don't understand, that doesn't matter. Sickness will mean nothing. That is why I have to get home.'

"What are you talking about?"she yelled, the concern in her voice was almost tangible, "You need to get to a doctor, you have an intense fever.'

"No!"I pleaded, "I have to get to Professor Redline, I have to discover it!'

"Discover what?'

"The secret to immortality—I'm so close.'

I tried again to lift myself but kept falling back down. Lights were turning on in my head and I was suddenly understanding things about life and death and I was desperate to get home so I could tell these things to Walter. I was sick and I realize now that the things I was saying must have sounded like the ravings of a mad man.

"Please stay here, "she begged, "If you won't let me take you to a doctor at least let me take care of you.'

I couldn't answer her.

"My name is Vivian Black.'

"Clement Thortan."I choked out.

I couldn't leave, even though I urgently needed to, I was too sick and weak. Vivian was kind; she patched the wound on my neck and cooked for me every day. It rained that night and my generous friend had lit a fire in the hearth across from my bed. I reached into the pocket of my jeans and pulled out the notebook I had used to jot down notes and write down discoveries I had found when working with Walter. Because of my delirium I couldn't understand them. I squeezed the tiny notebook in my hand and with a growl of fury, cast it into the fireplace and wept. Vivian came in and sat beside me on the bed.

"Why are you crying?"

"You wouldn't believe me if I told you.'

"You're still sick "she said softly, "Just rest.'

"I need to get home, "I said, "I need to tell Walter of my discovery; if I don't then I am going to die.'

"Who is this Walter you rave about?"she asked, "You call his name in you sleep and you talk about—well—about death.'

"You wouldn't believe me.'

"Just rest.'

"I'm not mad, "I told her, "really I am not.'

"I know, "she answered not sounding convinced.

"These ravings about scientific discovery, and the things I had said about reversing the curse of mortality—it is all quite true.'

She smiled and left the room.

"I'm not mad!" I screamed.

Before I slept that night Vivian prepared a warm bath for me and helped me stumble into the bathroom. She shut the door to give me my privacy but stayed close by to make sure I was all right. She washed my clothes and gave me some new things to wear. She mentioned something about her brother being close to my size.

"He left a few things here last time he came to visit," "she said, "you could probably fit comfortably.'

"You don't need to do this.'

She smiled, "I know.'

The next morning it was the sun that awoke me. The curtains were open and sun was shining into the room. With a groan and every ounce of strength and energy I could muster, I rolled myself out of bed. I hit the floor with a thud and groaned again. I crawled toward the window and opened it. I didn't feel pain. There was no burning, no blistering flesh—no pain. Redline was right. I remembered his comment about my mother being "just a crazy old woman." So she was just a crazy old woman after all. I started crying out in joy. It was the most miraculous thing I had ever seen. It was as if the Earth was swallowed up in this ball of radiant light and warmth, it was like the entire universe was filled with a sudden beauty that had never been known before now. My entire life I had been deprived of something so simple and ordinary, the everyday light of the sun. I was overwhelmed with joy. It was a miracle! I was on my knees now, throwing my hands into the air.

"Oh!" I screamed out, "Oh God! It's a miracle!"

Vivian came in as I expected.

"Clem?"

"Look!" I screamed, "Vivian look, it's the sun, the sun, my darling!"

"Clement, you're sick, go back to bed."

"No, look!" I began clapping my hands and yelling nonsensical things, telling her I was a genius, that I had discovered some divine power. I was laughing uncontrollably; it could have easily turned to a complete fit of hysteria. I was mad with joy, but undeniably—I was mad.

I yelled for Walter, telling him that I had discovered the secret of Victor Frankenstein; of course I was still delirious and didn't realize that these secrets consisted of patterns, intricate patterns in the world's design that change and shift and now my recordings were ashes in Vivian's fireplace. My gift had been destroyed by the flames.

I was mad for many more weeks and Vivian cared for me. She nurtured me the way a mother would nurture a son, and by the time I was well again I knew I owed her my life.

"I know I owe you something," I said, "And if you will let me tell you my story I can be sure it will be a payment you will never forget.'

She sat beside me, "I barely know you, Clem, and yet—I have become very fond of you. If you want to tell me what happened to you to cause your brain fever, I am willing to listen."

I told her everything, starting with Walter Redline and his teachings. I tried to explain to her that I had unlocked the secrets of nature and discovered things I was never intended to and then destroyed those discoveries in her fireplace. I would have to start from the beginning with Walter again. She didn't speak a word until I was finally finished with my story.

"You don't believe me, do you?"

"Of course I do," she answered sounding surprised, "Of course I believe you, but I also believe that your illness is what causes you to believe it."

I sighed heavily, "You don't understand," I said, "I tried to tell you before I had gone mad I tried to tell you that I don't have to be this way."

"Clem…"

"You needn't say anything," I said, "I am sorry for taking up your time. I am truly grateful for what you have given me, and one of these days I swear I will find a way to repay you. I have to get home to Walter and my father and mother. I'm leaving now, thank you again, goodbye."

I left that afternoon on my way back home. The sun was more beautiful than I ever imagined. It seemed to flood over the world like an unstoppable tidal way. I hated watching the people on the streets, and crowding the little shops and restaurants. I realized I was one of them—I was weak and mortal.

I got home close to evening time and luckily had my keys in my pocket. I stepped inside and the house was silent. Nobody came rushing to the door to rejoice my return. I saw a shape emerging into the entry. I turned on the light and realized I didn't know her she stared at me seeming as frightened as I was. She refused to avert her eyes and in an instant I was against the wall feeling an unnatural power emanating from her. She continued to walk toward me and I pressed myself harder against the wall unaware of what I was frightened of. Her beauty was mesmerizing and she walked very slowly. Her hips moved gracefully and her silken gown caressed her hands at her sides. It was easy to imagine a crown of gold on her head and flowers woven into her blood red hair. She reached out a delicate poreless hand. I shut my eyes prepared for pain but I felt a delicate coolness on my cheek. I opened my eyes and she was staring at me smiling.

"Ah," she whispered, "an intruder, how lucky that he must be so beautiful."

I tried to speak, but it came out in a pleading whisper. "This is my house.'

She froze for a moment, "You're Clement?" It didn't sound like a question.

I nodded.

"William Thortan is your father?'

I nodded again.

"Are you familiar with the name Mathius Castlebar?'

I couldn't respond at first. "Thief," I growled, "He destroyed my father.'

She nodded. "Yes.'

"What's going on?'

"I found him here, "she said, ignoring my question, "your father and your sick mother were approached by Mr. Castlebar.'

I stared, still shaking.

"I tried to stop him, "she said, her voice dropped sadly, "I tried to kill him, he destroyed my family as well, I tried so hard to kill him but by the time Mathius was dead at my feet your poor mother and father were as well.'

I froze and chocked on my breath. *Dead? Oh god if only I would have gotten here sooner, if only I had given Walter my recordings, I could have saved them, given them immortality possibly even cure my mother's illness, make her able to think clearly. It was my fault now, my fault that they were dead.*

"My fault.'

"No," the woman whispered, I hadn't realized she heard me, "It is the fault of nobody but Castlebar.'

I couldn't think I could barely breath I was numb with grief. How could I be so sure she was telling the truth? Perhaps she was the killer, after all what was she doing in my house?

"I came here for him, she said, "I have been following him for months, I knew he was planning a murder, I knew because he murdered my old father and other people alike.'

"Really?'

"I am no murderer Clem.'

I trembled when she said my name.

Her name she told me was, Luna, she never let me know her last name. She told me she could help me. I spoke to her about Walter and my fear of death so she explained to me that there was some place I could go, a place where life has meaning. I didn't understand at first but that is when she introduced me to Abraham. He was so kind and grateful to meet me. He gave me the name James West and took me in as his son; he is who I call Father. Alex who was his natural born son became my brother. Alex never showed jealousy or resentment toward me he greeted me warmly and instantly treated me like family. I was drawn to these people and manipulated into their way of life. They sacrificed people on the stone you have seen, the pure people the ones Abraham said were "made for us." He would serve their blood in silver goblets. He covers the stone with sheepskin and ties the victims down. He kills them with bone knives. It's barbaric and I knew this. I was terrified to believe differently, terrified to betray Abraham. It didn't take long for Luna to see the pain I entertained when I was forced to kill, it didn't take long for the pain to reach her. She took me away from the group who named themselves "The Sevren." I am still unsure of what the word means, something of a made language by the elder cult leaders. There was a fight between The Sevren and another group of people. There is one person who I will never forget... Ian."

"Ian is one of them, one of the good guys. He's a younger boy who helped Luna and me escape The Sevren. Of course I was not able to keep my betrayal a secret for long. I grew to love Abraham and Alex I grew to love them all as my family and for a long time I believed in the power of blood, for a long time I believed them to be right. Abraham is evil, I understand that now—he enjoys the killing and the feasting he's not sane."

He stopped there and pressed his fingers to his temples.
"Are you okay?" I asked.
He looked up and nodded, "Yes," he said, "It is just painful sometimes."
"I'm sorry."
"I do share your pain," he said, "My mother and father; I know how it feels to lose someone you love."
He could never understand; nobody understood the connection I shared with Danny.
"I'm so sorry, Aidan," I whispered, "For everything that happened to you."
"You must never tell anybody, Jane," he said firmly. His emotion changed and he was himself again, "You must never say a word about who or what I really am."
"What about Rudy?"
"NO!" he cried, "Especially not Rudy!"
"No—I mean. Rudy already knows."
He laughed and it was a relief to hear something other than tension in his perfect voice, "Rudy thinks I'm a—hunter."
"He told me where to find you that day."
He nodded, "and I knew that. remember?" he smiled, "I wanted you to see, I wanted something that would force me to reveal myself to you, I couldn't find the courage on my own."
"You wanted me to see?"
He nodded, "Otherwise I wouldn't have been there. Don't get me wrong, I didn't mean to frighten you but you don't seem like somebody who gets frightened easily. I didn't realize how terrifying I must have looked."
"You looked beautiful." I murmured.

He smiled, "and pathetic, crouched down like an animal."

"But you looked strong," I said, "I liked that. Even if it did frighten me."

"Were you afraid I was going to hurt you?"

"I don't know what I was afraid of," I answered, "But I don't think I was afraid of you hurting me otherwise I wouldn't have let you in."

"In a way Jane, I wish you hadn't," he said softly, "As much as I needed you and as much as I wanted to assure you I wouldn't hurt you, it is because of me that you are in danger."

I didn't know what to say, I couldn't tell him I was sorry because I knew that was a wasted effort and I couldn't tell him it was okay because it wasn't, but the silence between us was unbearable.

"Aidan?"

He smiled and locked his gaze into mine. He kissed my forehead.

"Everything will be fine," he told me, "I promise."

His words hadn't comforted me. For the first time his speaking was no more comforting than the pure silence and my fears rushing through my mind. There had to be some way out of this.

"Aidan?"

He looked at me waiting for me to speak.

"There is one more thing," I said, "That you haven't explained."

He sighed and dropped his gaze. "Rudy?" he muttered, "Is this about the day with Rudy?"

He looked at me again and I nodded slowly. "You don't have to tell me," I said, "If it's painful."

He half smiled and I wasn't sure what it meant. I just stared at him waiting for his response. His expression changed suddenly and I could see he was suffering. "I am only afraid of truly terrifying you."

Life Blood

I pulled my eyebrows together, "I really think it's better now if you tell me."

He nodded.

"Why were you covered in blood, but not cut?"

"As you know I came in simply because I wanted to protect you, the crazy thing is, Rudy and Eric both thought that the blood was from the garden rake— they came at me instantly, as soon as they saw me. The blood wasn't mine, Jane."

I choked on my breath. "What?"

"One of them found me." He continued, "One of The Sevren. A lower ranked member than myself. He was going to turn me over to one of the leaders—and he was going to kill you. I had to protect you!"

"So..."

He sighed and looked away from me "I killed him, yes" he said quietly. He sounded like he was forcing the words from his mouth. "With his own knife. I placed the body in front of the alter when I returned to the clearing."

"Which is why you were covered in blood?"

"Exactly. If they find out I killed him, which they probably already know—then they are looking for me."

I shuddered and felt him running his fingers through my hair. "Are you all right?"

"I'm fine," I told him, "worried."

He nodded, "I know. But nothing is going to happen to you."

I nodded and he grasped a lock of my hair and gave me a crooked smile. "Your hair has gold in it."

"Does it?"

"Jane—why don't you ever say what is in your head?"

"I do."

"I don't believe that."

"I'm—honest. Most of the time."

"Is that really what you were just thinking?"

I sighed. "No."

"Didn't think so," he muttered, but I could hear a smile behind his words.

"I thought you couldn't read me."

He laughed, "I can't," he answered, "But I *can* tell when you are saying something you are not thinking.

"I sometimes don't even know what I'm thinking, or what I'm supposed to be thinking."

"Now *that* was the truth."

"How about another truth?"

He nodded.

"I'm frightened.

XIV

Kidnapped.

"OF me?"

I shook my head. "I was telling the truth when I said I wasn't afraid of you."

He nodded, "Do you trust me?"

"I don't know."

"If you had to choose to trust me or not, would you?"

"If I had a choice, Aidan, probably not."

"That's probably best."

Words were becoming forced from me suddenly, like a scream I couldn't hold back. I swallowed my voice several times but the words kept trying to come out, I knew I didn't want to say it and yet I wasn't even sure exactly what I was going to say.

"But…" it came out in a choked whisper and he looked at me, "But I love you."

It fell out of my mouth. I couldn't believe I had actually said it.

"I know," he answered, "I've known that."

All the nervous feelings had vanished by his calm reaction. "Still," I said, "It feels good to say it."

"Feels good to hear it," he answered, "I told you that I need you, Jane, that in itself should have told you that I love you."

"You love me?"

He let out that smooth private laugh I was familiar with, "Of course. I thought you knew. That is why I always wanted to be close to you, since the first day I met you."

I smiled flaccidly it was clearly artificial. "This complicates things."

"Actually it may make things easier."

"How?"

"Love is strong," he said, "It gives speed."

That wasn't comforting at all. I had never felt so afraid. I couldn't decide what I was more afraid of, Aidan's lies or The Sevren. How could I know he was telling me the truth? Could I really trust him not to hurt me not to—kill me? I sighed before I could stop myself.

"What's wrong?" he asked.

"It's nothing," I lied.

"What are you thinking?"

"Why do you always ask me that?"

"Because you're one of the few who baffle me when you're in thought." He smiled.

I shrugged, "I'm not thinking about anything."

"Huh." He grunted. He gave me that warm smile, shaking his head.

I moved closer, feeling the need for his lips to close around my own but before I was able to take in a kiss a knock came at the front door.

Panic struck, "Should I—"

He nodded, "It's all right," he said, "It's safe."

I walked down the stairs slowly, feeling tense and nervous. What if it *wasn't* safe? What if it was one of—one of *them*?

I opened the door slowly.

"Hey!" she yelled full of energy.

I felt my breath explode. "Oh—um—hi, Becky."

"You okay?"

"Yeah."

"What are you doing?"

"Well—um—I'm a little busy."

She giggled to herself peeking behind me. "Is Aidan here?" her voice was quiet and she was suppressing laughter.

Life Blood

"Uh—yeah."

"You won't believe who I've spent the past three nights with."

I shrugged.

"Aaron. You know—he's actually kind of cool."

"Yeah."

"Oh—right—"busy."" She made the quotes with her fingers.

"Shut up," I laughed, "It isn't like that."

"Telling me it isn't like that when I didn't say it was "like" anything means it's *totally* like that." She chuckled.

"Right."

"Okay well—I'll leave you to it, but you are coming to opening night yes?"

"Opening night?"

She thrust her hand to her forehead, "Oh god, I forgot to tell you." She put her hand on her chest and exclaimed proudly, "I got the lead!"

I smiled, and it was genuine. I knew how much it meant to her, "That's so great, Becky!" I pulled her into a hug.

It was difficult for me to show my enthusiasm when there was a flawless, dangerous cult member in my bedroom.

"Aaron is taking me out to celebrate, seeing as you're busy I just want you to at least be there for the show."

"Definitely."

"Friday night—7:00 p.m."

"I'll be there."

"Bye, Janie." She leaned forward and kissed my cheek.

"Bye, Becky."

She skipped away but I nearly shoved her out the door. I felt bad not being able to celebrate with her and Aaron but the guilt didn't last long; I had other things to worry about.

I raced back upstairs and Aidan had suddenly become rock solid. His face was hard and emotionless.

"Aidan?"

"Wh—who..." he cleared his throat and I could hear his heavy breathing.

I had never seen him speak that way, stumbling over his words. I had never seen him so—imperfect.

"Who is this?" his voice sounded almost forced out of him.

He was staring at an old picture on my dresser.

"Who do you think?" I walked up beside him and pointed at it, "It's Danny."

"Short for Daniel, right?"

I nodded.

It was an old picture of him in his red baseball cap and red T-shirt. He wore that outfit a lot when we were kids. He was smiling the way he always had, the way I remembered. I was somewhere in the background—just a blur.

He cleared his throat, "Oh—of course."

"What is it?" I asked, "What's wrong?"

"It's nothing." He was suddenly perfect again, "he just reminds me of someone. Never mind."

I nodded. It was strange that he would have reacted that way, how could it possibly be anybody he knew? I tried to brush it off but it almost haunted my dreams that night. I felt like I was in the cold wood, saturated with rain. Aidan was there, looking terrified, holding the picture of Danny. The picture was different somehow. My brother didn't have that old innocent grin I remembered but his face was blank—stone cold. Not *my* Danny. I dropped to my knees on the cold, wet bracken and felt myself falling apart. I woke up frightened and buried my face in Aidan's chest.

"Did I wake you?" he whispered.

I shook my head.

He stroked my hair and kissed the top of my head, "Have happy dreams, love."

I smiled and shuddered when I heard him call me "love." Perhaps I had only dreamed that part.

"Are you going to school?" I asked him
He shook his head. "No, but you should."
"I'm not going without you."
"It's safe, you should go."
I shook my head. I could be just as stubborn.
"Will you go if I come with you?"
I nodded.
"All right. Let me get home really fast, I'll be back before you're ready."
"I bet," I laughed, "You have a way of appearing out of nowhere."
He smiled.

I showered quickly, actually feeling anxious over the thought that Aidan would be back. My feelings had turned so quickly. I tried to shake off the dream. I got dressed and actually used the blow dryer, stalling until I had to go back into my bedroom. I got dressed and walked back in. There was Aidan in a dark blue T-shirt and loose fitting blue jeans. He was staring at my brother's picture again.

"He was happy." He said quietly.
"Yes."

He turned to face me; he was smiling which didn't seem to match the tone in his voice. I half smiled back.

"What does Becky think?"
"I told her it isn't like that but she doesn't believe me."
He frowned, "Well—isn't it sort of—err—like that?"
I shrugged, "I'm not sure. I guess so."

School was a haze. Even as Aidan was there with me every chance he could be I wanted to get home. After school Aidan dropped me off. It was one of those days where I couldn't remember what I had done all day and didn't even remember the drive home.

"I'll be back," he said, "but I need to check something out first."

I nodded mechanically, my eyes glazed. I waited for his smile but I missed it. He'd turned away when I heard it in his voice.

"Don't do anything stupid, Jane."

I sighed and glared at him even though he couldn't see. I slumped into the chair in the living room; contemplating getting up to eat something hoping it would stop the knotting in my stomach. I heard the knock come at the door. That was *fast!*

I opened the door but it wasn't Aidan, silly of me to think he'd actually use the door. I turned and walked away. He closed the door and followed.

"Are you alone?"

"He's coming back, Rudy," I snarled, "I wouldn't stay if I were you."

He sighed and stood beside me by the kitchen sink. "Why don't you let me take you out?"

"What?" I cried overdramatically.

"C'mon, just dinner—you're obviously hungry.

I shook my head and closed the cupboard, "Aidan is coming back."

I turned away but he grasped my arm. I turned back toward him, I tried as hard as I could to strip every bit if expression from my face. He let my arm loose then placed his hands on my waist.

"Rudy...?"

"You know he isn't good for you."

"What?" I finally processed what he was doing, what he was there for. I flung his hands off of me.

"You *know* it. Jane!"

"Rudy, it isn't like that."

"But it is and everybody knows it. Just let me show you once."

"Show me what?"

"That I can be better for you." Despite my angry tone, he remained calm.

"No Rudy. Please just leave." I pointed toward the door and heard Aidan's car, "that's him," I said, "go."

"Not even two minutes," he hissed, "are you *ever* without him?" he mumbled something and stormed out, shoving past Aidan who was at that point at the door. He looked at me confused at first and let out a dry, half laugh.

"Don't start," I said acidly.

"Oh come on, Jane," he said too cheerfully.

"It's *not* funny!"

"Don't you like him at all?"

"Yes," I said automatically, "when he's not being his ridiculous self."

He smiled, "I think he's in love with you."

"Ewe!" I smacked his arm. He leaned against the counter on his elbows; he had his dark eyebrows raised and a smirk on his face.

"Oh *please,* Aidan."

I put the box of cereal back in the cupboard and headed to my room. He followed as if I was leading him there.

"You know, I'm not mad."

"You probably shouldn't be," I answered, "but if he tries that again you have my permission to be as angry as you want."

He wrung his hands together, "I would love to."

I instantly regretted saying that. Rudy was a good guy, just fatally jealous but he was a good friend to me, someone I could trust. Aidan sat beside me on my bed. I leaned against him and he automatically put his arm around me. I had already completely forgotten about Rudy.

"I don't want you to be afraid," he said, his voice was soft and serious.

"How could I not be?"

"If you had any conception at all of how much you mean to me, you would know that I would never let anybody hurt you."

"Don't promise me that, Aidan. You said yourself; Abraham is smarter and stronger than you are."

"Yes that's true," he said, "But I have my moments, if I'm doing it for you it's enough to give me strength."

"I'm not sure I understand exactly what you mean."

"I simply mean that my loyalty to you will kill me before anything bad happens to you."

"That's supposed to comfort me?"

"Just don't worry."

"I'll get right on that." I muttered.

He didn't answer. He pulled me into his hard chest and I concentrated on feeling the true strength of his arms. What did it mean for me to truly admire his strength and the broad build of his shoulders? I wanted him more than I realized, I couldn't lie to myself when he was this close to me not when I felt the feverish warmth of his skin when his desire for me heightened, not now that I needed him for my survival as well. He wanted me to need him in return and against what I would have chosen if the option were given to me, I did. I did need him, more now than ever.

"No matter what happens Jane—I love you."

It was the first time, he told me he loved me without me saying something first. I felt the blood rush to my face. How could somebody so perfect find *me* irresistible? How could Aidan Summers love *me?* I believed him, even though he had lied to me before, even if he was a member of The Sevren, I loved him. I didn't care anymore who or what he was, it was unconditional.

"I want to tell Becky so badly," I whispered.

"I know." He replied, without advising me not to.

"I don't mean about what's happening," I said, "But at least about us."

I could hear the smile in his voice as he tucked my head beneath his chin, "She already knows."

"Still," I muttered, "I wish I could tell her."

* * *

"Jane, do we *really* have to do this?"

"Aidan!" I hissed, "Of course. She's my best friend. You have *no* idea how much this play means to her."

He groaned

"You know—you don't have to come if you don't want to."

He gave me a sour look, "I do, Jane," he answered. "I hardly feel comfortable leaving you alone in your own home; I'm not letting you do this alone."

"Do you really think something bad is going to happen?" I asked, "At school?"

He shook his head, "Actually no," he said, "I don't. But I won't be able to relax until I know your home safe, so that's why I'm coming with you."

I nodded. "No more complaining please."

"Okay okay."

He smiled at me, forcing me to smile back.

"I'm guessing you want to drive?"

"You guess right," I answered, "I know my way at least to school."

He nodded and got in the passenger's seat. The drive to school was almost completely silent which made me uncomfortable. Made me wonder what he was thinking.

"Are you okay?" I asked.

He turned and gave me a weak smile, "I'm fine" he said, "Just a little bit anxious. I can't stop being angry with myself for not having enough self control to leave you alone."

I didn't know what to say so I tried to stay positive. "I trust you," I said, "I know you will figure this out."

The school was already flooded with students when we got there and we had to wait in line at the little window next to the theatre entrance. Aidan paid in cash and he followed me when I rushed inside to the center of the front row to make sure I had the best view. I was surprised at how excited I was. Shakespeare was always one of my favorites but *Romeo and Juliette* definitely seemed overdone. Either way, Becky would be fantastic. I heard someone call my name and turned to see Aaron.

"I'm glad you're here." I said.

"Wouldn't miss it for the world" he chuckled. He stared at Aidan for a minute and took the seat next to me. Ignoring Aidan as best he could.

"Hello, Aaron."

"Um...hi." Aaron stammered.

The tension was almost unbearable. I wanted to say something but couldn't find any words that would be helpful. I sighed and looked at Aidan. He shrugged his shoulders and looked straight ahead. The stage was high off the ground and I was getting impatient for the red curtain to finally move aside so I could watch Becky. The lights dimmed and the narrator, played by someone I didn't know recited his lines perfectly and the curtain finally came up.

I noticed Aaron wringing his hands together every time Becky's part called for her to kiss Jonathan Peirce. It made me laugh. I didn't realize what *I kind of like her* really meant. After the play the crowed exploded in applause and Becky instantly raced over to us.

"I saw you the second I stepped onto the stage," she shrieked out, "It was so awesome seeing you right in front of me."

I laughed, "Becky, you were so great!" I hugged her and she hopped up and down all excited and proud of herself.

"You did do really great." Aaron added and hugged her without a second's hesitation.

Aidan smiled at her, "Sorry to say we don't have any flowers for you."

Aaron thrust his hand to his forehead, "You know what," he started, "I actually do, and I left them in my car."

Becky smiled, "I'll come with you to get them if you want." She sang.

She skipped out to the parking lot with Aaron and I just followed behind. Aidan grasped my hand as we walked to my car and I let him. I waved to Becky, deciding to leave her alone with Aaron for a bit. I was so glad to see they liked each other.

"I have something I need to do once we get back to your place," Aidan said.

"Okay…"

"It's important, okay?"

I just nodded.

I drove us back to my house and Aidan got in his car, "You're coming with me," he said.

"Oh…I didn't realize I needed to."

"You do," he answered, "I got you involved rightly or wrongly."

I started feeling extremely paranoid and I just stood there beside the car unmoving.

"Jane—are you ok?"

I didn't answer, just stared at him. He got out of the car and walked toward me. I felt him grasp my hand.

"It's okay," he whispered, "Please trust me, it isn't a big deal. I just need to take care of something. I'm not going to hurt you."

Not going to hurt you. That was what I was waiting to hear. I nodded and hesitantly got in the car still feeling anxious and suspicious.

"You cannot turn around!" he snapped. He was more than testy, he sounded terrified. I held onto the door of the car as he skidded and sped all over the wet road.
"Aidan what are you doing?" I yelled, "You're driving like a lunatic, you trying to kill me?"
"Contrary. Jane, be quiet."
He advised me not to turn around so I glanced in the rearview mirror. Nothing but the road lined with trees—an empty road. Had he lost his mind?
"Where are we going?"
"I need to talk to Luna," he said, "That's where we're going."
I didn't say a word but we were driving the opposite direction of Aidan's house. We pulled into the driveway of a very small house; it was secluded off the road through a dirt trail, almost in the middle of the woods.
"Why are you so nervous?" he asked me, his tension had vanished.
"What do you mean?"
He touched my wrist and I realized I was wringing my hands together, "Don't worry." He said.
"What if—what if she doesn't like me?"
He chuckled and his eyes brightened, "You make me laugh, Jane."
He stepped up to the door and took my hand. He knocked lightly and I inhaled. A woman opened the door; I could only guess it could be Luna. She had beaming blue eyes and the most extraordinary hair I had ever seen. It was red, the color of blood and reached her waist in silken waves. She matched Aidan's description flawlessly. She was beautiful, but that didn't put me at ease, in fact it made me even more uncomfortable. She smiled and my anxiety lowered, she seemed very warm

Life Blood

and welcoming. The house was beautiful from what I could see. The front room was spacious with old fashioned upholstered furniture, a couch, love seat and chair, which all appeared to be from the mid 1800s. Most of it was framed with redwood and covered with floral patterns. It was amazing. The light was dim but not uncomfortably. There was a china cabinet to the left of the redwood door filled with beautiful artwork. I tried concentrating on the beautiful room to keep my thoughts away from apprehension.

"Come in," she said, her voice, sounded very young and feminine.

"He's in North Bend," Aidan said, stepping inside.

I turned my attention back to him.

"How do you know?" Luna asked.

"Many ways," he answered, "The stone has been used, and I destroyed my clean slate, Luna—forgive me."

"A bird?"

He nodded, "It was like he was inside of me," he said, "Like he had invaded my mind and controlled me." He sounded like he was suppressing tears.

Luna nodded and embraced him, "For a long time you believed in the power of blood," she said, "When you feel lost—lonely…"

He shook his head, "I was frightened," he said, "I was a coward. I did it because I was afraid to not believe anymore."

"Never be afraid to be who you are, James."

The name made me uneasy. James? There was no way I could ever look at him and see him as anyone but Aidan Summers.

"I'm sorry, Jane," he whispered turning toward me, "For making you a part of my problems."

"I'd stand by you no matter what," I said, "even if you tried to run from me."

He smiled that smile he only gave to me. "I know," he said.

Luna stared at me until I broke my gaze. "You look terrified." She said. I brought my eyes back to hers.

"I'm all right." I answered.

She nodded but didn't look convinced.

Aidan kissed my cheek, "Do me a favor Jane," he whispered pulling me into a hug, "and don't fight me."

"What?"

"I'm doing this for you."

I felt Luna remove my hands from around Aidan's shoulders and pull them behind my back. She was strong but tender at the same time. I tried to move away but Aidan's arms were too strong and held me prisoner in his embrace. For the first time I felt that freezing stab of betrayal. My eyes filled with tears.

"I love you, Jane."

His face was rock hard and Luna handcuffed me and dragged me away from him. I instantly started scrambling toward him trying to reach him, as if he was going to save me, but I wasn't strong enough against Luna.

"We really aren't the bad guys, Miss Doe," she sang, "He really does love you. This is just his way of doing what he needs to do."

She pulled me into another room and now that Aidan couldn't see, I let the tears spill over. What should I have expected? He warned me and I broke my own rules—I can't expect honesty and loyalty from *anybody* and yet I had trusted him. I was *so* stupid!

"Please don't cry," Luna coaxed, she still sounded sweet, "he is only trying to protect us all."

She handcuffed me to the post of a beautiful bed. The sheets matched the floral patterns on the furniture in the front room. There was a bookshelf to my left stuffed full of classic works and philosophy. I tried to struggle and even tried squeezing my hand from the cuff but it only tore through the flesh of my wrist. I cried uncontrollably feeling more deceived then I ever thought possible. I eventually exhausted myself and fell asleep. I didn't sleep for long, I was kept awake almost all night by disturbing nightmares. What was in Aidan's head? What was he thinking? I knew there was something more going on, something he couldn't tell me about. I tried to tell myself that Luna was being honest, that Aidan was doing this out of love. But how could I be sure? How could I be sure of anything? After all the lies and now this—it was like I truly didn't know him at all, which is exactly what I feared from the very beginning.

I wasn't aware I had fallen asleep but I must have because I was awakened by the sounds of unfamiliar voices. When I opened my eyes I met a white face and big, round eyes staring at me. I tried to scream but before any sound had escaped he had his hand over my mouth and I lost consciousness again.

When I came to, I heard muffled voices. I wasn't sure at first if they were speaking to me or someone else.

"You—*what*?" a deep voice bellowed

"I had to." A young and warm sounding one replied.

"Had to?"

"Yes."

"Why?" the older voice hissed. It sounded like he was speaking through clenched teeth.

"Luna had her,"

"You can't just go kidnapping girls," the older voice said,

"She can help us."

"Help us? How?"

"I'm not sure yet but…"

"But what?"

"She's in love with James West."

There was a maddening pause and then the older voice replied.

"In love?"

I strained to keep listening but it was almost impossible, I was slipping out of consciousness again and I still couldn't open my eyes. I heard the sound of a door squeaking open and I tried with every bit of strength I had to open my eyes. The first thing I saw was a young, charming face. He must have been the kind voice outside the door. The room I was in looked completely normal. There was a large bed with a floral mattress and white lace curtains. There was a wooden bookshelf and a nightstand with a little white lamp shaped like a lily. Nothing about the room was even the slightest bit odd, and the entire situation called for something a lot stranger.

"Are you Jane?" that kind voice whispered.

I didn't answer.

"I'm not here to hurt you," he said.

He was wearing a red baseball cap and had solid blue eyes. Tears began to form in my eyes—he looked like Danny and I suddenly felt enraged.

"Who are you?" I bellowed, "And why the hell am I here?"

"Please," he pleaded, "I'm not here to hurt you, I promise."

I ignored him and clenched my hands into fists; I wanted to tear him apart.

"Relax," he whispered, "I'm here to help you."

I remembered the conversation I had heard "Or am *I* here to help *you*?"

He smiled and nodded, "fair enough," he said, "forgive the —umm…"

"Kidnapping!"

He chuckled quietly, "I wouldn't say kidnap."

I sighed and shook my head trying to calm my anger.

"You know James."

I hesitated then nodded.

"I thought so."

This had all happened so fast. I had no idea how to react. I was furious and terrified. "

Why does it matter?" I asked, "If I know him?"

He stared at me. "Are you okay?"

"My God! Do I look okay?"

"I'm sorry," he answered softly.

I sighed and put my head down.

His voice suddenly changed and he sounded almost solemn. "You don't know do you?"

I looked up at him, "Don't know what?" I yelled, "That the boy I trusted and fell in love with lied to me about everything, betrayed me and will probably kill me? No, please explain."

He sighed, "Look, Jane. We need your help."

"How can I help?" I asked, "And with what? James hasn't told me anything. I don't know anything."

The look in his eyes weakened me; I could swear he was Danny.

"Abraham," he said, "He's back in North Bend. Do you know who I am talking about?"

I nodded, "The father of Aid—James."

"James has more strength than you realize."

"I realize more than you know."

"He's the worst one. James never listens to Abraham," he said, "He makes his own rules."

"Perhaps that makes him the *good* one."

He shook his head, "I understand that you want to believe more than anything that James…"

"Aidan!" I muttered.

"What?"

"Please—I know him as Aidan."

He nodded. "Understood. I know you want to believe that he's good, but he isn't."

I was too disoriented to even fully process what he was saying; I didn't know what I myself was even thinking. I finally let the tears spill over, why hide it now?

"I'm supposed to give you to Dorian."

"Who?"

"Dorian," he repeated, as if he actually thought my response was because I hadn't heard him, "He's sort of my boss."

"Why did you kidnap me from Luna's?"

"I told you," he said, "I think you may be able to help us besides, is it so wrong that I wanted to protect you from James—Aidan?"

My crying increased and the tears soaked my face now.

"You don't understand." I wept, "Aidan isn't like them.

"I know you want to believe that, darling, but it just isn't true. He's Abraham's right hand man, him being his son."

"What makes you think I will want to help you?"

"You will, Jane," he said smiling, "you will."

I couldn't answer.

"My name is Ian by the way."

I sat there expressionless. I remembered the name but I wasn't sure why. It took a long moment for it to process in my mind. Aidan had said something about him once. He was one of the good guys, that's what Aidan had said, and even though I knew at this point that trusting Aidan was foolish, I believed what he told me and I was slightly less afraid. I didn't want to get up. I was still trembling. I could feel my insides shaking, like I was cold.

Ian offered me his hand. I remembered that day in the woods when Aidan had offered me his. I remembered how warm and welcoming it had appeared and how cold, tense, and unfriendly it had felt. Ian's hand appeared soft and delicate and when I touched it, it was warm and smooth—purely human. For some odd reason I was almost disappointed by the normality of him as a person. The situation called for something a little bit more interesting. He didn't hold my attention. I think he noticed the look in my eyes, easily being able to tell that my mind was elsewhere.

"Don't worry," he said, "Dorian will explain everything."

I couldn't respond.

Life Blood

"We're the good guys here, Jane."

I had heard that before, how could I believe anybody anymore? I was trembling before Ian even opened the door. I saw the man who must have been Dorian. He was dressed all in black and had an extremely muscular build. He was dark skinned and handsome but didn't smile. He shook my hand,

"Sorry about how all of this happened." He said. His voice was deep and insincere. He must have been who Ian was talking to outside the door when I was barely conscious. He led me out of the house which I hadn't taken time to look at to a blue van parked outside. He held onto my arm and wasn't what I would call gentle.

"Hey!" I snapped, "Want to try *not* breaking my arm?"

He sighed heavily, "Just get in." He almost threw me toward the car.

"All right," I yelled, "I get it!"

I didn't even pay attention to the streets or which way Dorian was driving; I was too annoyed by the entire situation and still hadn't completely stopped crying. I sat silently, slouched down in the passenger's seat with my arms folded across my stomach.

"Don't think that James betraying The Sevren is a good thing for anyone." He grunted.

"*Aidan* was never part of The Sevren," I hissed back, "he was threatened into all of it."

He shook his head, "He never listened." He muttered, "Abraham would be furious if he knew what's going on with you two."

"What are you talking about?"

He chuckled, "From now on you're going to treat me with a little more respect."

"I think I deserve the same," I said, "If you still want my help."

He laughed; it was a dry husky laugh that sounded completely synthetic. "*Ian* needs your help," he answered, "I simply need to enforce the rules."
"What rules?"
He stopped the car in the middle of an empty road.
"What are you doing?"
"I told you—enforcing the rules."
I saw him lift a crow bar above his head and I gasped. My eyes went dark as I heard one last dry, husky laugh.

* * *

When I awoke it was very dark but I was still aware of the smell of dust and wood. My face was saturated with sticky tears and my head was throbbing. I remembered the crow bar in Dorian's hand and realized he has hit me to the point of unconsciousness. I moved to sit up, and suddenly gasped when I felt the flesh on my knee slice open from somewhere in the floorboards. I clutched my hand to the wound. The only sounds I could hear were my own whimpering, it was comforting, knowing I was alone and at least there was nobody there to hurt me—for now. I leaned my head back slowly, being sure not to hit another nail that may be sticking out of the wall. I closed my eyes, making more tears roll down my cheeks. Knowing that sleep was impossible here I spoke softly to the only person I felt I could trust.

"Danny," I whispered, my voice was almost throttled, "If you can hear me I just want to tell you that I love you. I want you to know that I am going to do everything I can to get out of here and to make it back to Dad and take care of him, but you are the only one who can give me courage. Stay with me, Danny, just this once; help me up just one more time. Be there for me like you were in life. I need you now more than I ever have before, I will see you someday soon but until then I want you to be proud of me, of my life. I know I am proud of yours."

Suddenly I felt calm and numb, almost the way I did years ago when I stole my mother's vodka hidden in the pantry. I felt almost like I could sleep. My eyes darted open when I heard the sound of footsteps. Light flooded the room and I could see a dark figure walking down the steps toward me. He stopped inches in front of me. The light was so blinding that I couldn't see who it was. He didn't even say a word before striking me hard across the face. I tried to stay silent to stay strong.

"You are the reason James has turned his back on us."

It was Dorian's voice. My chest shook with uncontrollable sobs. He struck me again and I let out a short, strangled yelp.

"You answer me, slag!"

"James was never part of your—group" I whispered.

"What the hell are you blabbering about?" he demanded.

I winced, thinking he was going to hit me again. "He hid behind the fact that he was Abraham's son." I said, "He'd never hurt anyone, not again."

"You mean the way he hurt your brother?"

I could instantly feel the bile pushing its way into my throat. No sound came out when I whispered, "What?"

He laughed, "What, he didn't tell you?"

I was silent.

"Your little boyfriend killed your brother."

It took a moment for me to process his words but when they ran through my head over and over I began to feel like I was spinning. I couldn't speak, I choked on my tears. I tried to remember who was saying this. He wasn't exactly somebody I could trust. But Ian's words came to mind, and Rudy's story and all of my suspicions before. Aidan *had* lied to me. Betrayed me. I cried hard, harder than I'd cried since Danny died. I tried to think about the good times with Aidan but my mind kept showing my brother dead in the forest and Aidan with his knife in hand. The grief and the visions were overwhelming. I held my breath to keep from screaming.

"If I'm in a good mood, I may decide to feed you tonight." Dorian hissed. He left me then to cry by myself.

My love had murdered my brother. I tried telling myself it wasn't true, but it connected with Aidan's reaction at seeing Daniel's picture on my dresser.

He just reminds me of somebody.

From the very beginning he had lied to me. I knew I shouldn't have expected anything different.

I had to keep my mind somewhere else, somewhere that wasn't a dark, cold basement or a forest where Danny died. Nothing was working. For the first time, Jane Doe's "active imagination" couldn't concentrate on anything peaceful. I was in agony.

Dorian did let me eat that night. Dry salad and warm water. He threw the plate at me, causing me to pick up lettuce and olives from the dusty floor, I didn't complain. I had to think of a way out I had to get home I had to do it for Danny. What if something had happened to Ethan, or Becky or Rudy—even Aaron, what if I didn't live long enough to ever see them again? Who was going to come to my rescue if not Aidan? He was my hero, my knight in shining armor—he was also my enemy now and the very reason for my misery. Danny's death wasn't my fault and I was able to accept that but if something happened to one of my friends it *would* be my fault and I would die—by my own hands if not by Dorian's.

I didn't want to believe that Aidan was a killer; I didn't want to believe that he had anything to do with The Sevren. But I knew deep down that he was one of them and he had been lying to me all along. How could I look at him again? How could I look into those enticing eyes without seeing my brother dead at Aidan's feet?

I curled up in a ball on the dusty wooden floor. I had no conception of what time it was, if even it was night, but I did my best to relax regardless. I thought that maybe I had been asleep because I was not disturbed by the light or footsteps but was startled to see him when I opened my eyes.

"Shh," he whispered, "I'm not here to hurt you."

I tried to let my eyes adjust. I could see he was small looking—young. Even in the dark I could tell that he was blonde and his eyes were cobalt blue. His face had that childish roundness to it and his voice was small and innocent. Even this didn't make me feel better.

"My name is Alex," he said.

The name caught my attention, "Alex?"

"Yes."

I hadn't realized I'd said it out loud.

"Aidan," I heard him laugh, "what a dreadful name to choose."

I squeezed my eyes shut, hoping maybe I was dreaming.

"It isn't true," he continued, "what Dorian said."

"What?"

"Your brother's death wasn't his fault—James, I mean."

"How am I supposed to believe that?" I asked, "I have been led to believe so many different things that I have no idea who's been lying and who's been truthful—if anybody has been truthful."

"James is my brother," he said, "I know him quite well. He was always the bad one in the family, he never listened to Father."

"Abraham."

He nodded. "I did everything that Father said. He hurt James a lot so I was frightened of him. He made me kill."

"Why?"

"Because," he answered as if he was shocked I had asked why, "because that is what's right, it's what needs to be done."

"Do you believe that?"

"Of course I do," he exclaimed, "it is James who does not believe, James is the one who doesn't listen or obey, or understand. His loyalty to you will kill him before this is over."

"Why are you saying this?"

"Oh I'm not lying," he said calmly, "He didn't send me down here to talk to you if that's what you're thinking." He was so comfortable speaking to me; it seemed unnatural, "What I mean by that, Miss Doe, is that he won't kill you."

"Oh well, thanks, I feel much better now."

He chuckled, "Though he did mention you were sarcastic."

"Perfect."

So he *hadn't* forgotten about me. I wasn't about to believe a word Alex was saying to me. I couldn't be sure if he even knew Aidan. I closed my eyes and leaned my head back against the wall.

"I didn't mean to wake you," he said, "But I don't believe you belong here. Neither does James but there is really nothing either of us can do for you—Dorian is always watching, I'm lucky I was able to get down here without being seen."

"Why *am* I here?" I asked.

"I couldn't tell you that, Miss," he answered kindly, "Even if I knew."

He handed me a brown paper bag, "Don't let Dorian see this, James begged me to do something for you—anything. So here it is."

My heart sank. It was filled with food, sandwiches and fruits all in plastic bags. "Thank you." I whispered my voice was caught in my throat.

"You're very welcome. I'm supposed to be asleep, so I will let you continue yours now."

I nodded. So it *was* nighttime.

"Sleep well Jane," he said warmly, "James—Aidan would want that." He tossed me a thin blue blanket, "I'm not sure what this will do."

It smelled like Aidan, which made me choke back tears. I buried my face in it pretending I was back in my bedroom with Aidan when I trusted him, when I loved him and things were—normal? Maybe not normal, but good. His scent and my memories of him put me to sleep. I didn't dream of him, in fact I cannot remember dreaming at all. I awoke to the sound of the door.

"Abraham told me to feed you," Dorian growled, "so here."

He threw a stale piece of bread at me.

"And don't complain. He just wants you alive for now, so I am forced to feed you."

I didn't say a word, I was alone in a place I didn't know and could very well be dying. This wasn't supposed to happen to me—but yet it was my fault, I got myself into this mess in the first place. It defiantly isn't supposed to happen to someone like Becky or Rudy and I hoped to god that they were safe.

I wanted to be somewhere else, somewhere in my mind. I drifted away into a forest with green rolling hills and trees that smelled like vanilla and peppermint, where the grass was soft like velvet on my bare feet and the sun shone through in thin rays through the branches. Where there was color and life—and beauty. I hummed quietly to myself staying locked away in this imaginary woodland.

I wondered what Becky was doing, what she was thinking at every exact moment that I was shivering in a dark, dirty basement. I almost wished she was there with me at least so I wouldn't be alone. I knew it was imperative that I concentrate on other things. Things that would help me survive this nightmare if I ever wanted to even see Becky again. I thought about hiding the food

Alex had given me. Where better than beneath the floorboards? I tried but the wood wouldn't break, I tugged at it and kicked at it.

"Damn." I grumbled, "Always works in the movies."

I pushed the paper back against the wall and tried to cover it with the blue blanket, without making it look too obvious. I was terrified Dorian would find it and beat me to the point where I wouldn't be able to move. I couldn't decide which I was more worried about, being murdered or simply starving to death when the food ran out. Which would hurt more? I crawled along the floor, looking for a place to hide the food and being careful not to catch another nail. I felt the brush of cool fabric against my arm and instantly turned to examine what it was. It was nothing but a shape in the darkness. I reached out to it and something cold and stringy wrapped around my fingers. I winced and shrieked, pulling my hand away and backing up. I tried to get my eyes to adjust but I still couldn't see anything more than a dark mound against the wall. I gasped when I heard the door at the top of the stairs crack open and I glanced that way. When I directed my gaze back to the dark shape I was completely blinded by the light. Slowly my eyes adjusted and the beam of light from the open door lit up the object, revealing dark, empty eyes staring back at me. Eyes that were clearly nothing I had seen before. They were almost protruding from the gray flesh of pasty, lifeless face. I covered my mouth with my hands, forcing myself to swallow the scream pushing its way into my throat. When the door opened farther I could see exactly what the horrific object was. The face was stiff and black matted hair still clung to my fingers. She hung there like a rag doll. Her flesh was the color of raw clay and a row of yellow, x-shaped stitches were pushed through her lips, sealing her mouth closed. She was naked and lanky, almost bony.

"She never knew what not to say." I heard

I shrieked and turned to see Alex, kneeling beside me staring at the corpse as if she was still alive. His voice was flat and emotionless, "foolish to be honest," he continued, "She'd seen it happen before, Abraham warned her not to tell anybody about us."

I only stared at his young looking face, a relief from the dead girl. My voice was impossible to force from my throat and my entire body was quaking.

"He didn't even drink her blood," he added shaking his head slowly, "he said it was impure."

I still couldn't find the strength to speak.

"I wish you wouldn't cry," he murmured.

If I was crying I couldn't tell—I could hardly breathe. I was finally able to choke out one word. "Blood?"

"Yes," he answered, "Aidan mentioned you call us vampires. Do so if you will. Blood is powerful, it is life."

"Yes," I retorted, "If it's left in your body."

I took another glance at the corpse on the wall and couldn't help but to ask one question.

"What was her name?"

"In death their names die with them," he answered, "she is nameless."

"Nobody is nameless."

"Well in life—her name was Sharon. Sharon Walters."

"Sharon." I whispered, "Such evil."

"You know," he started, "Your brother—wasn't *nearly* as rude."

My voice choked up again and the shock almost suffocated me, I felt paralyzed.

"Danny?" No sound at all had escaped my lips but he seemed to understand and nodded.

Rudy's story flooded back to my head again. Alex changed the subject so quickly I didn't have time to ask questions. "Your terror has really increased Dorian's desire for you."

I glanced at Sharon, realizing she was naked, "My body, or my blood?"

"Both," he answered, "neither of those options would be a pleasant experience."

I didn't know what to say if I should even say anything.

"The police won't catch Abraham," he said, "or any of us. Abraham is too clever. We aren't evil, Jane, I know you may not understand that, you are naïve and untaught, but I believe that is why The Sevren have existed so long—fate, karma. The evil are punished, not people like us—not the ones who understand the way the world turns. There are rules you know, rules that we follow. Ways we are to kill and whom to kill. Abraham decides the ones who are made for us. Only he can be certain of their truly deserved fate."

"Fate is dead," I sobbed out, "and I will be too if you don't get me out of here."

"I'm sorry," he said, "I can't do that, I just came to check up on you." He turned away, "there's a broken floorboard behind the stairs," he said, "Hide it there."

I did as he said, trying to ignore the corpse in the corner.

Your brother wasn't nearly s rude.
They dump their bodies in alleyways.

It made sense that The Sevren was responsible for Danny's death. Nobody ever let us know anything, all they asked us was, *Can you think of anyone who would want to hurt him?* But nobody would want to hurt Danny, everybody loved him, it didn't make sense.

Blood is powerful it's life.

Why Danny's? He was loved by so many. Why him?

XV

Ian

I started yanking on the floorboards and found the broken one Alex had mentioned. It was still difficult to lift and it hurt my fingertips. I finally broke it free. I reached down to see how deep the space was making sure I'd be able to get the bag of food out once I dropped it in. I felt something soft under my palm, like velvet. I gripped my hand around it and pulled it out. I couldn't tell what it was but in a moment my eyes focused more clearly and I could see it was a black velvet marble bag with a drawstring.

The bag was obviously filled with something, but the contents didn't feel large enough or heavy enough to be marbles. I opened the bag and poured the pieces into my hand. I studied them for a moment and felt them with my fingers. I instantly recoiled in disgust but refrained from dropping them on the floor. I saw that they were tiny gumdrop shaped teeth, some whiter than others some with gold fillings and caps. I wondered again what would happen to me. Would I end up a hanging corpse in a basement? How cliché. Would somebody break my teeth out and hide them in a marble bag? The teeth couldn't have all been from the same person, the shapes and colors were too diverse. Why would anybody keep teeth? I dropped them back in the bag and put it back under the floorboard. I just curled up in the blanket Alex had given me and cried. It was the first time I let myself go completely. I whimpered Danny's name and begged him to save me, begged him to help give me the strength to live so I could live for him.

I cried myself to sleep but was awakened several times by horrific nightmares of the corpse becoming reanimated and breaking out my teeth, there were visions of Aidan in the woods killing Danny over and over again. I cried most of the night and when I finally gave up and decided to stay awake, I decided it was time to search for a way to break the walls and escape. It was too dark to see much and I was so distracted trying to avoid running into the body hanging on the wall that I couldn't think of any logical or practical way to get out. It was all completely ridiculous. Why am I being kept in a basement anyway? Why haven't The Sevren killed me yet? Sacrificed me on that stone in the woods? I pressed my fingers to my temples and almost screamed in frustration. There was no way I was going to give up and surrender, I was going to do whatever it took to get out, but my body was drained and my mind was currently in ruins. I knew I needed rest if I wanted even the smallest hope of living. I wrapped back up in the blanket and tried to relax. I felt myself slowly dozing off and finally my dreams were peaceful. I dreamed mostly of memories of Danny and Becky, even good days with my parents and my childhood summers. When I awoke, the dreams kept me locked in my past. I felt that dreamy sensation of the past pulling me back to my childhood. I tried pushing the images away and find the strength to continue looking for a way out. Before I even got the chance to move, the door opened again and I sat up, praying it was Alex.

"Let's go." He said.

The Voice wasn't Dorian's but I knew it wasn't Alex either. I knew the tone and recognized the way he spoke but I couldn't make out the face.

"Jane?"

I squinted my eyes and stared. "How did you get in here?"

"Dorian left," he answered walking down the steps, "I'm sorry, I didn't know he was one of them."

"How can I trust you now?"

"Because I'm the only one who can get you out of here."

"Who are you, Ian?"

He smiled. "Come on," he said, "get up."

I stood up on my own, even after he offered me his hand.

"By the way," he started, "your friend—is a severe idiot!"

"What?" my voice finally sounded more normal.

I heard a quiet laugh shake through him, "you're loved, Jane."

"Aidan?"

"Well—him too, but he isn't nearly as foolish as the other one."

"Other one? What *other* one? Who?"

"Don't remember his name at the moment, "he said, "Light spiky hair, taller than Aidan."

I gave him a blank stare.

"Wow let me tell you—those two do *not* get along."

I gasped, "RUDY!"

"Ah," he chuckled, "there ya go, Rudy, that's the one."

"What the hell is *he* doing here?"

"Well, from what I gathered he claims he loves you, so Aidan asked him to help."

"This is crazy!"

"Come on," he said, "before Dorian gets back, we have to get you out."

He led me up the steps. I was dizzy and fatigued, but as soon as I heard that familiar voice call my name, it somehow brought the energy rushing through me and I ran to him and fell into his arms.

"My god, are you okay?"

I didn't answer I just clung to his shirt and cried. "I'll take care of you," he said, "You'll be fine."

He was so warm. I didn't want to let go.

"We have to get you out, Jane," he said, "We have to move."

"You're crazy," I told him, "coming here."

He smiled, "Not crazy, Jane—I just can't leave everything up to Summers, I don't trust him an ounce."

"Where is he?" I asked, "Rudy, where's Aidan?"

"Shh—he's just around the corner, come on."

He took my hand and led me down the hallway. I saw him standing there, waiting for me. My eyes hadn't fully adjusted and before I even knew for sure it was him, I raced to him and wrapped my arms around his neck. I pressed myself close and constricted my arms tighter.

"Can't breathe, Jane." He whispered.

I moved away and he was smiling. My memory had forgotten how beautiful he was. Everything that Dorian said about Aidan being a killer and the words of Ian, even Rudy's story were at the time, erased from my mind.

"We have to go," Rudy said, "We have to keep moving."

I nodded, drying my eyes with the back of my hand.

"I have my car," Aidan announced, "It's just outside. We have to get you home."

"Is Ethan okay?"

He nodded, "As far as I know Ethan is fine."

We walked down the dark hallway passing several rooms. All the doors were closed and I could hardly tell what the house even looked like, though nothing appeared unusual. As we neared the end of the hallway I heard the familiar breathy whimpers and pleas of sobbing. I halted and turned toward the door. My blood ran cold and a dark foreboding flooded over me.

"No! Jane!" Rudy whispered, "Bad idea. You're safe now, we can't save everyone." I could hardly listen to him, only the violence behind the closed door in front of me.

"Rudy, listen," I said.

"No," he whispered. He grasped hold of my hand, "let's go."

"I can't," I demanded, "I have a very bad feeling Rudy, like I need to do something."

"You have a bad feeling?" he echoed, "You have a bad feeling because if we don't keep moving you're going to get yourself killed. Don't do it. Please!"

"*She* doesn't have to do anything," Aidan started, "but I think you should let me do the right thing—for once."

"Since when are you the good guy?" he snapped.

"Since you tried to steal my girlfriend."

"What? Your…"

"Both of you stop," I growled trying to keep quiet, "I *know* that voice."

I listened intently to the sounds, almost able to make out words.

"You're making this into something it isn't," Rudy said, "why don't we just get Jane out of here. Be logical for once."

"Look," Aidan demanded, "we have to at least try to get along. You can hate me if you want to—that's fine but until this is over. Please at least *pretend* to tolerate me, I will show you the same courtesy."

I looked at Rudy, trying to have a "way with my eyes" as Aaron had once said, a way, which Rudy couldn't refuse. It seemed to work.

"Fine," he growled, "but I'm not doing it for you."

"I'm not asking you to."

Aidan sighed and reached into the inside pocket of his jacket and pulled out a knife at least four inches in length.

"What the hell are you doing?" I spat.

"Jane—close your eyes."

I began shaking and tears formed in my eyes. I looked to Rudy and he nodded. I wanted to bury my face in his chest. He squeezed my shoulder and pressed his lips together. Aidan yanked on the handle of the door a few times before cursing to himself and kicking it in almost violently.

"Jane," Rudy whispered.

I turned toward him and his arms were open. I nodded and pressed myself against him. I put my hands over my ears and hummed quietly to myself. I felt the blood returning to my numb fingertips as Rudy stroked my hair. I tried my best not to listen but a growl and a deep gasp of pain found its way to my ears. I pressed myself harder into Rudy's chest.

"It's all right," he whispered.

What was happening to Aidan?

"James...?" I heard in a cracking voice, it was almost drowned out by the sobbing I had heard before. A voice cut through the air like a knife through steal.

"JAAANE!"

It was a desperate, miserable sounding voice, choked with horror. But I knew the voice, even poisoned with fear. I would know it anywhere. It had been my comfort and my shelter on the rainiest days in my life.

I pulled away from Rudy, even when he tightened his arms around me. She ran to me stumbling and almost falling over. She was a haggard mess, naked and shaking furiously.

"Oh my god!" I wept. "BECKY!" I joined her tears and embraced her, hiding her exposed body.

"Shh," I coaxed. "You're okay now."

I heard Rudy mumble something so I looked at him.

"I told her to stay behind," he said, he covered his face with his hands. "She wouldn't listen."

She was bawling uncontrollably and her legs were shaking so violently that I had to hold her up. My eyes were open and I was peering into the room. Aidan stood over a body covered in blood. It was exactly the way I saw him in the darkest nightmares that woke me up and brought me into his arms in the deep mornings when I loved him. More tears spilled from my brown eyes when I remembered that love and all of Ian's words came back to me along with Rudy's story. I saw the blood and it was no nightmare. I was awake this time. I couldn't open my eyes and find perfect, beautiful Aidan lying beside me, I was no longer the heroine in this story, I was nothing.

Aidan pulled his knife from the man's back and turned away from him. The body moved and the man stumbled to his feet. He had long dark hair and thick stubble of a forming beard. Blood clung to his hair and soaked the back of his shirt, but he could still move.

Rudy chocked out Aidan's name but it was too quiet for him to hear—it sounded like concern. I couldn't help but to cry out when Aidan turned back toward the man and shoved him to the ground, splashing blood on the walls and driving his knife across the stranger's throat. He turned to look at me.

"Why are your eyes open?" He was calm. His eyes expressed pure distress and agony. I was half expecting him to cry, but he didn't even move. He pulled the bloody shirt over his head and used a clean sleeve to take a couple of wipes at the impossible stains on his jeans. I stared at his shimmering skin and long thin lines of muscle. His beauty captivated me the way it always had and I almost forgot about my beautiful sister in my arms until I felt her grip my shirt.

"Aidan," I said, "get her something—please."

He nodded and pulled a clean white sheet off the bed and put it her over her shoulders. I wrapped it around her twice and tied it off in the front so Rudy could carry her. She was too weak to walk.

"No," she sobbed, "no, Jane."

"I'm right here," I said, "I'm right behind you."

She sighed lightly and fell unconscious in Rudy's arms.

"I'm sorry," Aidan whispered, "That you had to see that."

"How badly did he hurt her?"

"I'm not sure," he answered, "She may be slightly concussed but he was fully clothed when I walked in. She's mostly just scared."

"Abraham?"

He stared at me for a moment, then broke eye contact and nodded. He continued to lead us down the hall to the car parked right outside the house. I couldn't pay attention to anything, not even where we were or what anything looked like, just on the fact that I was alive and so was Becky. Other thoughts were haunting me, Aidan had just killed his own father, it was an act that seemed completely deceitful and worth fearing him for.

Becky was still unconscious. Rudy put her in the back seat with her head rested in my lap. Aidan drove while Rudy sat in the passenger's seat seeming completely dazed and disoriented. I couldn't say anything to him there was this thick, obvious tension and coolness between him and Aidan. I felt Becky stir and looked down to see that her eyes were open.

"It's okay," I told her, "I'm here and we're going home."

"Correction," Aidan interrupted, "hospital."

"No," Becky whispered, "You'll be in too much trouble."

"We don't have to tell them exactly what happened, do we, Aidan?"

"No, we don't Jane, but either way, in this situation I am innocent."

"You killed Abraham."

He nodded, "self defense."

I didn't answer.

"Thank you." Becky whispered.

Rudy turned to look at me, "My god," he yelled, "Jane—have you eaten *anything*?"

I nodded, "I'm okay, I was fed."

"Not as much as I had hoped," Aidan answered, "But Alex gave you food, right?"

"Yes," I answered, "Thank you for that."

"I'm sorry I couldn't get you out sooner, I am so sorry I let this happen to you."

"It isn't your fault."

"I should have never gotten close to you."

"I tried to tell you that." Rudy murmured.

"Not now!" I snapped back.

"When?" he mumbled under his breath. I could still hear the anger in his tone.

Aidan answered, "how about when Jane is coherent and Becky is conscious? Sound good to you?"

"Jeez," he snapped back, "a little hostile, are we?"

"For the love of god, man, I just found my father attacking my friend and the love of my life half starved to death in a dirty basement so I think it would be nice if you could just shut the hell up before I crash this car into a tree. Yes?"

He didn't answer just slouched down in his seat. I had never seen Aidan so angry and it actually scared me. It made me realize that he could be capable of anything if he got angry enough—but at the same time he let Rudy beat the crap out of him and never moved an inch to fight back. I shook off the confusion to try to rest on the car ride home. Resting ended up being more difficult than I imagined. I couldn't let myself stop listening to Becky's breathing, making sure she still felt warm and alive. I heard Aidan curse as he pulled over to the side of the road.

"What's wrong?" I asked.

"Damn car's out of gas." He murmured.

"What?" Rudy growled, "It was completely full just before we got here."

"Abraham," he sighed under his breath, "Damn—we really do need a car."

"That's not exactly an option," Rudy chimed in.

"Nonsense."

"Okay—another question then. How do you propose we *get* a car?"

He looked at Rudy and smiled. For the first time I had noticed something other than anger and resentment. Aidan shook his head.

"It won't be too difficult."

Aidan drummed his fingers on his cheek and hummed quietly a few times.

"Okay." He whispered.

We waited for the actual beginning of his sentence.

"Rudy," he started, "I need to go back inside. Stay in the car and look after the girls. Lock the doors. If Dorian gets back, I'll take care of it."

He nodded.

I sat there silently. Becky was still asleep and Rudy didn't even turn to look at me, he was so quiet that it made me nervous. I was shaking the entire time, terrified that Dorian would appear out of nowhere, but Aidan returned as quickly as he always did. He walked back to the car with something in his hand he looked completely content and emotionless. Rudy unlocked the door.

"Let's go," Aidan said, showing us a small silver key hanging from a keychain.

I smiled and stepped out of the car. Rudy carried Becky and followed Aidan and me around the house. I lost my breath for a moment when I spotted a black mustang in the open garage. I stepped closer and saw the familiar license plate. Aidan turned and looked at me.

"Are you okay?"

I nodded, but I think he knew I was lying. I was pretty far from okay.

XVI

Ethan

HE got in and started the car. Rudy put Becky in the back seat. She stirred silently and it was a relief to see her move. A breath escaped her lips and it seemed like she was trying to say something.

"Becky?"

She didn't wake up but whispered Aaron's name. I smiled.

Rudy got in the passenger's seat and Aidan sped off, driving like a lunatic the way he usually did.

"Slow down," Rudy sputtered. I could tell he was trying to hide the tension in his voice.

"Sorry," Aidan laughed, "It's simply out of habit."

"I wouldn't mind getting home a little sooner," I said.

Rudy turned around and looked at me, "Are you *going* home?"

I shook my head, "I guess not, but the sooner Becky gets to a hospital, the sooner we all get home.

He nodded, "She'll be okay," he said, "you should get checked on too."

"This is silly," I said, "Take her to my house. Ethan's a doctor you know."

"Ah," Aidan chuckled, "that's right, he *is* a doctor."

"Hmm," Rudy muttered, "thought he was a shrink."

"No," I answered, "He's the one who fixed my ankle when I got hurt in the woods that night."

"Oh, we'll take her to Ethan then."

"I'm still not sure about it though," I said, "We're going to need a pretty good cover story."

"Don't worry about that." Aidan answered.

I leaned my head back to rest. What seemed like seconds later, Rudy was whispering my name. I opened my eyes to see his smiling face.

"You're home, sweetie."

Aidan pushed him aside, "You all right, love?"

Rudy glowered.

"I told you, I'm fine."

"That never means much coming from you."

I tried to smile.

"Becky," I whispered, "Becky, honey wake up."

She opened her eyes for a second, then closed them again, "Are we at the hospital?"

"We're at Ethan's," I told her.

"Good." She whispered.

"How are you feeling?"

"Not sure," she said, "tired."

"Anything hurt?"

She shook her head, "Just a little sore."

He must not have hurt her as much as I imagined. "Can you walk?"

She nodded and sat up slowly.

"Don't try!" Rudy demanded his concern was tangible.

"Really, Rudy, I'm okay."

"I should carry you."

"Rudy, I'm not even dizzy—I'm fine."

She stumbled toward the porch, "Is—this a different car?"

Aidan laughed, "Yes," he said, "The other one was out of gas."

"How long had I been out?"

"A while."

"Ethan isn't home yet," I said, "Which is good, gives us time to come up with a plausible story.

"Already taken care of," Aidan said, tapping his finger against his temple, "just let me do the talking."

I should have guessed as much. Becky went straight to the living room to lie on the couch. "Can you call Aaron?" she asked, "Please."

I nodded and picked up the phone on the kitchen wall. He picked up after one ring.

"Becky?"

"No, it's Jane."

"Is she with you?"

"Yeah, she's here."

"Is everything okay? I've been calling both of you all day."

"Things are complicated, but we're both okay."

"Can I come over?"

"Of course," I answered, "That's why I'm calling."

"Okay," he said, "be there soon."

When he said soon, he meant it. In ten minutes a knock came at the front door. Becky perked up. "Lie down." I said.

I went to open the door but before Aaron saw me Becky shoved her way through and into his arms.

"Oh my god," he choked out, noticing the dirt and the blood, "Becky, what happened? Are you okay?"

She moved away and avoided eye contact, "I'm okay," she said, "No worries."

He pulled her chin up to his level and stared into her eyes. She instantly started crying and moved into Aaron's chest.

"I'd rather Ethan didn't know exactly what happened." I said.

He nodded, "Can you get her some clothes?"

"Of course. Come on, Becky," I said, "Upstairs; you need a shower."

"So do you," she said, wiping her eyes.

"I'm a little more worried about you at the moment." She nodded and I helped her up the stairs. She went into the bathroom and I went to my room, fumbling through my drawers for something I could let her wear, something that would at least fit her and her lengthy limbs. I found a pair of loose fitting sweat pants and a black tank top. Becky would probably look good even in my "cleaning the house" clothes.

I knocked on the bathroom door.

"I'm alive, Jane." She called.

"Just checking. I left you some clothes on my bed; I'm going to use the other bathroom."

"Okay," she called back, "Thanks."

She sounded completely content, as if it was just one of our normal weekend sleepovers.

I went to use the master bathroom down the hall trying to ignore the voices downstairs. Aaron would blame this on Aidan for sure, Rudy did, even I did, but it really wasn't his fault. I tried to focus my mind on something else but I was haunted with the memories of the basement, the hanging corpse, the bag of teeth, the man I saw being murdered and my beaten sister in the other bathroom. Of course I couldn't forget the killer of a boyfriend I had, and the fact that he may have killed my brother as well. I suppressed the tears and enjoyed a hot shower. I had never felt so dirty in my entire life. I washed my hair twice and stood there in the water longer than I ever had before. After I was clean I wrapped myself in a towel and headed to my room. When I heard Becky yell my name I picked up my pace and raced to my room as fast as I could and Aaron was up the stairs in ten seconds. I walked in and she was sitting on my bed in my clothes, holding a small slip of paper in her hand. She handed it to me.

Jane Doe,

We know who you are and we know that you are the reason for James West's betrayal of The Sevren. We also know that because of your love for him your blood is tainted so it is not yours that we want. We have your father, bring us Rudy Thompson and his life will be spared.

~Dorian.
P.S. I think it best that you do not disregard this note.

"My god." I whispered.

"What do we do now?"

"Ask Aidan," I heard Aaron say, "Sorry to intrude," he continued stepping into my room, "but I think the new kid is the only one who *can* know what to do."

"They have Ethan," I said to Becky, "They want Rudy, they took Danny; they kidnapped me and tried to kill you."

"This is personal," Becky whispered anxiously, "It must be."

I nodded, "Aidan came to North Bend for a reason, he came to North Bend—for me."

* * *

"Before anything else is done, Jane, you need to be taken care of."

"Aidan, I'm fine, we don't exactly have time. They're going to kill Ethan."

"No," he answered, "They won't."

"And why not? How do you know they haven't already?"

"One," Aidan said reaching into his pocket, "They wait for Abraham's call." He pulled a tiny, silver cell phone out of his pocket. "Two—he's bait to get to Rudy and to get to me."

"We have to find Ethan."

"We'll get him back Jane and nobody will be hurt in the process—except maybe me."

"Not *one* word, Rudy!" I demanded.

He put his hands up and nodded.

"Now please," he continued, "Aaron brought some food, eat something."

I had forgotten about the knotting cramps in my stomach. "Thank you."

Aaron smiled and pulled his arm a little tighter around Becky's waist.

"I doubt she's going anywhere." I chuckled.

"Eh—you never know."

"Why me?" Rudy asked, his voice was shaking, "Why me and not somebody else?"

Aidan shook his head, "Because they can't use Jane," he said, "her blood is tainted. To them you are the next best thing."

"I don't even like you."

"Yes, but they don't know that." Aidan was perfectly composed, "They are using you to get to me—and Jane."

"Me?" I yelled.

He nodded, "Even though they do not want your blood does not mean you won't end up like..."

He stopped.

"Like what?"

He was silent and obviously distressed. My mind replayed everything I had been through. I realized what he was saying.

"Aidan?"

"Like—one of their victims."

"Oh my god," my voice was completely throttled "You know about Sharon."

He bowed his head and sighed. The nod came later and was hardly a movement at all, but I knew he was saying yes.

"I promise," he said, "I won't let anything bad happen to any of you!"

XVII

Just Friends

RUDY sank into the cushions of the couch. I wanted to comfort him but I really didn't know what to say. Aidan was right when he said we shouldn't be friends. If he would have simply done what I asked and left me alone who knows what I could have been doing. Maybe I'd be out to a movie with Rudy or maybe Becky could drag me along to another party or shopping trip. I'd been locked in a basement for three days; I can hardly comprehend how sick Ethan must have been with worry. Of course I couldn't completely blame this on Aidan could I? After all it wasn't *him* who captured me or hurt Becky, it wasn't *him* who took Ethan.

I couldn't stand the look Rudy was giving me he looked like he was struggling just to keep from fainting. I could see how terrified he was. I stuffed my fries in my mouth and went to talk to him.

"Jane?" his voice was trembling.

"Are you okay?"

"Can I talk to you for a minute?"

"Of course."

"I mean—umm—alone?"

I nodded.

He stood up and walked around the corner so the spying eyes in the kitchen wouldn't make him so nervous. His eyes were trembling and his entire body seemed like it was shivering.

"Rudy…"

"Really. I'm okay," he said, "I'm just confused that's all. This was all thrown on me for no reason."

"I'm so sorry for letting you become part of this."

He moved his gaze to the floor shaking his head. He cleared his throat, "No," he said, "I was the one who didn't trust Aidan, I wanted to protect you, I got myself involved."

"I should have listened."

He smiled, "*should* have—yes. When do you ever do what you should?"

I tried to smile but felt slightly insulted. I always tried to do the right thing.

"If I go," he started, "I think that if I just go—willingly…"

"No!" I yelled, "Rudy, don't please!"

"It's better than getting us all killed, and Ethan too."

I shook my head mechanically, "Stop that, Rudy, Aidan will figure this out."

His voice turned acidic, "I know."

I sighed but before I could say anything, he took one long stride toward me and locked his eyes into mine erasing my thoughts completely and leaving me wondering what he was thinking.

"If I die, Jane, I want you to know something."

I tried to look away to hide the expression on my face. I knew this was coming.

"I love you," he said. His voice became soft and sad, "I'm *in* love with you." He paused and cleared his throat, "just know that."

I couldn't answer.

"That's why I have to go. I've loved you since we were kids," he continued, "everything about you, Jane. Your courage and your love…your beauty."

I still couldn't say anything but I shook my head. He was doing this on purpose. What did it mean that I was so desperate to keep him alive? I cared about him yes but the thought of him strapped to that stone ate through me like acid, making me feel as if I would do anything to keep that from happening. There was this nervous stinging in my stomach. I touched his hand trying to get him to say something—anything. He moved his hands to my waist, but this time I didn't fling them away.

"Rudy…"

"I know," he said, "I know as I knew from the beginning that I can be the one to stand beside you—to protect you. You love me Jane, I know you do."

He leaned forward almost touching his lips to mine. I closed my eyes and exhaled softly. When I opened them he hadn't changed position but there was this stronger desperation in his eyes.

"I don't want to die without feeling you close to me at least one time."

"That isn't fair." I growled.

"I never claimed it was." His voice had changed and I almost heard a smile in it though he wasn't smiling, his expression remained serious. "I love you and so does Aidan, that means there will be a fight Jane so here I am—fighting. And I don't fight fair, there's little gain in that." It was then that he smiled, making me unsure how serious he really was.

His hands were still on my waist and I was beginning to feel this sort of heat from them piercing through my skin, scorching me. I wanted to pull away from him, but I couldn't.

Rudy had always been there for me on the days I needed to forget about home and Danny and Aidan, he held me together when I felt like falling apart. He was like the last leaf on the dying tree that was my life. And after all of that I was still resisting his affections. This time it was more mentally than physically, I didn't move away at all but I refused to let my mind drift into thinking this was okay. I knew I couldn't betray Aidan even if he *had* betrayed me in some small way. Yet even as I was resisting him mentally I still didn't push him away when I felt him stroking the back of my neck. He twisted my hair around his hand and leaned in toward me again. He found my lips and kissed me softly at first but when he realized I wasn't stopping him his passion heated and he began kissing me almost violently and I found something somewhere in me to push him away and slap his face—but I ignored it. I suddenly found myself kissing him back. My lips moved with his in ways they never had with Aidan. Aidan had always stopped me before letting me get too involved and that's when I realized that this could go on as long as I wanted it to, this could lead to whatever I chose. I wrapped my arms around his neck and he pulled me close against him. I could feel the hardness of his chest and the strength in his arms as he wrapped them around me. I never realized the thin lines of muscles I could feel in his stomach. I found myself admiring the feel of his body near my own. I found myself wanting him closer to me but there was no way that could be right and I knew it. I tried to pull away but I wasn't strong enough against his passion. I pushed on his shoulders with the heels of my hands and arched my back until I was free. He stared at me. His expression was a collogue of confusion and triumph. I sighed and looked away from him.

"I'm sorry," he whispered. He touched my face and I closed my eyes, waiting for him to kiss me again, wanting him to but he walked away. I opened my eyes to find that he was back on the couch. I ran up to my room and locked the door. I didn't even have time to lie face down on my bed and scream before a knock came.

"Go away!" I called.

"We both know you are going to let me in, so either open up now or argue with me for fifteen minutes."

I opened the door and was once again reminded how stunningly beautiful Aidan was. I pressed myself against him and he returned my embrace. I took his hand and led him through the doorway and into my room and shut the door. He stared at me unmoving.

"What's wrong?" he asked.

"Nothing." I retorted.

He gave me that look again where he leaned forward and raised his dark eyebrows at me.

I sighed, "I don't want to talk about it," I said, "Just be with me."

I moved closer to him and leaned against him, I met his lips and felt his resistance.

"Stop it, Aidan," I hissed, "just kiss me."

I pushed him harder against the door but he pushed me away.

"Jane, what's with you?"

"I love you," I whispered, "that's all."

I was a terrible liar and he knew it but he took advantage of the situation and for the first time let himself give in. He let me push him against the door and not only accepted, but welcomed the kisses I was giving him. I couldn't let what happened with Rudy mean anything. I am unsure whom I was trying to convince, Aidan or myself. He pulled away from me.

"I love you Jane," he whispered, "but just tell me again that you're okay—besides the obvious issues."

I stared into his eyes and noticed genuine worry; he almost seemed to be expressing suspicion. "I'm okay." I whispered. It was honestly the truth, I *was* okay besides the obvious and since I was such a terrible liar, Aidan realized it was the truth and his desire heightened. I led him to my bed and found myself desperate for him, as I had once been—desperate to be close to him. I pulled my shirt over my head and he moved away.

"What's wrong?" my heart sank into my stomach.

"If you want to do this…" his voice dropped, "I'm sorry, but if you want to do this I think we should wait until things settle."

"It may be too late by then" I murmured, touching his face "What if you don't come back?"

He smiled, "I'll come back," he said "I know you love me; I am not worried about that. I am not going to let one kiss from Rudy make me even as much as nervous."

I gasped and he was staring at me almost laughing.

"Damn Aidan. How do you do that?"

"You ask me that question a lot."

"Well—it's like you have eyes that come out and follow me wherever I go."

He chuckled dryly but it was that ringing sound I loved that trailed through me, "I wish. Neither of you were being very discrete. Becky and Aaron noticed too I'm sure."

I grumbled and pressed my face into a pillow.

"It's okay," he laughed, "I won't kill him. He loves you; I was prepared for him to fight."

"He doesn't *love* me," I said lifting my face up again, "He just thinks he does."

"Jane—stop being so modest. He loves you but you *know* I love you and you don't need to prove that to me and you shouldn't have to prove it to yourself either not any other way than being with me."

I nodded and pulled my white tank back on, suddenly embarrassed.

"But don't think I don't want to, he continued, "I do—of course, but I would rather it not be because of Rudy or The Sevren or your fear of me not coming back—for no negative reasons but because we care for each other, is that fair?"

I nodded and forced a smile. "I understand," I said "but—don't leave."

He smiled and laid beside me on my bed and took my hand.

"Rest your mind," he said, "Everything will be fine."

I couldn't even rest my eyes, so it was obviously impossible to rest my mind. Aidan rolled over and propped himself up on his elbow. I turned to look at him. His eyes were darker than usual but still shone with that almost unnatural brilliance. He whispered my name, that way that never seemed to be my name but some foreign word he was speaking meant only for himself.

"I know," I said, "we should go back downstairs. I don't want to leave everybody when they are just as scared as I am."

"We all need to be there for each other," he said almost annoyed, "I wish there was some way I could make you believe me that I won't let any harm come to you—*any* of you."

I closed my eyes and sighed, "I wish that too."

* * *

I needed some time by myself. I sat on my bed, flipping through the scrapbook my mom had packed for me. It hadn't even crossed my mind a single time since I had moved. I stared for a long time at an old picture of me and Danny at the beach when we were about eleven years old. I remember that day completely but at the time I couldn't think about it. I slammed the book closed and dropped it on the floor.

I lied back on my pillow and closed my eyes sighing.

"Jane, you gotta occupy your mind."

I didn't even flinch at the sound of his voice. "I really wish you'd just knock on the door like a normal person."

He chuckled softly, "normal." He mumbled, "Where's the fun in that?"

I just shook my head.

"Are you angry?"

"No," I sighed, "I'm sorry. Just irritable."

"I have some ideas in mind," he said, "just to break the ice."

"What kind of ideas?" I asked, propping myself up on my elbow and turning to look at him.

"I'm prepared for several outcomes but—we are going to need your attic."

"Umm—okay. Why?"

"I would rather *not* have Walter asking questions."

"What are you not telling him?"

He waved his hand at me, shunning my question. "I need to keep some stuff in the attic for a while. There isn't anywhere at my place to keep it."

"What stuff?"

"Just some things we may need, please, Jane—I would rather not tell you yet, just trust me."

I nodded. "Okay."

He actually used the door to carry three bags into the house. He opened the attic door and slowly unfolded the ladder. I tossed one of the bags in and crawled in after him.

"So really, what's all this stuff for?"

"I told you," he answered, "For plan A, plan B and plan C to get us all out of this mess."

"Why don't you just let me see what it is?"

He sighed, "The only reason I'm keeping it here is because you have an attic. Remember, I can't have Walter asking questions."

I nodded. "Wow," I laughed, "my dad is *such* a pack rat."

Aidan laughed lightly and glanced at all the stacks of boxes and books covered in dust.

"I wonder how much of my old stuff is in here."

"Whoa," he whispered crawling to the other side, "What's in *this*?"

I saw the old chest I had asked Ethan about when I first moved in. "According to my dad, nothing."

"Hmm, I think it needs a key."

"Eh maybe," I answered, "But it's probably empty."

He shrugged. "Promise me something?"

"I won't open the bags, Aidan, okay?"

He nodded, "I'm just trying to keep things from getting any more complicated."

I nodded, "I miss Ethan." I whispered.

He turned me so I was facing him and gently squared my shoulders. "I will get him out of this, love—I swear."

I sighed and rested my head in my hands. He wrapped his arms around me and I let myself lean against him."

"I wish I could tell you not to worry."

"You can."

Yes—but what good will it do?"

"I'm not sure," I answered, "I'm not sure it will make me feel any better at all but it's worth a try."

"Don't worry," he said, "I swear to you that things will end up okay."

I sighed, "Thanks." I whispered sincerely, although his effort really had been wasted. His own worry was almost tangible. I moved away from him so I could look into his eyes.

"So when are you planning on locking me up at Luna's?"

His mood completely shifted when I heard him laugh. "Nothing gets past you, does it?"

"I know you too well to think for even one second you don't have something planned—or *plotted*."

He smiled, "I just want to keep you as safe as possible. And thank you for not complaining you tend to not trust me enough."

I glared at him.

"Okay I understand why," he answered, "but honestly, Jane, you're too clumsy to deny you're in danger when you aren't moving."

Irritation rocked through me. I wasn't in a mood to laugh.

He pulled me into his chest, "I'm sorry," he said, "I'm doing a terrible job of trying to cheer you up."

I sighed, "I feel better just being with you; you don't need to try so hard."

He smiled, "It's my job now to protect you in every way that I can."

"I just can't stop thinking about Danny," I whispered, holding in tears "They killed him, Aidan. I want them dead—all of them."

"I understand but this isn't the time for revenge."

"How did I know you'd say that?"

"You know me too well," he said smiling, "In all seriousness I just need to focus on getting Ethan away from The Sevren. You need to stay at Luna's. I don't want you here, especially by yourself, they'll find you, Jane."

"They found me at Luna's, too. They can find me again."

He shook his head, "They won't," he said, "We weren't careful enough before. She'll keep you safe this time. I promise."

I nodded. "I love you, Aidan."

"It's okay," he said calmly, "You don't have to tell me that."

"I want to."

"Then next time—don't say it like it's the last time."

I ran my fingers through his hair and sighed. I thought it would be the last time. He hadn't even left yet and I was already saying goodbye.

I had no idea what he had planned and wasn't sure if I wanted to but at the same time I didn't want to let him lock me up at Luna's either, I didn't want him sacrificing himself for me. Everything was falling apart, fraying at the ends and becoming unraveled.

"Why Rudy?"

"I told you—because you love him." He turned to look at me.

"And Ethan?"

He hesitated before responding "They took Daniel," he said, "You and Ethan were supposed to stay safe, but I got involved. I had no idea he was your brother if I did—well, I don't know."

My mind replayed the day in my room when he stared at Danny's picture seemingly stone cold terrified.

"This is all about me," he continued, "my betrayal of The Sevren and murder of Abraham. My involvement with you as well—especially because you are related to one of our victims—*their* victims."

I shuddered, realizing he just included himself. There was so much suspicion now that flooded me every time I looked at him, and it kept getting worse.

"I cannot tell you why they chose him either, Jane."

"Why?"

"Well, because I don't know," he answered, "If I did I would explain it to you in unmistakable clarity."

"Even then it wouldn't make sense, would it?"

"Probably not," he answered, "It never makes sense for people to be so evil. Stop driving yourself mad trying to make sense of something that there is no sense to be made of."

I nodded shedding slow tears. Before I even realized I was crying he was catching my tears with his kisses. I heard quiet knocking coming from downstairs.

"You should get that," he whispered in my ear.

We climbed down the ladder and Aidan closed the door. I dried my eyes and walked down the stairs.

"It's probably Becky." I muttered to myself.

I opened the door to see Rudy. Before saying a word to me he peered behind me.

"Good," he breathed stepping inside, "You're here."

"You're happy to see me?" Aidan laughed.

"Not happy," he corrected, "but relieved."

"What's wrong?" I asked immediately.

"I've been feeling anxious," he started, "I've been spending too much time worrying about myself and now I'm beginning to worry that we are waiting too long for Ethan, if you have a plan, I'm ready to hear it."

"I don't exactly have a plan," Aidan answered, "but I'm prepared for a few different outcomes."

I interrupted, "What about plan A, plan B and plan C?"

"I meant mostly that I am prepared for what might happen."

"Which may be what?" Rudy asked, his voice sounded muffled.

"I don't know," he answered, "But blood will be involved which is why…" he shifted his eyes to me, "*you have to stay with Luna.*"

"They can find me there."

"Nobody will steal you from Luna," he told me, "we just need to be more careful."

"How can you be more careful then handcuffing me and locking me up?"

He glared at me. "Be quiet, Jane."

I sighed and walked to the living room. Aidan and Rudy followed and sat beside me on the couch.

"Let's go, then," I announced.

"What?" Aidan bellowed.

"Let's go," I repeated, "Take me to Luna's and go save Ethan."

Aidan smiled, "Are you ready?" he asked Rudy.

"I'm ready for anything," he answered.

"Rudy, meet me here tomorrow morning, Jane, I will take you to Luna's early."

I nodded. "What about Dorian?" I asked.

"Don't worry about it," he said, "They wait for Abraham's call. Dorian doesn't know of his death just yet; if he did he would have found me by now."

"And if he finds you?"

"I just can't be here when he does." He said, "I won't let him find you again."

"So tomorrow?" Rudy asked.

Aidan nodded. "Tomorrow."

Rudy left and I sighed falling into a more comfortable position on the couch."

"You look exhausted," Aidan whispered.

"I haven't been sleeping well," I answered, falling into a deep relaxation.

He nodded, "Rest then, if you'd like I'll stand guard." He smiled that certain way letting me know he was serious.

I nodded and cushioned myself into a sleeping position. I felt the weight of a blanket drape over me and Aidan quietly hummed to me until my body and mind drifted into unconsciousness.

It was light that disturbed me. Light from the streetlamps flooded into the living room casting a shadow on Aidan's flawless features as he peered outside. He turned to look at me.

"Oh I'm sorry," he let the curtain fall back into place to darken the room again, "I didn't mean to wake you."

"It's okay." I groaned, sitting up. "I need to be awake."

He smirked, "why?"

I shrugged, "I don't know. I guess I just don't really feel safe."

He nodded, "I know." He walked toward me, "You know I care about you and you know…"

He broke off, whirling around back toward the window.

"What is it?"

"Shh. Jane, get your shoes on."

"What?"

"Just do it," he snapped, "comfortable shoes, running may be involved."

I ran upstairs and put on a pair of running shoes I can only recall wearing a few times. It was nearly impossible to tie the laces with my shaky hands. He followed after me.

"Shit." He grumbled.
"What's wrong?"
"We'll have to sneak out through your window."

I couldn't answer, the blood had rushed to my cheeks and I was shaking.

"What's going on?"

"It's okay," he said, "But they found me. I knew they would."

"Who?" I asked.

"It's okay," he told me, "but it's him—it's Dorian."

Just the sound of his name sent chills through my body. He opened my bedroom window and stepped onto the roof, pressing himself against the house. He stepped slightly to the right and offered me his hand. I stared at the paleness of his fingers for a moment watching the shadows play upon his skin. His hand looked warm, but I had expected that cold tension I had felt in the woods. I took his hand and all the uneasy feelings vanished. His hand felt normal, so normal I wasn't surprised that it felt normal. I watched him grip the oak tree and whirl his legs around almost spider like and crawl down to the lawn. He signaled me to be quiet. I reached for the tree but my shoes slid across the shingles making a horrible scraping sound and the slanted roof almost made me fall to the ground. I fell slightly forward and grabbed the branch. I clumsily climbed into the tree. I looked down to see Aidan, silently signaling me to hurry. My limbs were shaking and I couldn't quite make it to the bottom of the tree before my hands slipped and I fell to the ground.

"Oh," Aidan whispered, "are you okay?"

I sat up with a groan "Yeah," I said, surprised he hadn't been right there to catch me like Aidan usually was. I pressed my hand to the back of my head trying to stop the throbbing. "I'm fine."

I stood up and Aidan crouched down, leading me into the neighbor's lawn.

"When I tell you to, you're going to need to run, okay?" he whispered, "as fast as you can. Just follow me."

"What about your car?"

"I can't get to it without him finding us, don't worry about it; just run when I say."

I nodded.

We crouched down, inching across the lawn. The houses on the street were dark so I wasn't worried about being seen by suspicious neighbors, but nor did I have any conception of what time it was. Aidan continuously peered over his shoulder at my house. He made eye contact for a brief moment then turned around to look at my house again.

"Okay, Jane," he started, "run."

I ran as quickly as my legs could carry me imagining a dark figure chasing after me I still lagged pretty far behind Aidan. By the time we reached the end of the cull de sac I was slightly out of breath.

"What do we do?" I asked him, "In case you haven't realized. Rudy lives only a few houses down from me."

"Oh my god!" he yelled, pulling Abraham's cell phone out of his pocket, "do you know his number by heart?"

"Yes, of course."

"Call him right now."

"And tell him?"

"Tell him to lock the doors and stay inside until tomorrow. We're changing plans; tell him to meet us at my place. I can give him directions."

"You mean Luna's."

He shook his head, "I mean Walter's. Dorian doesn't know where that is. We can be safe at Walter's until the morning."

I nodded and dialed his number.

"Rudy?"

"Jane?" He sounded concerned.

"Yeah, it's me."

"Are you okay? Should I come over?"

"No!" I yelled, "Rudy, lock your doors and tomorrow meet us at Aidan's."

"What's going on?"

"I'll explain tomorrow, just please don't leave your house."

"Are you okay?"

"I'm fine."

He sighed, "Are you with Aidan?"

"Yes."

"Good," he answered, "If you end up hurt, I'll kill him."

"He's only trying to keep us all safe."

"Let me talk to him."

I handed the phone to Aidan and he immediately told him exactly what to do.

"Tomorrow morning at around ten, meet us at my place. Get a pen, you'll need directions."

I stared trying to hear Rudy on the other end but I couldn't.

"Do you?" Aidan asked, "Yes, Gallagher's. Right but it's the other house, yeah the beige one. Okay, see you then." He closed the phone and put it back in his pocket. "Well this will be interesting." He mumbled. I wasn't sure if he was speaking to me or to himself.

"What?"

"I don't want Rudy involved any more than he has to be," he said, "but he wants to help, and I'm sure I will need it at some point."

"Why can't I stay with Walter? Dorian doesn't know where that is."

"Yes that's true, but Walter isn't the type to kill—Luna is."

"Kill?"

"Yes."

"I don't understand."

"If Dorian found you there, which is a possibility, he would kill you as soon as he saw you. You're safety is more important than anyone's right now. I would be able to save Rudy, and Ethan—you? Not so easily. Walter wouldn't be able to protect you the way Luna could."

"So take Rudy to Luna's with me. You don't have to have him help you do you?"

"Yeah, that's funny Jane."

"What?"

"Rudy has a car and I'm aware of that, meaning if I tell him to meet us at Luna's, you will escape." He tapped his finger to his temple.

"What if I promise?"

He shook his head.

"Then when *you* drive me to Luna's or—whoever does, Rudy can come along. That simple."

He narrowed his eyes. "I don't know, Jane."

"Please?"

He sighed, "Rudy won't have it," he said. "He's persistent about helping me save Ethan, and you have to promise me to just do as I say."

I nodded. "Fine," I said, "but if he wants to stay with me, I would feel much better."

"Okay."

"I'm sorry, for being so difficult."

"It isn't your fault at all. I'm so mad at myself," he whispered, "I was mad at myself for getting you involved, now I have gotten, you, Rudy, Becky, Aaron and Ethan all involved as well. I wish I would have never come to this town."

"Please don't say that, Aidan," I pleaded. I changed direction of my thoughts and tried to lighten the mood a little. "Hey, maybe it's about time for something interesting to happen."

"You aren't frightened easily, are you?" he asked smiling thinly that went nowhere near his eyes.

"I don't know—maybe not."

"This is my last chance to do something good," he said. I thought he was trying to smile again. "I'm going to save you all I swear to it." His movement seemed almost choreographed—rehearsed, "You are my last chance, Jane," he said, desperately, "The last leaf on a dying tree."

XVIII

Michael London

AFTER over an hour of walking I was beginning to feel sore. "Aidan, where are we going?"

"We need a car," he said, "Unless you want to walk the entire way."

"So…?"

"So—how do you feel about grand theft auto?"

"I'm sorry?"

He laughed; it was one of those laughs where I could tell he was actually amused. "Would credit card fraud suite you better?"

I groaned and covered my face with my hands. I murmured his name under my breath.

"There's no way we're walking all the way to Walter's," he continued, "We need a car."

"Aidan, I'm sore and tired yes, but that doesn't mean I want to commit a crime."

"Though you don't seem to object when it serves you." He spat.

"Excuse me?"

He began listing things but broke off, "Abraham, the Mustang…I'm sorry," he said, "I don't mean to be such a grouch. Just please try to trust me."

I didn't respond, I couldn't find it in myself to argue. He was the only one who could get any of us out of this mess and crazy as it may have been I did trust him. I knew he wouldn't let us get in trouble. He stayed hidden from the law for years already, who knows what he had done that he never told me about.

He used another name to rent the car, charging it to a credit card—which he had a ridiculous number of. It was a white Toyota pickup truck—odd choice.

"What about the stolen Mustang?"

He shrugged his shoulders. "Eh—don't worry about it. I have to go back and cover my tracks after everything is settled anyway."

"Cover your tracks how?"

"I'd rather not tell you."

"Why?"

"Just because…"

"Because I won't like it…?"

"Yes."

"At this point, Aidan, I don't think there is anything I can't handle."

He sighed, "Aidan Summers can go back to not existing, just as easily as Michael London rented this car."

I pulled my eyebrows together.

"I told you you wouldn't like it."

"So, by covering your tracks I'd never see you again?" Although I had asked it as a question it was more of a statement, I didn't want him to answer.

"Perhaps—most likely."

"You're right," I said, "I don't like that at all."

I climbed into the passenger's seat and fastened my seat belt, crossing my arms in front of my chest.

"So," Aidan started, his tone now even and casual sounding, "are you hungry?"

"Hungry?" Maybe I would remember food when I find out if my dad is alive or not. "I don't know."

"Hmm, well, I know I am and you have to eat *something*. There are coffee shops open 24 hours. At least eat some soup or something."

I nodded. So it *was* late. I couldn't tell. There was no clock in the truck.

He drove to a tiny 50's style café that was dimly lit by lamps hanging from the ceiling. It was too dim to be comfortable for me but I ignored it. It was quiet and empty. We took a seat at the bar. Aidan ordered coffee and smiled at me when he noticed the waitress flirting with him. I settled for some soup and a glass of water.

"Do you realize the effect you have on people?"

He chuckled and shrugged his shoulders, "Sometimes. The reaction I'm used to people having at seeing me isn't normally as positive."

I smiled. "Well, maybe that means there's no threat."

He laughed. "Like there would be anyway, Jane."

"Well, she was very nice, and quite pretty."

"Was she?"

"Like you didn't notice."

He shrugged his shoulders.

"Ah, come on Aidan you don't have to be that nice."

He shrugged his shoulders again and sipped at his coffee. He smiled at me and shook his head.

I smiled back. It was feeling good to be able to smile, but I think he could tell it was a very weak attempt at looking happy.

"Are you okay?" he murmured.

"I'm fine," I answered, "why?"

"You seem distracted."

"How far is Walter's house?"

"It's not far," he said, "don't worry."

I tried to smile, veiling my uncertainty of anything he said.

When we finally did get there it was well into the morning. It must have been later than I thought when we left. Aidan had a key so let himself in. I lingered on the porch for a moment before mustering the courage to step inside. The house was dark, but dimly lit by an old fashioned yellow lamp set on a wooden desk. There was an old man sitting at the desk, writing slowly. He had thick white hair neatly trimmed and white stubble of a beard. He was very cliché.

"You're late." He sputtered.

Aidan smiled and approached the old man, "I usually am," he chuckled.

They embraced and the man removed his glasses, "You must be Jane." He said.

I nodded as he shook my hand. He held very hesitantly, as if he thought I was made of glass.

"A great pleasure to meet you. Walter Redline, as I'm assuming you know."

I nodded, "Good to finally meet you, Mr. Redline."

"Ah—this isn't a classroom," he sputtered in laughter, "Call me Walter."

"Walter." I echoed, trying to smile through my nervousness.

"Clem, you mind giving me a hand?" he asked.

Clem? How many names did he go by?

"Sure, what do you need?"

"To rearrange the guest room; it's become my storage unit." He exploded in a dry, sputtered chuckle again.

"Sure." He winked at me and followed Walter around the corner. "Make yourself at home," he called.

I sat on the brown, leather love seat that was placed beside the desk and stared at the painting of a brown horse running through a field hanging on the wall next to the front door. I folded my hands in my lap and just made up a story about that horse. Maybe it was the painter's pet horse or maybe he had seen it running free through a field one day and he remembered it. Maybe Walter knew the horse. I wondered how important it might have been to the person who painted it and wondered if it could ever be that important to me if it were hanging on my wall.

Aidan interrupted my thoughts. "You must be exhausted." He said. "Come on."

I took his hand and felt that cold tension again, but he gripped tightly and even through the coolness of his skin, I felt a sense of security. He led me down the narrow hallway lined with bookshelves to the spare room. There was a lovely queen-sized bed against the wall with an old-fashioned floral comforter. To the left was a bookshelf and a nightstand with a little yellow lamp like the one in the front room.

"I shouldn't sleep." I told him.

"It's late."

"What if Dorian finds us?"

"He won't. I'll take care of any problems—I'll stand guard."

I shook my head slowly.

He sighed, "I'll lie beside you."

I nodded and brought myself into his arms.

* * *

I was still half asleep but aware of Aidan's arms around me.

"Jane?"

"Hmm?" I mumbled out.

"Jane—wake up—now."

I instantly became alert when I recognized the tone in his voice.

"Aidan, what is it?"

"We can't stay here."

"What?" I whispered sternly, "What's going on? You said we'd be safe here until morning."

I could scarcely see him but could tell he was nodding, "Yes, but something has come to my attention, something I was a fool to ignore. We should leave to Luna's now, and not later."

I sat up and switched on the lamp. I gasped when I noticed small pin drops of blood splattered on his right cheek.

"Jane, I'm all right," he said, "I've been betrayed, we need to leave here."

"Betrayed? By who?"

"To be honest—you've met him before."

"What...Aidan what happened?"

He sighed, placing his head in his hands. "I heard something," he started, "A voice, coming from outside. When I recognized it was my name, I went out to see who it was. I found a friend of mine who is a member of The Sevren; he's of lower rank than myself so always listened to me, that's why I believed he would never betray me. He told me Dorian threatened his life so he confessed that he knew where I lived. He came here to warm me of this."

Who?"

"Do you remember that night at the bookstore—with the wolf?"

"Yes of course—"

"So you remember Mike."

"MIKE?" I cried, "He's—he's one of them?"

He nodded. "Mike and I were enrolled in school here—sort of like an undercover thing."

"Oh my god," I grumbled, covering my face with my hands and smoothing my hair back. "This keeps getting weirder!"

"Come on," he said, "I'll make sure Rudy gets to Luna's safely, unless I decide I really need his help."

"I'd rather him stay with me," I said, crawling out from under the sheets.

He nodded, "I would, too," he whispered, "but he wants to help and to be honest, I may need it."

"Walter will take you to Luna's," he said, "but don't worry, I'll be right behind you with Rudy, okay? I need to get you out of here first."

I nodded, trying my very hardest to trust him, if that's what Aidan said the plan was then I was going to trust it was the best one. "Okay."

Walter took me to his little car out front, he was saying something but I couldn't listen to it. I gathered enough to respond telling him I was fine.

"Clem's a good kid," I heard, "Just got mixed up with some bad things."

I didn't answer.

"To Luna's then."

* * *

I awoke slowly to the sound of her voice.

"Jane?" she sang, "I made some breakfast."

I shook my head, "Thank you, Luna, but I'm not hungry."

She sighed, "You can't let yourself get sick over something you cannot control."

I nodded, "I'm fine."

She left the room, closing the door on the way out. I was a terrible liar but I didn't care, I kept up the act. I stayed in my room all day contemplating what could happen and driving myself near mad with the possible thoughts of never seeing Aidan again and without telling him one last time before I left that I loved him.

Luna came in again without knocking.

"Please at least eat something," she pleaded.

I could feel how annoyed she was becoming, but remained unconvinced that eating would make me feel any better.

"Thank you for caring, Luna, but I'm really not hungry."

She just shook her head but didn't bother arguing.

I stayed on the bed with my knees drawn up to my chest. I wrapped my arms around my legs and silently begged for Aidan to come back. It was almost mid-day and Rudy wasn't with me. I could only hope he would be safe as well. I kept the curtains in the bedroom closed and barely took my eyes off of them. Dorian found me here once, he could find me again, and I was sick with fear every second that he would. I wanted Rudy here, at least for comfort if nothing else. I knew he would tell me that everything was fine and offer to stand guard so I could rest. I waited all day and by sunset I began to fear the worst. The smallest sound of a leaf falling off a tree made me peer out the window to see if Aidan was coming, but I didn't see him. I let a few tears escape. I was in no mood to do any real crying, I had been doing plenty of that the past few weeks.

I almost dozed off after exhausting myself with my uncontrollable thoughts; I didn't hear Luna knock a single time so I guessed she was letting me be. I shut my eyes and let my thoughts swim and race through my head. I saw visions of blood but also pictures of me dancing in the woods with Aidan. I saw Ethan cooking dinner and Rudy's smiling face. I saw Becky and Miranda. I saw Danny as I did every time I closed my eyes, he was happy in my mind this time. I was able to remember him the way he was when he was alive and happy. I didn't want the images to stop but when I heard a knock at the door I instantly sprang up in bed. I raced to the door of my bedroom but before I opened it I heard a loud popping sound. I knew that sound, I had heard it on T.V. enough times to know—gunshots. I backed away from the door already sobbing and unable to breath.

Dorian.

I knew it. It had to be him. I *knew* he would find me. My body was trembling and I tried to find my voice. I pushed with all the effort I had, trying to scream, trying to call for help. But what good would it do me now? Who would hear me? It would make more sense to stay silent. I couldn't think clearly and I suppose I didn't even have to think to know that Luna was dead and I was alone with—with *him*. I hid beneath my bed like a little kid; there was nowhere else I could think of hiding. I watched from under the bed and saw the handle on the bedroom door turn slowly. My breathing increased and I had to clasp my hands over my mouth to keep from crying out.

Life Blood

Small sounds still seeped from between my fingers and I held my breath, trying to keep quiet now. Maybe he wouldn't see me. The door opened and I shut my eyes.

"Get out!" I heard. It wasn't his voice, "Get out from under there *now*!"

I crawled out from beneath the bed and stood there trembling and crying. It wasn't him. It was somebody I didn't know, somebody I had never seen before.

"I found something." He said.

His voice was almost metallic sounding. It was unnatural. His eyes were black and his skin was the color of burned sepia. His hair was jet black, greased, and smoothed back. My teeth started chattering.

"Yeah," he said, giving me a crooked smile revealing crowded, blackened teeth, "You heard me; I found something and was wondering if you wanted it—if it was yours."

I couldn't speak. I tried to ask him what he was talking about but no sound came out of my mouth. He seemed like he knew what I was thinking.

"It's all right," he chuckled, "You can have it, I won't keep it from you."

I stood there, waiting. He reached for the strap on his shoulder and held out a brown bag. The bottom of the bag was stained a darker color, telling me there was something—wet, or even bleeding inside. He reached in and I saw his fingers grasp something un-solid. He pulled his hand out revealing what it was.

"Do you want it?"

I choked on the last bit of breath I had left. It was there—in front of me and it was real. His fingers grasped a chunk of lovely hair. I saw empty eyes that were once full of hidden emotions and deep secrets that I would never know.

It was *him*.

It was Mike, or—part of Mike. It was his head completely severed and still bleeding. His mouth was open but his face didn't have an expression of pain, which was better than if it had. I fell to the floor on my knees and tried to look away.

"Come on, don't be shy," he said, "You can be just like him if you want, I can take you and James together if you would prefer a Romeo and Juliet type execution. Yes?"

I heard footsteps behind him. There was another, there was no doubt in my mind at that point that it was him. It had to be Dorian. I squeezed my eyes shut and heard that loud popping sound again of gunfire. I covered my ears and screamed. Three shots one after the other without a second's delay between them but I didn't feel any pain. I opened my eyes and she was there, staring at me seeming completely calm. I ran to her arms, I didn't know what else to do.

"Luna." I choked out.

"It's all right," she said, "You're fine."

"What about you?" I gasped, moving away from her.

"I'll be fine." She said.

I noticed she was bleeding. It was covering the entire side of her pink T-shirt. "Fine?"

"It's only my shoulder," she said, "I'll be fine."

"We have to get you to someone."

"Jane, it's all right," she said calmly, "I know what I'm doing, ok?"

I nodded.

"You're a wreck," she demanded, "I'm making you some herbal tea and I'm not taking no for an answer all right?"

I nodded. I couldn't do anything else. I stepped over Mike's head and the thin, lengthy frame of the stranger with the gun trying to pretend it was nothing more than a plastic movie prop or something from a dream.

"He's a lousy shot," I heard Luna say as I approached her in the kitchen. "Apparently this isn't one of his usual jobs."

"How are you so calm?"

She smiled, handing me a warm mug, "It's something you get used to after a while, I guess I just realize that at the time there is nothing to worry about, he's dead and we're not so—it's all right." We took at seat on the couch in the living room.

"Mike is dead." I choked out.

She sighed, "You knew him?"

"Not well," I answered, "and from what I did know I didn't like but still—he's dead now. He's—gone."

She nodded. "I understand," she answered, "sometimes you just have to let things happen. Things will fall into place as they are meant to."

"Meant to?" I questioned, "Do you really believe that?"

She nodded resolutely, "I do."

"I don't," I answered.

"Why?"

"Things are *meant* to happen as you say. Like I was *meant* to lose my brother, the only person who ever truly knew me, my parents were *meant* to get divorced I was *meant* to fall in love with a boy who was a member of some insane cult and *meant* to lose him in a fight to save my life. *Meant* to."

She nodded softly. "I'm sorry," she said, "I know I can't understand what you're going through. Drink your tea, Jane, it will make you feel calm, I promise."

I did as she said. It tasted a bit like grass but had a sweet flavor that lingered.

"What exactly is this?" I asked.

"Just some herbal tea," she answered, "Like I told you. It has rosemary and other herbs from my garden. I picked up the recipe from a witch I met down at Coos Bay about a year ago. It does wonders for stressed minds."

I nodded.

"I need to ask you a question," she said.

"…Okay."

"Do you know how to sew, Jane?"

I stared at het for a moment, not entirely sure what she was getting at. "Umm—my mom taught me a bit when I was young…I couldn't make a dress or anything."

"But you know how to thread a needle."

"…yes."

"good." She said, "Here." She handed me a needle a thread.

"Luna?" I questioned, my hands were quaking, "Why…?"

"Thread the needle," she said, "I'm going to need you to be brave all right?"

"What?"

She pulled her T-shirt over her head and I saw the injury on her shoulder. Jagged edges of the wound were protruding from the torn flesh.

"I need you to sew this up for me."

"What?" my voice raised an octave and came out trembling. That's when I noticed the aluminum case with a red cross on it sitting on the coffee table in front of me.

"Jane, I cannot do this myself, ok?"

"Can't we get you to a doctor?"

"And tell them what?" she raised her eyebrows at me.

I nodded reluctantly. I threaded the needle with trembling hands. It took me at least three tries before I succeeded and moved the needle toward the gash.

I started to cry, "I can't!" I sobbed, "Luna-- I'm sorry, I…"

"Jane, listen to me," she said, "I need you to do this. I know you can. I know you are strong enough."

I shook my head and my chest started shaking with my sobs.

"I can't."

"Yes you can," she said sternly, "I know you can. I need you to."

I couldn't just do nothing could I? The thought of pushing a needle through skin sickened me, but I knew I had to do it. I moved the needle toward the wound again and pressed it into her skin. I groaned in disgust at the popping feeling of the needle penetrating. She winced but didn't make a sound. I tried my best to stay strong and keep myself from being sick. I pulled the needle through and continued, trying to ignore the lines of blood streaming from the holes I was putting into her.

"Jane," she started, "there's a small bottle of alcohol on the counter in the kitchen." I could hear the pain in her voice even when she tried to hide it.

I nodded and got the alcohol. I opened the first aid kit and used a cotton ball to clean her wound. She gasped.

"I'm sorry." I said.

"Are you okay?" she asked me.

I nodded, "I told you, I'm not very good at sewing." I looked at the crooked stitches even some overlapping others." I put a thin piece of gauze over it and taped it down.

"I hope this is good enough."

"It's fine," she told me, "It will do the job until I can get James here."

"You think he's coming back, Luna?"

She smiled, "If you think he isn't, you don't know James."

She was a very lovely person, easy to trust but no matter what she said or how sensitive she was, there was nothing she could do to put me at ease.

IXX

The Misty Morning.

IT was well into the morning of the next day when I was finally almost asleep. I tried to imagine Aidan beside me, back in the days when things weren't so messed up. It did little to help, not even my imagination was active enough to feel his arms around me. I sighed rolling over and instantly found myself sitting up in bed when I heard a knock on the front door. I raced to the door and almost shoved Luna out of the way to get there first.

When I opened the door the picture I had in my head of what I was expecting was torn to shreds. The morning was dark but a small gleam of sunlight was peeking over the hills glistening through the trees. It was moist outside like it had been raining all night. Clouds ringed the sky and the patch of clear sky was gray. It was very misty and fog sheathed the grass. It made what was coming seem even more like a nightmare. My words were suppressed by sudden terror. I tried to speak but my voice was caught in my throat. He was frozen stiff, not moving, I couldn't even tell if he was breathing. The look on his face told me he didn't want to look at me, like he was dreading what was coming. Finally I was able to speak one word.

"Rudy?"

He seemed to understand me even when I was sure no sound was coming out when I asked, "Where's Aidan?"

He pulled his eyebrows together and a sound escaped his lips like he was trying to speak but was as numb as I was.

"Rudy?"

It was then that I finally noticed that his brown shirt was covered in blood and a deep gash on his forehead dripped blood slowly down his check. He shook his head slowly. He had confirmed my nightmares with one small gesture. Before I realized it I was in his arms, sobbing uncontrollably and smelling the blood on his clothes. There was this pain tearing at me, clawing through my chest.

"Jane."

I was able to pull away and look at him.

"Ethan is ok." he forced a crooked smile.

My heart rate sped up and I could feel myself shaking, the relief and the pain all at once was too much to handle and all I could do was cry. I couldn't decide if the tears were happy or sad, Ethan was alive—but Aidan was gone.

Forever.

And again as I should have expected, I heard that word, the word that was only ever meant for me the word that only he would say. It was my name, but never sounded like it. It was like some resonance in my brain that shook through me and tore away my sanity for a brief moment. Though it always left so soon it kept me wondering if it had ever really been there in the first place. I couldn't move at first when I saw him but I forced my legs to unfreeze. I ran through the wet grass as fast as I could, as if he was going to disappear into the fog if I didn't get to him soon enough. I pressed myself into his chest and cried.

"I thought you were dead."

"I promised you I'd come back didn't I?"

He was smiling. He didn't appear hurt. That's when I remembered Rudy and the blood on his clothes. I gasped and glanced back at the doorway. He was staring blankly but I thought I saw him suppressing a smile.

"The blood isn't his." Aidan said.

"You're both okay?"

He nodded.

"And Ethan?" I peered behind him.

"I convinced him to wait for you at home. He'll be there."

He wiped the tears from my cheeks. "We're all okay…"

His words faded and he peered behind him.

"Aidan?" I whispered.

"Oh God." His voice swelled in his throat, "LUNA!" he screamed.

I looked toward the doorway and saw Luna frantically running into the house.

"Hurry!" he called. "Jane. Jane, go to Rudy."

"What?"

"Go!" he demanded, "Now. Run to him."

I turned and started running. My legs lagged behind my body but I pushed myself to move as fast as I could. As soon as Aidan's cry reached my ears I halted and turned in his direction.

I felt my chest burning and my blood ran cold. I had never seen Aidan look so helpless. This time it really was Dorian. He held Aidan effortlessly in his grasp and yanked his head back by his hair.

"When will you learn to do as you're told?" he spat.

"I will kill you first," he groaned, "I swear."

"Oh will you now?"

I just stared not sure what to do.

"Run!" Aidan called.

Run? How could I run? It was me he wanted wasn't it? It had always been me. I couldn't let Aidan take the fall for me, I refused.

"Why don't you just admit it's me you want!" I called.

Dorian's eyes darted to me and I felt my breathing quicken.

He pushed Aidan to the ground and stepped toward me.

"I'd rather make *him* kill you." He snickered, pointing to Aidan as he continued to move through the fog closer to me.

I took a step back. What could I do now? I glanced at Aidan, still on the ground unmoving.

"He can't kill me if he's dead." I demanded.

Dorian laughed that dry, husky laugh I remembered, "Oh he's not dead," he answered, "not yet anyway. He'll wake up in a bit with nothing more than a bad headache. It would only make sense for him to kill you. That's his job, Miss Doe."

I felt my limbs shaking in fury. I wanted to tear him apart with my bare hands. He wouldn't kill me. I knew he wouldn't. He wanted Aidan to do it. He couldn't take my life himself.

"He isn't one of you," I said, "he never truly was."

He smiled devilishly. He was so vile, "If only you knew," he started, "If only you knew what he's done."

Don't listen; he's trying to distract you.

He was inches away from me now but I didn't back up.

"Maybe I'll just kill you myself after all," he said, "Just for my own comfort and enjoyment."

"You wouldn't," I taunted.

"Do you want to test that little theory of yours?" he sneered back, still with that foul smile on his face.

He reached into the inside pocket of his jacket and I braced myself, prepared to be staring down the barrel of a gun, but he pulled out a knife. The blade was tarnished; I could easily see the blood that had never been washed off. All Dorian ever wanted was to kill me, so what was stopping him now?

He took another step forward and froze for a moment. He opened his mouth to speak but no words came out.

"Not her!" I heard, "It can never be her!"
Oh God! Luna!

I saw her emerge from behind Dorian to stand beside me with a knife in her hand, dripping with his blood. Why not use the gun?

Dorian stumbled toward me again.

"Jane," she whispered, "run."

I did run this time. Into the house, ignoring Rudy's pleads for me to slow down. I even felt him grab my arm at one time but I tore him away from me. I scrambled around frantically; searching for the pistol Luna had used to shoot the man who killed Mike. I grabbed it off the table by the china cabinet and raced back outside holding it in position the entire time. I was no longer frightened, I was angry. I shoved Luna out of the way and fired. Not once, not twice, not even three times. I just kept shooting like I couldn't stop.

"Jane!" Luna screamed. Her words tore me out of my fury and I lowered the gun.

I didn't even look at her. I couldn't take my eyes off Dorian. He was on the ground soaking the grass with blood. It pooled out of him the way I never thought blood could. It spread rapidly to my feet soaking my shoes. I never knew there could be so much blood in one body, no matter the size. I didn't even know how many times I shot him and I didn't care.

"Jane," Luna whispered.

I glanced at her this time.

"Guns aren't our way!" she spat and tore the pistol from my hand.

"What?"

"The gun was meant only for emergencies." She demanded shaking the weapon at me.

"And this wasn't an emergency?"

She sighed, "Guns aren't our way," she repeated.

I heard Rudy as he approached Luna, "She just killed a man," he said, "try to show a bit of sensitivity."

She huffed and shoved passed him walking quickly back to the house.

"Are you okay?" Rudy asked.

I nodded. "I think so."

My eyes were fixed on Dorian again. I couldn't take my eyes off of him. I couldn't see *him*, not the way I used to. He was a mess of flesh and blood, like he had never been anything more than that.

"Aidan." Rudy announced, rushing toward him. I followed behind him and knelt beside my love.

"Aidan?" I whispered.

He groaned and lifted his hand, sitting up "I'm all right," he said, "I'm not hurt."

I wrapped my arms around him.

"Okay," he groaned, "Not completely unhurt. Gently, Jane."

I moved away from him, "I'm sorry."

"Dorian's dead," Rudy whispered.

Aidan nodded, "I heard the gunfire."

"That was Jane," he said.

"What?" he mused, "I told you to run."

"I—didn't listen,"

He sighed, "of course you didn't."

Rudy grasped Aidan's arm and helped him stumble to his feet. "Come on," he said.

I felt my breath explode. I didn't realize I had been holding it. I forced a whisper, "thank you." And found myself in Aidan's arms once again.

"Rudy will take you home." He whispered.

"What about you?"

"You'll see me soon." He chuckled, "I promise."

His laugh brought me back to the days when I wondered about him, when everything he did was mysterious.

Rudy came up behind me and tenderly took my hand. "Come on." He whispered.

I couldn't take my eyes off Aidan. Rudy practically dragged me away from him. Aidan was smiling the entire time.

"What did Luna mean?" I asked Rudy, "about the gun..."

"The hunters don't—believe in guns."

"Believe?"

He nodded not taking his eyes of the road, "They kill with knifes. According to Aidan, killing an enemy with a gun is only acceptable when the enemy has first broken the rule."

I nodded, remembering the man in my room who had in fact used a gun.

"But Luna, she isn't one of them."

He nodded, "I know, Jane, but I've talked to Aidan and I understand what he means when he says that it's hard to shift your beliefs when you believed something for so long. She felt Dorian should have died by his laws."

What are they?" I whispered, unsure if I really wanted to hear more horror stories.

"Insane," he spat, "evil, vile, sick people who believe only what they want to believe. They're people who live by their own laws."

It was clear to me then that Rudy had never truly known before what the hunters really were. He really *did* believe those crazy stories.

I cried on the car ride home. Again, I wasn't sure if it because I was happy or sad, I finally decided it was both. Rudy spoke to me but I couldn't tell what he was saying. I managed to pick up "It's ok," and "everything is fine." Things of the sort.

He was at my side the entire time, up until my hand reached for the door of my house. Just the sight of the house in the mist of the early morning made everything seem normal for a brief moment. I felt like I was back to the first week I had been in North Bend. I hesitated before opening the door; as soon as I managed I slowly opened up and stepped inside, still with Rudy beside me. Ethan instantly ran to me and pulled me into one of his brace tight hugs like the one he gave me when he picked me up from the airport what seemed like ten years ago.

"Are you okay?"

"I'm fine," I told him, my voice muffled against his chest.

"Are..."

"I'm sure, Dad. I'm fine. And you?"

"A few bumps and bruises but nothing to be too worried about."

"Are *you* sure?"

"I am."

"Dad?" I started, moving away from him, "Even after all of this, I'm glad I came to live with you." For the first time I had said something to him that I meant one hundred percent.

He smiled, but it wasn't one of his *I'll accept that* kind of smiles, but more of the way he smiled when he was happy. He *was* happy and I was finally able to tell.

I remembered Rudy and turned around to see him returning the smile. I laughed and brought myself back into his arms again.

"Thank you." Ethan said to him, "For everything you've done."

Rudy nodded. He tucked my head under his chin and rocked me for a moment before pushing me forward and looking at me grinning widely.

"I love you, Jane." He said. It wasn't meant the way it was the first time he had said it which made it mean even more than it ever had before.

"I know." I answered, "I love you, too, Rudy."

His grin widened which didn't seem possible until I saw it happen.

Ethan didn't want to talk much about what had happened.

"I really would rather not burden you with it," he said, "I'm all right and that's what matters. I don't want to add any fuel for your nightmares."

I half smiled, "Dad, I'm seventeen, I can handle it."

"And I'm your father."

I just looked at him, unyielding.

He sighed heavily, "All right," he started, "I got off work a little earlier than usual and decided to get some sleep. I figured you were with Becky so I didn't worry. That was my mistake and I'm so sorry."

I put my hand up, "You have nothing to be sorry for," I said.

He nodded but I could tell he had this guilt, gnawing at him. "I woke up when I heard someone in the room. I thought I may have been dreaming until I felt my mouth covered and I was blindfolded. I tried to scream but I was gagged. They took me—right from the safety of my own home, dragged me out of my house and into the trunk of a car. The drive wasn't long but when the car stopped and they let me out, they took the blindfold off and I was in the woods somewhere—somewhere I had never been before. There was a large, dark skinned man who led me into the trees."

I knew instantly he was talking about Dorian.

"They led me to others. There were at least a dozen people all cloaked and hooded in black like monsters from some demonic folktale. They were chanting or singing I'm not sure which. It must have been very late because the sun was starting to come up when they strapped me to this stone…"

He broke off and looked at me, "Jane?"

"I'm fine," I lied. My heart was physically aching with the images I was seeing in my head.

"You don't need to hear the rest of this."

I nodded, "I'm fine," I said.

"Your friends saved me," he said.

I nodded, "I know."

"That's all you need to know."

I shook my head, "How long, Dad?" I questioned, "How long were you there, strapped to the stone?"

He sighed and bowed his head. His voice was so quiet, "Over night," he said, "when I got home, Rudy said I had to wait at home while he went to get you. He was crying for some reason. He mumbled that he didn't want to tell you something." I remembered the way he shook his head when he went to get me from Luna's. He thought Aidan was dead.

"He was just scared," I said, "when he came to get me there was nothing wrong," *except the blood on his clothes which Ethan seemed to not have noticed.*

"I just wanted you back," he said, he pressed his fingers to his eyelids under his glasses, "I just wanted you back, Jane. I couldn't lose you, too."

My eyebrows pulled together and it took everything I had not to cry. He saw the look on my face and being my dad, decided that hugging me would help. It was then that I cried.

"I didn't want you to feel this way."

"It's okay," I said, "I needed to know."

"They said I was—pure," he added, "Innocent. Things like that."

I nodded, "I know." I whispered before I realized I shouldn't have said anything.

He looked at me for a moment then narrowed his eyes, "You—know."

I nodded, "They told me..." I decided it was best to lie, keep Aidan out of the story, "They told me the same thing."

"Oh," was all he said.

* * *

I went up to my room simply for the sake of being in my room, to be at home again. I spotted a folded slip of paper on my bed. Panic struck. My palms started sweating and my heart was pounding. I picked it up and shook it open. It was hand written in his beautiful writing.

Jane,
I'm sorry I lied to you. There is something you need to know. I couldn't bring myself to tell you before, but now you need to see for yourself. Check under your pillow. I love you.
Yours,
Aidan.

I sighed in relief and reached under my pillow, feeling the coolness of the room from the icy temperature of the fabric. I felt something and pulled it out. It was a tiny silver key, intricately designed like a Celtic knot attached to a lovely blue tassel. It took me a moment. Why would I need a key? I replayed a few events and I heard Aidan's voice in my head, telling me about plan A, plan B, and plan C. And the chest in the corner of the attic flashed through my memory. I raced out of my room and brought myself to the attic; I switched on the light and stared at the redwood chest still in the corner where I remembered it.

I think it needs a key.

I eyed the tiny silver lock and crawled over to the chest, terrified of what may be inside. I thought it better to get it over with. Thoughts were racing, what if it was another bag of teeth, or several bags of teeth? What if it was filled with bones or vials of blood? I sighed and turned the key. The clicking of the lock was like an attack on my nerves. I opened it and the smell of dust and wood assaulted my nose. When the dust cleared I peered inside relieved to see that the chest was filled with papers and photos. I picked up the photo on top and thought my eyes were playing tricks on me. The picture in my hand was in color but I could still tell it was old and the colors had faded. There was an older man sitting on the steps of a porch next to a young boy. I could swear it was Rudy. He didn't have the spiked hair and I couldn't see the eye color, but the smile and the rounded shape of the face—it looked exactly like him. His story replayed in my head. I recognized the older man in the photo as well though I couldn't decide why. I stared at his round eyes and childlike face, trying to decide who he looked like. I could tell even in the photo that his eyes were a light sky blue. The name came to me slowly and I didn't know I was going to say it until I actually did.

"Oh my god!" I choked out, "Walter!"

Rudy's grandfather *was* alive—he was Walter Redline. My god. What kind of secrets could be hiding in an old chest? The next thing my eyes caught was a leather bound journal. I opened to the first page.

"September 26, 1948,

The killings are getting worse. People all over the city are going missing. I know they will end up like Jack, I can't take it. The Sevren are too powerful. We are no match for them. They are clever. If these pages are ever read I hope you know how to defeat them, if you don't, then get out—run! They are evil and will stop at nothing to put an end to The Silver Wing once and for all. They wanted a war and they are winning the one we gave them."

The Silver Wing? There was talk of war in the pages. My thoughts were instantly shattered and I shrieked, dropping the journal from my hands.

"Jane?"

"Oh." I breathed.

"I'm not used to startling you anymore. I'm sorry."

"Aidan, explain this! Now!"

He sighed and sank his head low. "How angry are you?"

I chocked on my voice before responding. "I—don't know yet."

"I can't explain everything, all that I can tell you is it was better for you not to know until now."

"Why?"

"I didn't want you worrying over any more than you already were. But you had a right to see this."

"How did you know about this?"

"It belonged to another member of The Silver Wing—the ones who were trying to stop…"

"I know about The Silver Wing!" I yelled, "How did you know about this?"

"It belonged to somebody I knew. It was given to your grandfather."

"My grandfather?"

He nodded.

"And Danny?" I yelled, "You knew about Danny! Tell me why they killed him! You knew. The entire time you KNEW!"

"Jane…"

"Tell me Aidan—James—Clem. Whoever the hell you are. Tell me now!"

He shook his head slowly and his voice remained calm. He was sad—genuinely sad. "Rudy's great grandfather, Peter knew about The Sevren," he started, "He constructed a group to try to stop them. The group called themselves The Silver Wing. They were never able to defeat them and Peter's son; Rudy's grandfather took over the group after Peter's death. Your grandfather, Jane, he was also a member of The Silver Wing. They killed him and they killed Danny. They lost track of you, your mother and Ethan when the person instructed to find them disappeared. That's why I was enrolled in school here. Abraham found me and threatened my life, ordering me to finish the job, I was sent to find you. It was my job— to kill you."

"What?" my voice was muffled.

"I would never hurt you, Jane," he cried, "I swear it! When I first met you I didn't know who you were, if I did…"

"If you did you would have stayed away? You would have left me alone?"

"Yes."

"You lied to me Aidan, about everything. *Everything*!"

"No," he answered calmly, "Not everything. I love you, Jane, that was and always has been the truth."

"Aidan, leave." My voice was so soft, I could hardly hear myself, but I knew he heard me.

"What?"

I handed him the picture of Walter, "Leave!"

"I can explain this." He said.

"You don't need to." I wept, "Just leave me alone like you should have in the first place."

"I'll leave because you're telling me to," he started, "But I *will* be back, Jane."

"Don't bother!"

I wept uncontrollably into my hands. I left the key on top of the chest and headed back to my room. I cried myself to sleep.

Around 4 a.m. I was disturbed by the feeling of a warm hand on my face, I awoke slowly un-startled and switched on the lamp on my nightstand.

"I left because you told me to," he said, "but I thought maybe you were calm enough now to let me explain."

"Aidan, there's nothing to explain."

"How can you say that?"

"I know about The Sevren and The Silver Wing; I don't care to know more."

"The Silver Wing no longer exist," he whispered sadly, "The Sevren killed most of them, and most of the people who were connected to them. That's why Rudy was also in danger."

"What about Walter?" I asked, "Were you *ever* planning on telling Rudy his grandfather was alive? That's why you didn't want him there, and that's why Dorian wanted him."

He nodded, "Walter left Rudy's life to protect him from the Sevren, the hunters as he calls them. It seems Dorian found out who Rudy was after all, but Dorian is dead and as long as Rudy doesn't know, he will be safe. Walter did everything he could to protect him. That chest belongs to him. Your grandfather couldn't stand watching Walter shuffle through all those old pictures and letters, it was making him miserable. So your grandfather took it—simply so Walter would stop tormenting himself. The Sevren kill the beautiful and the pure. Those are the ones Abraham taught us were "made for us." After the construction of The Silver Wing, it was our job to stop them, to destroy their alliance so we could continue our way of life."

My mind took another path, one away from The Sevren and back to the old tugging pain that I had finally been able to push aside.

"You—you killed Danny." I whispered, locking my gaze directly into his eyes. My heart felt like it was slowly chipping away, like acid was eating away at it. My entire chest burned. I am unsure how, but somewhere in me I knew it had to be true. I had known all along somewhere deep within me.

"Danny's death—I couldn't have stopped it if I tried, if Abraham did it he would have suffered. I had to."

I nodded, "I want to tell you it's okay, Aidan, but it isn't. Danny is dead—by your hands. That's all that matters."

"Jane, he was innocent and I understand that it was wrong. My killing of him was mercy. I wish I could help you see that. The Sevren are not who I am, Jane, they are who I *was,* who I will never be again."

"You're a killer," I sobbed.

"I love you," he said sternly "Please. We don't have to hurt anymore. We can leave North Bend—together."

"What?"

"In the morning, open the bags I left in the attic."

"Why?"

"Just do it," he said, "I will see you soon."

He was gone in seconds and it took me at least an hour to fall back asleep. I contemplated looking in the bags right after he left but decided to trust him one last time, though I knew I shouldn't. Danny's death replayed in my head over and over again making it impossible to relax.

When my body finally shut down into unconsciousness I was assaulted by a series of strange dreams that I couldn't remember as soon as my eyes opened but left a lingering feeling of anxiety. It was still dark when I awoke but lied in bed until the sun came up and I heard Ethan leave for work, sure that he had been in to check on me several times. I didn't want to do what Aidan had said about the bags in the attic but my curiosity got the better of me.

I crawled into the attic and opened the dark blue duffel bag Aidan had brought over. I gasped and with shaking hands, shuffled through the contents. It was stuffed with clothes and wigs of all different colors and styles, bottles of hair dye. There was a plastic bag filled with fake IDs and passports. His plans A, B and C, were to help me cover my tracks as well. Help me become somebody different, but perhaps he was right, maybe I really couldn't stay here, I didn't even bother opening the other bags, it wasn't worth upsetting myself any more.

By covering your tracks I'd never see you again.

I wondered then if it was avoidable, could I really stay in North Bend as Jane Doe? The Sevren were everywhere widely spread and clever. North Bend wasn't the only place, it couldn't have been. Nowhere was safe—*nowhere!* But there had to be somewhere safer than here. The name on one of the IDs became distorted and I realized I was crying. I dried off the plastic and left the attic.

    I never intended to fall in love with him. I never meant to be hopeless and foolish for him, but I was and after everything Aidan had put me through even the lies and the murders, after I wanted nothing more than to hate him —I wanted him with me. I wanted to touch him and hear his voice. After everything he had done—I loved him.

XX

Goodbye

I never thought about how my life in North Bend—at Ethan's home would end. It wasn't my true home, it never could be. But now that it was ending, I realized it should have occurred to me before I even moved here, that it would come to a screeching halt. I couldn't stay even if I was with the people I loved; my heart still wasn't in North Bend. It was in California with my beautiful mother, the place where I last saw Danny. I wanted to escape my past so I came here—to the place where I spent most of my childhood summers, how could I have thought that would be the right solution? I couldn't run away anymore. It was time to go home.

Now that it was over, I thought of every reason I should be sad. It confused me that I wasn't sad at all. I shouldn't have been ready to leave; I shouldn't have been relieved to be going home. I should be terrified to leave Becky and Ethan—even Aaron and Rudy as well, but I wasn't.

"Are you ready?"

"Physically or mentally?"

He smiled, "both."

"I'm not packed," I told him, "but I'm ready."

"I'm sorry," he said, sitting beside me on the end of my bed "I didn't want it to end this way."

"I know." I answered forcing my voice to stay even and strong.

"So this is it then?"

I nodded, "I go home, you go home and it's all only a memory." I wondered for a fleeting moment where home was for him.

"Why won't you look at me?" I could feel him move closer.

"If I look at you this will never end, Aidan."

"I don't want it to end."

"Then don't look at me either."

I stood up and turned away from him. A light rain was falling and I listened to it, trying to ignore the burning in my heart, the pain of wanting him and being forced to leave him. The only solution that can keep me and everyone I loved safe.

"What did you tell Ethan?"

"Honestly…nothing." I answered, pushing aside the pain in my voice, "He already knows."

"Nobody is going to hurt him," he said, "They won't hurt you either, I won't let them, I can protect you."

"No, Aidan," I answered sharply. I finally turned to look at him, confirming that all of this was real and right in front of me, "You can't. You don't have to sacrifice yourself for me. If I stay here, everybody I love will be in just as much danger as me."

He sighed and nodded. "I love you, Jane."

I broke my gaze staring at the floor, "I know. But I can't let that matter anymore."

The pain at that point was impossible to hide. Every time I looked at him I was reminded of how beautiful he was and how much I loved him. I stared at my bedroom window, studying the patterns of rain drops on the glass, looking for a deeper meaning, for something to make sense—to be in order. I couldn't choose this ending, this was the *only* ending. I was anxious to get out, to leave these feelings of Aidan as far behind as possible. I still didn't understand completely, all I knew was that The Sevren were after me because my grandfather was a member of The Silver Wing. They would be after Rudy if he knew about Walter. But what about Ethan, and my mother? They were in danger as well.

"What else can I do?" I asked, "Ethan, and my mother."

"We—Ethan and I, agreed that we don't want your mother to know about this. I will help your father cover his tracks, as I promised. He won't even have to leave North Bend. I will keep The Sevren away from California, away from you and your mother until I can stop them and I swear to you Jane—I *will* find a way. I'll come back to you when it's safe."

"I can't look at you that way anymore." I told him sadly, "It's too painful."

"Jane…"

"Don't" I snapped, "Please. If you love me, really love me; just let me do what I need to do. Let me go, Aidan, let me live my life and let me forget you so that someday—I can remember you."

He nodded solemnly, "Can you do just one thing for me?" he asked.

I didn't answer but the look in my eyes confirmed that I would do anything for him.

"Help me make things right?"

"How?"

"I know I can't make everything right," he said, "With you. But I want to make things right with Rudy, if that's all I can do, let me redeem myself in one small way."

His words had touched me to be honest. I couldn't say no to a request like that. I nodded. "Of course."

"Thank you."

* * *

"Why can't you just tell me what this is all about?" Rudy asked.

Aidan smiled, "Well, it's sort of—a surprise."

"A surprise?"

"Mmhmm."

"Huh—Jane?"

"Its fine," I told him, "It was Aidan's idea and I promise you'll love it."

"It's a thank you for helping me," Aidan said, "Don't worry."

He sat silently occasionally glancing at one of us. Aidan kept his eyes on the road but his face looked happy. I was able to ignore the pain I felt when I looked at him, trying to make things seem a little more normal for Rudy. This was his day. Aidan drove slower than usual and pulled into the driveway of his house."

"What are we doing here?" Rudy asked.

"You know this is where I live," Aidan said, "But you've never been inside." He smiled crookedly and raised his eyebrows. He unlocked the door and stepped inside.

Rudy glanced around like he knew where he was. Almost like he had been there before but couldn't remember when. He looked so confused.

"Are you all right?" I asked.

"Jane…" His voice was so quiet I could hardly hear him, it was almost throttled. He pointed to the painting on the wall. The horse.

I just stared at the look on his face. He knew that painting. I could only imagine how important it must have been for him to have reacted that way. Walter entered the room but Rudy didn't notice yet, he kept his eyes locked on the painting.

"Ah." Walter said. Rudy turned around, "I always liked that painting."

Rudy was silent. I could see he was already crying.

"You've grown." Walter said, "It's all right. I'm not a ghost."

Rudy stumbled toward him and fell into his arms. I could hear him quietly sobbing against Walter's chest. "I thought you were dead." I heard.

"Oh but I had to be," he whispered, "I had to be dead to protect you."

"And now?" Rudy asked moving away.

"Now it was time for you to know the truth, we can protect you now. We know so much more about The Hunters now than we used to my boy."

"So you aren't going to leave me again?" he sobbed, "You won't disappear?"

"I won't disappear."

"What about Mom?"

"Oh she'll find out," Walter laughed. It was that dry sputtered laughter I had heard before, "But don't you go telling her just yet."

Rudy nodded, "Okay." He turned toward Aidan. "Thank you." He whispered.

Aidan gave him that formal bow and smiled.

I wrapped my arms around Aidan's shoulders. "Thank you for doing this," I whispered in his ear.

"I had to."

"I know."

"So after today, you will be all right?"

I nodded, "I'll be all right, Aidan. You need to let me go. You need to let me forget everything. That way I can remember it someday."

He nodded. "I'll miss you."

My chest burned, I couldn't answer. I looked at him and nodded telling him *I know*.

* * *

"So, "I'll see you again?" His sobbing was becoming ridiculous.

"Dad, I'm not dying," I said, forcing a smile.

"He pulled me tightly into his chest. "Tell your mother 'hi' for me."

I nodded; refusing to let myself seem sad, it would only makes things harder for Ethan. Becky was even worse; she wouldn't let me go even when I choked out, "Can't breathe." It didn't seem fair that I had to hurt her this way, Rudy and Aaron as well, for my own selfish reasons. That's when my thoughts halted and I remembered that I was doing this for them, to keep them safe. Standing by me would put them at the top of The Sevren's hit list. I chocked back my own tears there was no need to make this worse for her. Aaron stepped forward once he was able to pry Becky off of me. He led out his hand and I laughed, "A hand shake?"

He shrugged his shoulders smiling and embraced me.

I slowly turned to Rudy who was just stepping inside as I was letting go of Aaron. He just stared at me for a moment giving me a synthetic smile through his tears. I held out my arms and after one step, his lips were crushing mine. I pulled away instantly. "Rudy, I—"

"I know," he said. He sounded perfectly content, "you're leaving, it seemed like a good excuse."

I laughed and shook my head. "Bye, Rudy." I said and hugged him.

"You'll come and visit?"

"Of course."

I slung my backpack over my shoulder and grabbed the handle of my suitcase. I walked past my friends and waved as I stepped outside, leaving my childhood home once again. They followed me out to the car where Ethan was waiting. I couldn't look back at them again; my entire face was burning with my attempts to hide my emotions. Tears still spilled over and I didn't want any of them to see that.

"You come back any time you want." Ethan said, shoving my things into the trunk.

I just nodded.

He took off his glasses and pressed his thumb and index finger to his eyelids, "You're always welcome here."

"I know." I answered.

I wore the red raincoat Ethan had given me when I moved to North Bend, sort of as a farewell gesture you could say. The car ride to the airport was silent which saddened me quite a bit more than I would have otherwise expected. I wished my father and I could have bonded more over the time I had spent there, but I supposed it was my fault, I never answered his questions and avoided conversation with him until he either gave up or decided to leave me alone, thinking I wasn't interested in what he had to say, which wasn't it at all really. It was just difficult for me to open up to Ethan; I'd never talked to him about personal things before. I sighed at these thoughts.

"Doing okay?" he asked.

I tried to actually answer him, let him into my head a little bit, "I'm doing okay, Dad," I answered, "just going to really miss everything about this place."

"Hmm, didn't expect that." He said smiling and glancing over at me.

I laughed, "Neither did I."

I was suddenly aware of everything, every single sound, the wind whipping by as each car or motorcycle passed by, I could hear the buzzing behind the turned down music on the radio and Ethan's slow, deep breathing. I could almost hear my own pounding heartbeat, my god—it was really ending. I was able to contain myself and was beginning to feel a great sense of relief. Now everything can go back to normal. I could spend my summers at Ethan's and the school years with my mother. That relief lasted only until I boarded the plane after about three more of my father's tight hugs. As soon as I settled into the uncomfortable airplane seat, I felt myself break down and quietly wept until I exhausted myself enough to relax and fell asleep. All of the emotions of the past month had paralyzed me and even in the uncomfortable seat of an airplane I slept deeply and dreamlessly. The stewardess awoke me; she had dark cropped hair and large round eyes. Her voice sounded sweet, and natural to me.

"Miss?"

I opened my eyes and she was smiling at me. I immediately got up and grabbed my bag from above me. I was almost a zombie as I sat in the terminal with a romance novel I had daydreamed through, getting to the bottom of the page and starting over again at the top. I sighed heavily and slammed the book closed. I leaned back in the plastic seat, sleep was impossible but I tried at least to relax, that proved impossible as well. I gave in and let my thoughts run wild, everything came to mind, from Danny's death to that first date with Aidan, Andrew Gallagher's Halloween party—to this—the end. The end of the only thing that let me believe trust was possible, that I was capable of love without Danny. The rest of the time I sat there waiting, that hopeful mood came back, I was looking forward to seeing my mother and my old room again, my old town—everything I missed, and sunny California that I loved.

As soon as my mother saw me she ran to me and hugged me the way Ethan had, to where I almost couldn't breathe. She was crying more than she was when I left. It was different than it was with Ethan; it was always easy to talk to my mom. Though Ethan and I didn't talk much we had talked about what I would tell her and we both agreed that she didn't need to know about any of the terrible things that had happened. Amazingly I still looked like me, instead of aging fifty years premature. My mother always asked a lot of questions, but this time I felt bombarded by them.

"I'm so sorry I'm late, sweetie," she said, "so what ultimately sealed the deal for you to move back out here?"

"Mostly homesickness," I said, "Also—nothing really felt right in North Bend, and of course Danny's memory is stronger there."

She nodded, like she was unable to answer. She never talked about him.

"I'm glad to be home."

She smiled, "glad to have you home."

"How is everybody?" she asked on the car ride home, "Becky and Ethan…?"

"Great," I said, "Becky is finally with a really nice guy her own age, one of my new friends actually. Name's Aaron, he's really cute."

"Well that's a relief. Her mom still a mess?"

"I'm guessing so, she never really talks about her and I haven't seen her."

My mom nodded. She cared more about Becky than Becky's own parents. "But she's doing all right?"

"Yes she's all right."

"So have you made any other new friends?"

I decided to leave Aidan out of everything for the rest of—well—forever. "No," I lied, "Just got reacquainted with Rudy Thompson from across the street and his brother Eric. There are a few people I talk to, but nobody I really got close to save for Aaron."

"Well at least you have a nice circle of friends."

I smiled, "Can't wait to visit them again."

"Oh I'm glad to hear you say that Jane, you haven't been at all social in so long."

"Well—I guess I changed a little bit."

She smiled at me, knowing there was something I was hiding but she didn't push it. It was so good talking to my mom again. I had missed her a lot more than I realized. When we finally got home it felt like I had never really left in the first place. She helped me carry the rest of my bags into the house.

"So is my room a weight room now?" I teased.

She laughed, "Of course not, I knew you would be back at least to visit again."

I smiled. "Did you at least paint the walls?" I never liked the pale pink color.

"It's all the same, honey."

"Hmm—nice."

I went upstairs to my room and just like my mom had said—all the same. Everything was empty but the bed was in the same place with the floral comforter and pale pink pillows that matched the walls. "The Friday The 13th" poster was still on my door and the dresser and bookshelf hadn't changed at all. It was a relief to have nothing different; it was like I had never left, like North Bend was all a dream and nothing had changed. I was just Jane Doe and I smiled as I placed Danny's picture on my old wooden dresser where it had always been before. He was happy in that picture, just how I wanted to remember him. In the red picture frame that matched the red baseball cap he was wearing. I unpacked slowly, placing the pictures Becky had taken off to the side, planning to put them on the walls somewhere later. I came across a picture she had taken of me and Aidan in the cafeteria. It was in the beginning when things were more normal.

It was a nice picture but I didn't like the way I looked next to Aidan with his flawless skin and perfect eyes. I hated looking so average. I shoved the picture under my bed and stared at another one, this one of me, Rudy, Becky and Aaron. That was the one worth keeping, it made me smile. My mom knocked on the door a few minutes later.

"It's open." I called.

She came in and instantly smiled at me; she knelt on the floor next to me. "Oh pictures." She said. I was glad I had shoved that other one under the bed. My mom would love to add these to her scrapbook.

"Yeah," I answered, "thank Becky for that." I handed her the stack and she looked through them as I told her about Aaron and what was going on in each picture or why all of us were laughing at the same time. Becky loved snapping pictures when I was laughing about something stupid. I already missed her but planned to call her later that evening, hopefully she'd tell me she was fine as was Aaron and Rudy. I finished unpacking most of my clothes and some of my old books but everything else was still shoved in my suitcases. I decided I'd devote a few days to that until my mom got me reregistered back at my old school. It would have made more sense for me to wait through the summer to come home, but I couldn't stay there another minute, not with The Sevren so near. So now I'd be coming back to school, middle of the semester with no idea how I was to catch up.

Time passed and it was a while before everything had finally gone back to normal. I got my job back, but Amber was still the only person I really talked to except for a few people in my English class usually asking me for help. I was happy being home and even happier that summer was close and I would get to see Becky, Rudy and Aaron again, also I missed Ethan more than I thought I would. It would be nice to go back to North bend for a little while but even now I wasn't sure I could be safe, so my friends had all planned on coming to California instead. My grades were back to the way they should be and I was pleased I was able to catch up without too much of a problem. Aidan didn't usually cross my mind and when he did it was easy for me to push it aside and think of something else. I didn't have a lot of room left in my head to miss him, but if I were to stop and think about him I figured I would cry myself to sleep for hours. I realized a couple weeks later—that I was right and that suppressing his memory only lasted so long and all I could do was cry over him for nights on end, wishing he was lying next to me like he used to. Just so I could bring myself into his arms when I awoke every night from those strange nightmares.

    My mother had asked me to help her with some grocery shopping the morning after another dream of Aidan and The Sevren. Amazingly enough I was able to hide the pain it had caused me. I drove to the grocery store without even noticing the streets, everything still looked exactly the same, and the warm air from the approaching Summer was comforting. I hadn't seen the rain a single time since I'd been home. I was constantly aware of every voice and every face I passed by, hoping that maybe one of them would be his. Every time I heard someone behind me I'd turn around, only to feel ridiculous when I realized it wasn't him. After all how could it be? I left North Bend to get away from The Sevren but also to get away from Aidan. I left because I could no longer bear to look at him. Daniel was dead and there was nothing I could do now to bring him back but if there was even the smallest chance that I could help make things right I would. How can I love a boy who killed Danny? How could I live in a way that would honor Danny and make him proud by being with his killer? I asked myself these questions searching for an answer that could justify me and Aidan being together— nothing came to mind. There was a way there had to be and now it was only weighing on whether or not I could find it and so far it didn't seem like I would. Being by myself never bothered me before so I guess it shouldn't have then either. I knew it could be possible to live the way I had before Danny died and I made that terrible decision to move to North Bend. I knew it would take a lot of work suppressing memories and tucking away old pictures. At the same time that all sounded wonderful in my head, I found myself unable to take Becky's goofy pictures off the walls of my room and couldn't bear to hide the notes she had written me about Aidan when she was bored in math class. I wanted to remember even if it hurt me, even if it killed me—I didn't want to forget. I never had people in California the way I did in Oregon, not people who had shared once in a lifetime experiences with me. I would never find friends like them again and I couldn't forget what we had been through. Me having friends and being listened to and even understood in even one small way was like a miracle. There *was* life after Danny after all and I was determined to live it.

My mind wondered from Aidan, to Becky and back again. Wondered through every day I had suffered in North Bend and every day I had been in love. I realized the memories didn't hurt so much after all. Most of it seemed so surreal, like a dream long ago that never made much sense. I tried telling myself that it wasn't a dream, that it was real and all of it had happened—to me—Jane Doe. It made things worse of course but again, I would do anything to not forget even if that meant inflicting old pain.
    The thoughts of Aidan had mostly stopped haunting me. It was a relief to be able to stop thinking about him. I was able to take refuge in the bookstore without thinking about the first day in North Bend, the day that Aidan had rescued me the first time. It was like a memory being in that place again, it wasn't one of those normal every day things anymore but more something that *used* to be a normal everyday thing. It was a strange feeling but a good one at the same time. All of the time I spent in North Bend had faded in my mind seeming like nothing more than a vague dream.
    I let out a long sigh letting my mind swirl and wrap around peaceful daydreams as my eyes slowly unfocused on the bland black text in front of me. I had no conception of what the words were, nor did I care. I waited for that face again, for the softness of his blue eyes and the kindness of his smile. As the image began to take

form I was ripped almost violently out of my dreams and into the vacant, dust of the bookstore.

"Jane."

It was soft, almost hesitant. I knew it wasn't him, but the voice was familiar and my mind told me against what I knew that it was. I almost whispered his name as I turned around.

"Jane?'

"Y—yes?'

"You don't remember me."

It wasn't a question. I did however. I knew the softness of his hair hanging slightly in the left side of his face, and his dark blue, round eyes. There was so much I had blocked from my memory.

"I do," I said, "only, I'm unsure why."

He led out his hand. "Ian." He said.

Visions in my head spun and flashed rapidly. Dorian. The basement. The bag of teeth. The hanging corpse. It assaulted my mind leaving me gasping for breath and almost brought me to my knees.

He dropped his hand. "Come on," he said, "We need to talk." He sounded calm and composed but his eyes were tense.

"What are you doing here?"

"Not now, Jane, wait until we get into the car."

That told me it wasn't something he couldn't mention in public, meaning it had something to do with all the horrors I had left behind. Instantly I began to feel a sense of anger tugging at my nerves. I shoved passed him and walked quickly to my car. He followed me without hesitation.

"Jane, we need to talk."

He reached for me and tore the keys from my hand.

"You must be joking," I snapped. I held out my hand, "Give them back to me. NOW."

He sighed but handed them back. I climbed inside and sat stiff for a moment. What was he doing here?

What was so important that he'd come from North Bend? I couldn't just drive away—could I? I was immediately outraged at these thoughts and gripped my fingernails into the plastic if the steering wheel. Ian didn't even move he was frozen stiff next to my window just waiting for me to do what he knew I would, what I wanted more than anything to *not* do. I sighed and slammed my hand into the steering wheel. I climbed out of the car and slammed the door as hard as I could.

"What the hell are you doing here?" I demanded, "If this has anything to do with Ai..." I couldn't finish my sentence. I didn't need to.

"Just follow me." He said calmly. "Please."

I sighed heavily. "Fine."

He led me to the other side of the parking lot and my stomach grew tight as he approached a black mustang. He sensed my discomfort.

"Just a bad choice I suppose," he said. He was smiling which didn't seem at all like the appropriate reaction.

I nodded and got in the passenger's seat. He instantly started with the questions. His relaxed attitude had vanished and his eyes almost looked turbulent.

"Where's Aidan?" he yelled, almost bellowed.

His mood had startled me and that name—that dreadful name; it made me cringe.

"How should I know?" I retorted, in response to his yelling.

"Jane, don't play games. You have to tell me."

"Ian, I don't know."

"What? When was the last time you saw him?"

"What do you mean?" I snapped, "In North Bend, where else? Aidan and I—we aren't—we aren't like that—anymore." I forced the words from my mouth as my eyes burned with the tears I was fighting back. I couldn't stand thinking about him.

"What?'

"I left him." I answered. My voice has lowered almost to a whisper.

"How could you do that?"

"He killed my brother..."

He interrupted me. "You let him go?"

"What the hell is going on?"

"You know who he is, Jane—*what* he is."

"I believe *you* don't."

"What are you talking about?"

"If you're worried about *me,* don't be. I'm fine, if I'm in danger Aidan can find me."

"And you think The Sevren can't?"

"What?" the terror in my voice was unmistakable.

"Your brother was killed here—in California. Just because Abraham and Dorian are dead doesn't mean the others don't know your previous address."

"Aidan wouldn't let them. He'll protect me. He promised."

"Jane, wake up!" he yelled throwing his hands up, "He's been ordered to kill you. It's who he is, Jane; he will never be anything but the bad guy. He'll come for you, and with him he'll bring the others. Stop fooling yourself into trusting him."

"He's saved my life, Ian, more than once."

"He is what he is." He said firmly, "He will always fall back into his old ways. He's coming for you; we have to get you out. Just come with me, trust me."

"How can I trust you?"

He sighed. "Because you know I'm right." He answered sadly, "Because I'm your only hope."

"If they're coming for me, then what about my mom? What about Ethan?"

He put his hands up. "Both of them are safe, I took care of it."

"Took care of it how?'

"My friends are keeping them safe. You're the one they want the most, you're the one who's connected to

Aidan. We need to *hide* you. The others will stay near your parents. They're standing guard in every direction."

"I really think I can handle myself after all that's happened."

"Jane, you and I both know that isn't true."

"How much time do we have?"

"A couple weeks."

"Weeks? Why are you here?'

"I'm not patient." He said smiling.

I sighed. "Not cute."

"I'm sorry," he answered, "I got anxious. We need to act fast is all."

"How do you even know when they're coming?"

"I had connections with Dorian remember? I didn't know he was one of them. The others recognized me, remembered I had been seen with Dorian. I'm a pretty good actor when I need to be."

"Are you insane? Are you trying to get yourself killed?"

"Jane, relax," he chuckled, "It's not a big deal."

"Have you spoken to Ai—to him?'

He shook his head, "No." he said, "He wasn't around. But don't think that convinces me he's not involved. Mike wasn't there either. Those two usually work together."

"Mike?" I yelled, "Ian— Mike's dead!"

"What? When?"

"When I stayed at Luna's..." I broke off, remembering his severed head in the brown bag and that creepy man in my room. I shuddered.

"I'm sorry," he answered, "I didn't know."

I nodded, "You know maybe…"

He cut me off, "Put the possibility of his innocence out of your head please, at least until we get you safe okay?"

I nodded, "Fine."

I sat quiet for a minute, it seemed like the silence lasted hours and I was almost startled when he started the car. I didn't ask where we were going, it didn't seem like it mattered at the time. Everything was still replaying in my mind making my pulse race. I felt like I could hardly breathe. All of the horrific images that had finally stopped haunting my dreams were attacking my brain. I sighed and closed my eyes. Even with my eyes closed I felt dizzy and disoriented. I tried opening my eyes but I was weak and suddenly extremely sleepy. I didn't know I had fallen asleep—or fainted but I awoke in a room I didn't recognize. Great! Just great, at least this time it wasn't a dark basement. I was on a soft, white couch with blue pillows. The room was bare save for the couch I was on and a round coffee table in front of it. No T.V, no chairs, no cabinets—nothing. The walls were even bare. Bland off white with not a single photograph or painting. Things were coming back to me and I remembered Ian, but didn't see him.

"Ian?" I called. There was no answer and I instantly regretted trusting him for even a moment. "IAN!"

"It's okay," I heard him say. He walked into the room from around the corner, "I'm right here. I wouldn't leave you alone. I was just waiting for you to wake up."

"How long have I been out?"

"A few hours." He answered putting his hands up and walking closer to me. I sat up.

"Where are we?'

"A safe place."

"Which is...?"

He sighed, "Arizona."

"Arizona?" I was instantly filled with nervous worry, almost furious. "Why?"

"We aren't staying here. We'll be staying with my brother in Maryland."

I got up but almost collapsed back onto the couch I was so dizzy.

"Jane?"

"Forget it, Ian!" I yelled, "I'm not going to Maryland."

"We have no choice."

"WE?" I yelled stepping toward him, "There is no 'we'"

"Jane..."

"Don't." I yelled, "I was already mad at you for dragging me out of the bookstore and bringing all of the North Bend horrors back to me once I was FINALLY able to live my life without constantly looking over my shoulder. And now? Now you want to take me to damn Maryland? It's not happening, Ian."

"So what are you going to do, Jane?" he yelled, "Stay here? Not come with me?"

"No. You are going to take me home."

"To hell I am. I was sent to protect you. That's what I'm going to do."

My voice calmed. "Wait, what did you just say?"

He sighed, "I was sent to find you and to get you away from The Sevren."

"Sent by whom?"

"I don't remember his name," he said, "An old man. A doctor I think and a woman."

"Luna?"

He nodded, "Yes, Luna and an old man."

It came to me and I knew before I even asked. "Walter?"

He shook his head, "I don't know," he said, narrowing his eyes, "Mr....Wingline...or something of that effect."

"Redline." I corrected, "Mr. ...or, *Professor* Walter Redline."

"That's it," he answered thrusting his hand to his forehead, "You know him?"

I nodded, "He's my best friend's grandfather."

"Ah right," he answered, "The severe idiot who came with Aidan to rescue you from Dorian."

"Right." I said sarcastically, "The severe idiot who has stuck by me through everything even when I almost betrayed him in the beginning."

"Right." He muttered, "Sorry."

"Yeah, Rudy's great grandfather was the one who established The Silver Wing in his early twenties."

He nodded, "So I heard. The professor is at the point now where he wants to avoid violence with The Sevren, and create a treaty."

"A treaty?"

"Yeah…what are you thinking?"

"That The Sevren aren't going to agree to any damn treaty, Ian!"

He sighed, "I'm not going to respond to that because an argument is not going to get us where we need to be."

Something Aidan would say.

"So if you can stop being your difficult, hardheaded self we will leave to Maryland tomorrow morning."

I didn't say a word. I sighed and flopped back down on the couch. "Can you get me some water maybe?" I asked, "Or does this place not have any cupboards or sinks?"

He smiled. "I'll get you some water Jane."

He ended up bringing me water and a bottle of pills.

"What are those for?" I asked.

"Oh these?" he questioned shaking the bottle, and laughing, "These are for me. You're giving me a headache."

"Funny."

"I thought you could use something to relax you. You don't have to take any if you don't want to."

"It's fine, Ian," I answered, "If you say taking one will help, then I'll take one."

He nodded and handed me a small white capsule, "Just drink plenty of water with it, it's a little strong."

Well he was right about it being a little strong because I ended up falling asleep for about an hour in the car, but it also helped relax me mentally and I wasn't feeling so anxious anymore. Maryland, I didn't even know where it was, or what the weather was like. Being the way I am I was never one to travel. I liked staying in one place. Why over complicate things?

XXI

SMALL, squeaky ceiling fans and tiny glass ashtrays with no smoking symbols. Bland white walls with water stains and scratchy blankets on two cleanly made beds. For three days this was all I knew. The days when home wasn't an option. He never said anything before about a hotel, and wouldn't answer me when I asked him why we hadn't left to Maryland, and why we were still in this cheap hotel room. It had become clear to me that he realized there was no safe place.

The Sevren aren't going to agree to any damn treaty Ian.

It was obvious then that a treaty had never truly been his intentions, not even in the beginning, so what was he really planning? Ian was sitting in a wooden chair next to the bed reading the paper.

"Where are they?"

"Who?" he asked. His voice was calm. He looked up from the newspaper and sighed, "Jane..." he put the paper down, "we have to stay here okay, just for now."

"Where are they, Ian?"

"Walter and his people are in North Bend. The Sevren is weak. Their loss of Abraham and Dorian along with the regrouping of The Silver Wing has weakened them more than we could have hoped. They have already lost sixty percent of their members."

"How?"

"People who have wanted out and who left out of fear, without Dorian and Abraham; nobody is really strong enough to stop them from getting away. And..." he broke off.

"And?"

He sighed and nodded, "And a large percentage were killed by The Silver Wing."

I nodded, "So what now?"

"We wait."

"That's it?" I snapped, "We wait?'

He nodded and picked up the paper again. "We wait."

I just sat still, with my knees drawn up to my chin.

"Jane, I really wish you wouldn't do that."

"Do what?"

"That—thing you're doing, thinking silently. It worries me."

"Why are you worried?"

He laughed, "I never know what you plan to do."

"I plan to listen to you," I answered, "Even though your ideas are making me crazy. We should be doing something, not just sitting here."

"Walter and his people are doing something. *I* am keeping you safe."

I sighed. "I know." I said, "I just wish we could help."

"Like I said," he started, putting the paper down again, he sat beside me on the bed, "The Sevren are trying to regroup. There's no order anymore, that's why the members weren't afraid to flee."

"They're brainwashed," I answered, "too many of them still believe in what they practice. Enough of them to hurt the people I…"

He put his hand on my shoulder and leaned in close to me. "Nobody is going to hurt them, Jane," he said sternly, "Understand?"

I nodded, but couldn't keep the tears from coming. He sighed and pulled me into his chest. "This won't be forever. It'll go away."

"I hope you're right." I sobbed.

"I am right."

I barely slept that night, I kept waking up after disturbing nightmares, and every time I was reminded that Aidan wasn't there for me to find comfort in. Aidan would never be there again, and that's the way it had to be. I looked to the other bed and saw that Ian was out cold. I couldn't understand how he was so relaxed. Either way I was glad it was him that found me rather than somebody else, he was sweet and easy to trust. Of course there was that possibility he wasn't who he was making me believe he was. That had happened to me too many times already. I only hoped it would all be behind me soon and I could go back to California, to my normal, boring, comfortable life. I always wanted adventure but this—this wasn't one of my cheap romance novels, this was a real life horror story and it may not have a happy ending after all.

When I awoke the next morning after barely sleeping I almost screamed when I saw Ian sitting beside me. I instantly recoiled when my mind woke up the rest of the way. I could have sworn for two seconds that he was Danny.

"You ok?" he asked smiling.

"Fine." I said, "You—startled me is all."

He chuckled, "Oh I'm sorry. Are you hungry?"

"I don't know, I guess."

He led out his hand, "I'm going to bring us something."

I took his hand and crawled out of bed. "Can't we go out? Please?"

"Jane, you know that isn't a good idea."

"Please," I begged, "I can't stay cooped up in here any longer, I swear I will go crazy!"

He sighed, "It isn't safe."

"Ian, you even said The Sevren is weak and we are miles from California."

He shook his head, "I don't know."

I gave him a pleading look.

Life Blood

"Gosh I hate it when you look at me like that."

"Does that mean yes?" I smiled.

He tossed his arms up and turned away. "Don't take forever getting ready." He muttered.

I shrieked and hugged the back of his shoulders. "Thank you."

I showered in the tiny bathroom with the tiny bottles of shampoo and conditioner mixes and little bars of soup wrapped in papers with the name of the hotel (which I didn't bother reading.) I didn't even feel nervous about leaving the perceived safety of the hotel; I *had* to get out, if only for a while. I took some extra time fixing up my hair a little bit and almost thought of putting on some makeup when I realized that of course I didn't have any with me. The thought left as soon as it came anyway. I never cared for makeup. Ian drove us to a nice little coffee shop that seemed so normal and peaceful to me. I was all smiles.

"You seem overly happy to be here." He said laughing.

I took the seat next to him, "It's been a while," I answered, "Like I said, I was going to go crazy cooped up in there."

"Well, try not to do anything to attract attention to yourself."

I laughed, "When have you known me to attract attention to myself?"

He nodded. Sometimes the looks he gave me reminded me so much of Danny that it hurt to be around him. It was a relief that he didn't wear that baseball cap he wore when I first met him. I kept my eyes off of his face for a moment, reminding myself continuously that he wasn't Danny. I inhaled slowly and brought my gaze back to his. I smiled falsely, veiling the thoughts and feelings he wouldn't understand. A stern voice interrupted us suddenly.

"Excuse me."

I looked up automatically at the man standing beside our table.

"Yes?" Ian replied.

My hands started shaking; I realized instantly that we were in trouble. It was a cop. He flashed his badge and stared at me until I averted my gaze. How did he find me?

"Can I help you?" Ian asked calmly.

"Yes." The officer answered handing him a photo, "I believe you can."

"Whoa!" Ian laughed, "Lisa, take a look at this."

I realized what he was doing instantly and leaned over to glance at the picture. I felt dizzy like I was going to faint. It was a picture of me. A picture Becky had taken of me in the cafeteria. My mother. I knew she'd worry sick over me.

"This girl looks just like you."

I tried to relax and play along, "Yeah I guess," I said, "But honestly Josh, her hair is hardly even the same color."

He laughed.

"So you don't know her?" the officer asked.

Ian shook his head, "This isn't Lisa," he answered, "But I understand the mistake."

The officer just stared at me again and took back the photo. "Are you sure?"

"We're sure."

"Sorry to bother you then."

He left us then but the look on Ian's face was almost distressing. "We need to leave," he whispered, "now."

"Why?"

"Why?" he hissed, "He didn't buy that for a split second and he's going to bring someone else in to haul us off and drag you home."

"It's my mom," I started, "She's..."

"Of course she's worried, that's why we weren't supposed to leave the hotel. Come on. Quickly now, we've gotta get out of here."

Life Blood

I sighed and followed him out to the parking lot.

"I am proud of you though," he said after starting the engine, "The way you handled yourself in there was great. I was terrified you wouldn't catch on."

I smiled, "I'm not *completely* clueless you know."

"I know," he laughed, "just naïve."

We got back to the hotel without a problem, but Ian immediately started scrambling around the room, almost frantic, shoving his things into his suitcase.

"Jane!" he yelled, "What are you doing? Get moving."

"We're leaving?"

"Yes," he whispered sarcastically, "Of course we're leaving. We can't stay here."

I sighed, "I hate this."

"Just get your stuff."

I did as he said, trying to not think about why, but I kept hearing him mutter things under his breath.

"Shit!" he announced, peering out the window.

"What is it?"

"The damn cops."

"What?"

"Just do as I say. Can you do that for me?"

I nodded.

"Ok, get your things, and we'll take off through the window and out to the car. They're a few blocks away, so we have a bit of time, but we still have to hurry. Come on."

I followed him out to the car around the back of the hotel, avoiding any spying eyes, to not leave witnesses for the police. We shoved our things in the back seat and Ian didn't even buckle his seat belt before bolting out of the driveway as fast as he could.

"Way to be discreet." I teased.

"Not my concern," he muttered, "Trying to be quick."

Definitely something Aidan would say. They weren't so different and my thoughts of him raced. I began finding myself thinking about him again and hoping Ian could find some good in him somewhere. We were headed to a different hotel. I didn't need to ask him to know. I figured that all of my "what's" and "whys" had really gotten me nowhere. I already knew the answers.

The hotel room was almost exactly the same as the other one. The same twin beds in the tiny room and the cramped little bathroom with the bars of soup that I was almost afraid to use. I hated it. I couldn't wait for things to change.

It was time to move on. To move forward, this was my life for right now and I couldn't go back to being Jane Doe in sunny California. That couldn't be my life anymore. I had to move forward and stop looking back. Ian was who I had right now. He was my guardian and my protector— almost like I was with Danny again. He was warm and kind like Danny, but with a lot of hidden secrets I would never know. I had to stick by him now, he was the only one that could help me move on, and stop looking over my shoulder at what used to be.

XII

Trackers

IT was late in the morning when he awoke me.

"Hey, sleepy head," he muttered.

I yawned and rolled over.

"Come on," he said, "I need to talk to you."

"So talk to me," I groaned, "Why do I need to be up for you to talk?"

He chuckled, "okay, just don't fall asleep on me."

I rolled back over to look at him.

"Something needs to be done about you and your mother."

"What do you mean?" I asked, suddenly terrified of what was going to happen next.

"I was just thinking—now that The Silver Wing has taken care of most of the problem, we need to make sure the few radicals left won't try coming after you again."

"You think they would, Ian?"

He nodded, "I *know* they would, which is why you need to be kept safe."

I nodded and sat up, "okay…?"

"I'm not sure what we are going to do yet," he started, "but The Silver Wing is stationing a small group in a few areas so you and your mother need to go somewhere they will be standing guard."

"So I can't go back to California?"

He shook his head, "That wouldn't be best, no," he said, "Perhaps after The Sevren are no longer a threat at all…"

"I understand," I interrupted, "fine."

He nodded and leaned down to kiss me softly on my cheek, "I'll take care of you," he whispered, "You'll be fine."

I shuddered. Ian just kissed me and worse than that—I had enjoyed it. It actually gave me chills. I shook it off, no need to get infatuated with Ian that would only complicate things farther. Either way—it almost felt wrong. He was too much like Danny. I tried to change the subject and veil the feeling he had forced into me.

"Do you think the cops are still looking for us?" I asked.

He nodded. "Yes."

"So—what are we going to do about that?"

He sighed and went to sit on his bed. He opened the newspaper.

"Ian?"

"Right now, nothing," he said, "they wont find us for a while, and by the time they do, you will be back with your mother."

I smiled. "I can't wait for that." I said.

He glanced at me then back at his paper.

"What?" I questioned "What are you thinking?"

"Nothing, Jane."

"I may not know you that well," I started, "but I can still tell when you're lying. You're a really lousy fibber."

He smiled half-heartedly. "I am still just a little concerned is all."

"Concerned about what?"

"Everything," he answered, "I'm not going to tell you things aren't a mess."

I nodded, "I know things are a mess. But—Ian?"

"Yes?"

"I'm glad it was you that found me."

He smiled. "Thanks, Jane. Now let me read the paper. There's some bread and things in the fridge."

I nodded. I didn't feel hungry at all; I hated that tiny fridge and crummy microwave. I wanted to go home more than anything.

* * *

The days passed simply enough. A quiet, maddening routine. Ian only left at night to run down to the liquor stores and gas stations for food. I was living like a fugitive, and in reality—I was a fugitive wasn't I? Making up elaborate lies to tell the cop at the restaurant and then running away in an unregistered vehicle when he didn't believe me. I sighed at these thoughts.

"Are you okay?" Ian asked.

I just looked at him, didn't respond.

"I'm sorry," he said.

A knock on the hotel door interrupted and both of us looked at each other not knowing what to say. Ian signaled me to stay silent. I nodded. Fantastic, they must have found us. But what if it wasn't the cops? What if it was something—worse? Much worse? My limbs started trembling.

Ian looked through the peephole on the door and he had the strangest reaction.

"Jane?" he whispered, "Have you spoken to anyone? Told anyone where we are?"

"I don't even know where we are." I whispered back, "So—no."

"Well," his voice was no longer a whisper, "Then explain *this*."

He opened the door and there he was, expressionless, frozen still. I tried to think straight, to say something, but everything was spinning. I tried to sit down but it was too late. I fainted, landing on the floor of the hotel room at Ian's feet.

It was Ian's face I saw when I came to. It took me a moment to remember where I was and what I had seen.

No, no, no. I thought. *Please let this be a dream, please let me wake up.*

"Jane?"

Oh god, that voice, that word. My head was spinning again. He came to sit beside me.

"Jane, I'm here to help," he said.

I couldn't look at him; I didn't even know who he was anymore. I tried to respond.

"Aidan..." no sound came out.

"Yes?"

I shook my head.

"I'm here to help," he repeated.

"Couldn't you have sent someone?" Ian said.

Aidan shook his head, "You know me," he said, "I needed to do this myself."

"How did you find us?"

"I followed the man who is tracking you."

"Tracking us?" I yelled.

He nodded, "That's why I'm here."

Just perfect, more trouble, more running, more danger. More, more, more of everything I was praying to have end. Just prefect! I was almost enraged.

"Please," Aidan started, "I know that look all too well."

I noticed I was practically bearing my teeth at him.

"Goddamn wonderful." I muttered under my breath. He seemed to have heard me, but just sighed and stood up, turning toward Ian.

"We—well—*you* anyway, need to leave."

"Well, if they are tracking us, they'll just follow." He answered.

Aidan nodded, "Yes well—do you know how to fight?"

Ian nodded, "I can take care of myself for the most part."

"But—what about her?" Aidan asked, pointing to me without looking at me.

God, was he real? I felt like I was going insane seeing strange apparitions of the past or, perhaps just visions from a fading dream— or nightmare. I didn't even hear Ian's response.

"You can't tell me you didn't know this could happen..." Aidan said forcefully.

I saw Ian just shake his head. "I did know it was a possibility." He said, "How many?"

Aidan sighed, "Well I didn't get that past you." I heard him containing laughter—so like him.

Ian just nodded, "If there were only one, I would believe you'd take care of it."

He nodded, "I would have yes. Dorian and Abraham are both dead, which puts my mind at ease; but the radical followers are trying to regroup, which is why Walter and the others are regrouping as well. For now we have a few more to take care of."

Ian's face was blank, which confused me. I was going half crazy trying to figure out what he was thinking. Then he nodded—that was all, just one delicate almost feeble nod. I was having difficulties keeping my thoughts sane. Aidan was so beautiful; he had his back to me but I could still see the softness of his hands and the long slender build of his legs and torso. He was perfect. It wasn't possible for my mind to comprehend his beauty until I saw him again. My memory never quite did him justice. I sighed heavily and Aidan turned to face me.

"Are you all right?" he asked.

I couldn't make eye contact, I just ignored. I felt like I was having trouble breathing. I was almost gasping for air.

"Here," I heard Ian say. He handed me a bottle of water from the tiny 'fridge in the corner of the room.

"Thanks." I whispered weakly.

"I'm sorry," Aidan whispered.

I finally looked into his eyes, and noticed they were dark, not the vibrant green color I was used to. He sighed and put his hand over my own. I didn't react, at least not out loud, but my mind was assaulting me with a loud screeching sound. Like the sound of a car burning rubber on a highway. He moved his hand away.

"I didn't mean to barge in on you like this…" He stopped speaking and moved his gaze to Ian.

Ian stared back at him with an almost nervous chaos in his eyes.

"Wait…?" Aidan stammered, "Are you…?"

Aidan moved his eyes back to mine.

I narrowed my eyes at him slightly shaking my head trying to tell him without speaking that I didn't understand what he was saying. He looked at Ian again then back at me.

"You're…Are you and Jane…"

"Oh!" Ian cried, "No, no. it isn't…Jane and I aren't…"

I chuckled, realizing what he was thinking "Ian was sent to protect me," I said, "It isn't like that."

Aidan nodded, and stuttered an "okay."

I shook my head smiling.

"I'm sorry," he said, "It isn't really my business."

I didn't respond. It wasn't his business, but I liked that it bothered him, liked it a lot more than I should have. I tried to change the subject.

"So what do we do?"

It was Aidan who replied. "I have some things I need to see to," he said, "People I need some words with."

"When will you be back?" Ian asked. He sounded very calm yet I could see he was reluctant to trust him.

"Soon," he answered.

"Well, here," Ian started, handing him the key, "Take this."

Aidan nodded and slipped the card into his pocket.

"Thanks." He said.

Life Blood

I couldn't stop the tears that started streaming down my face. Though they were slow and silent, I still couldn't hide them from Ian. He came to sit beside me.

"I wasn't even sure if he was real." I said.

He nodded and put his arm around me. I automatically leaned against his chest and he stroked my hair. It felt wonderful to be comforted.

I looked at him and he had this strange look on his face, it was like he wanted to ask me something but was terrified of what I would say. He just stared at me solidly, not averting his gaze and remaining unnaturally stagnant. It almost felt like I knew what he was thinking, like I could hear his thoughts but was unable to detect the words. He moved closer and held my face in his hands. I saw a very timid smile slowly spread across his face, softening his features. I half smiled in return. He leaned forward, and our lips met. It was soft and brief but when he realized I hadn't pulled away he moved back toward me. His lips were warm and inhumanly soft, even as he deepened the kiss and parted his lips I didn't pull away—I couldn't. Something felt right. I ran my fingers through his hair, it wasn't like Danny's; his skin wasn't like Danny's. He wasn't Danny in any way, was he? So why couldn't I let myself care for Ian, what reason was there for me to deny my infatuation for him? He wasn't Danny and he never would be.

I deepened the kiss again and his tongue passed between my lips serpent-like and my heart rate quickened. He moved his hands from my waste to my back and pulled me closer. I felt my body heat rise in temperature at the same time I felt his. What was this sudden urgency I was feeling? It had only ever been Aidan I had wanted to be this close to. Why was this okay? But it was okay, it was better than okay. Before I had even felt his weight over me I felt the soft bed beneath me. The heat of his body was piercing through my clothes feeling as if it would burn me alive—but I loved it.

His skin was almost shimmering in the dim light of the room, and it shown tawny or russet. It was maddening. I could feel the muscles in his chest and stomach harden and move against me until I wanted him so much it was driving me half insane. I wanted all of him and only for myself. For long minutes we remained kissing almost violently with him on top of me. It seemed innocent enough, except for the thoughts in my head, the longing for more. My thoughts were quickly stripped away when I heard the door open. Ian quickly moved away from me and toward the door. There was only silence and awkward stares. Nobody could say anything. I wanted to yell out *I didn't lie to you, I swear!* But I couldn't say anything yet. I was humiliated by what he saw, by what he must have been thinking. *What a tramp, to get over me so quickly.* That must have been what he was saying to himself. But it really wasn't like that. I would never be over Aidan, but I had to move on didn't I? I had to eventually let myself care for someone other than him. I had to leave him in the past, that's what was right. It didn't seem to matter what was right, not when I saw the devastation in his eyes. Ian cleared his throat.

"Umm, you're back. Did—did you take care of what you needed?"

I sat up and looked away.

"Uh—yeah." He answered "Yeah it's taken care of."

"What did you find out?"

"That leaving wouldn't be the best idea," Aidan answered, "That staying here and fighting would be better."

"Fighting?" I cried, forgetting the discomfort that was consuming me only minutes ago.

He nodded, "Yes, Jane, fighting."

I could hear the irritation rocking through him and his eyes were still dark. He didn't look curiously innocent as he sometimes did, but more—agitated and hurt. Hurt over what I had done with Ian. But it was nothing to dwell on right? Aidan had walked in before I made a mistake. It would have been a mistake, as much as I wanted it to be right, it wouldn't have been. Ian wasn't the one.

My thoughts raced. Thoughts of embarrassment, regret, and fear. Ian and Aidan and the obvious tension between them was bad enough but on top of that discomfort, was the realization that I didn't know how to fight. What was I supposed to do?

"What…"

"Jane, don't worry about it." Aidan interrupted. That was always a dead giveaway that I *should* be worried.

"I hate when you say that." I replied quietly. I drew my knees up to my chest and rested my chin.

"Aidan and I will take care of it." Ian started, "You don't need to worry about a thing."

Great I thought *another day of sitting alone waiting for people I care about to return not knowing for sure if they would. Just like the days at Luna's when Aidan almost didn't come back.* I couldn't stand going through that again.

"You can't leave." I yelled it before I could stop myself. I was on my feet instantly, almost clinging to Ian.

"He's not," Aidan hissed, "I am."

XXIII

One Last Fight

HE left Ian and me alone in the hotel. I could hardly look at Ian. I felt terrible about what had happened between us, and even worse—how much I had enjoyed it, how much I wanted it to lead to more. It couldn't be that way. He pretended as if nothing had changed. He sat there calm and composed reading the paper as always.

"Where is Aidan?" I asked, interrupting his reading as usual.

"I don't know," he answered, "He'll take care of Abraham's men, don't worry about them."

"I'm not," I murmured, "I'm not worried about them at all; I'm not worried about myself…I'm worried, I'm worried about him."

"He knows how to take care of himself."

"Ian?"

He looked straight into my eyes.

"He's protecting me," I said, "He's protecting *us*."

He smiled and nodded, "So perhaps I was wrong," he chuckled, "Is that what you wanted to hear?"

"No," I answered, mirroring his smile, "no, I just wanted you to see some good in him."

He smiled. "I have."

I laid back down on my bed, staring at the ceiling, waiting for Aidan to come back. He already came back once, what if he won't come back again? What if this was the task to ultimately claim his life? What if this one fight would surely be his last?

"Jane?"

I looked over to see Ian sitting beside me on the bed. "What's wrong?" I asked.

"Nothing," he said smiling, "but you're doing it again."

I sighed, "I'm sorry," I answered, "I'm worried."

He touched my shoulder, "I know, but sighing and fidgeting isn't going to help." He chuckled.

I just nodded, trying to calm my thoughts. Aidan would come back. He had to come back—right?

S. Jean Brenner

Three Months Later

Life Blood

I walked through the store with the shopping cart picking up everything my mom had asked for as I went, thinking about Becky and what we would do as soon as she got here. She and Aaron were still together and actually doing great from what she had told me, maybe she had actually found the one. I was relieved that my mom didn't ask too many questions about everything I had told her. She simply accepted it as fact, and understood that it wasn't Jane Doe's active imagination this time. I couldn't fabricate a single event or person, I told her everything. From meeting Aidan, to running from the cops with Ian. I was terrified she wouldn't believe me. She stared at me solidly, completely emotionless, even when I began to softly cry. It wasn't until I was finished with everything I had to say that she cried and hugged me until I couldn't breathe. It was all okay though, she understood better than I could have hoped. Becky knew everything and why I hadn't been returning her phone calls—she wasn't at all surprised.

Things just keep finding you. That's what she had said.

The town here wasn't too different than California, as far as where everything was, it wasn't too hard to get used to it and find my way around. A reclusive town in Florida is where I was forced to stay. This time however, it didn't seem forced upon me. I liked being here. I had no choice, why dwell on what you cannot change? I was finished with that stage of my life. I just walked through that normal, neat little store, looking ahead and no longer behind. When I ended up in the shampoo isle, I glanced at the shopping list again and noticed that the very specific brand of shampoo my mother wanted (typical) was on the very top shelf. Perfect. I could barely bring my fingers to brush the bottle. I stood on the lower shelf, softly kicking the paper towels over and brushed my hair from my face. Typical of me I stumbled down, off the shelf, bringing the entire thing with me. I put my arms up in front of my face when I saw the shelf leaning toward me. A few moments later I realized nothing had happened and I lowered my arms and opened my eyes. I saw pale, soft-looking hands easily reaching the bottles and reorganizing the shelf. He handed me the purple bottle and smiled a flawless, breath-taking smile. His green eyes had me captivated to the point where I couldn't speak at all. I choked on my breath.

"Hi," he said, in that perfect voice, lending out his hand, "I'm Morgan Wright."